By the same author

ANTICIPATION

GILBERT

the real right way

A NOVEL

Frederick

McPherson & Company

GREEN:
to dress for spring

OF 1968

Ted Castle

New Paltz, New York · 1986

Publication of this book has been assisted by grants from the New York State Council on the Arts and the Literature Program of the National Endowment for the Arts, Washington, D.C., a federal agency. Designed by Bruce McPherson. Manufactured in the United States of America. FIRST EDITION.

1 3 5 7 9 10 8 6 4 2

Library of Congress Cataloging-in-Publication Data

Castle, Frederick Ted, 1938-
   Gilbert Green—the real right way to dress for
spring.

   I. Title.
PS3553.A8143G54   1986   813'.54   86-2634
ISBN 0-914232-76-2 (alk. paper)
ISBN 0-914232-77-0 (lim. ed. : alk. paper)

ACKNOWLEDGEMENTS
The song "Gilbert Green" by Barry, Robin & Maurice Gibb, is published in the U.S.A. by Gibb Brothers Music, copyright © 1967 by Abigail Music Ltd., Unichappell Music, administrator, with All Rights Reserved and Universal Copyright Secured, and is used by permission as the epigraph of this book, and is excerpted on pages 4 and 45.

Although the many coincidences with reality in this book are intentional, whatever resemblance there may be between the characters here created and actual persons is purely coincidental. All such places as New York, Chicago, and Los Angeles are completely fictional. The year 1968 did exist at one time. F.T.C.

I dedicate this little Book,
written when he was two years old,
to my one and only son,
Jesse George Frederick Craver Castle Winston

F.T.C.

Gilbert Green

On a hill inside a house at Thornwell Reach
Stands a man who's feeling very tired;
Looking at a song he wrote some time ago
Could have made it big inside a Broadway show.
Every day I go away and find ideas
Think I'll climb on top of somewhere high:
Couldn't I write a song about a man who's dead,
Didn't really know if he was off his head?

> Everybody knows
> That's the way it goes
> Too bad for Gilbert Green—
> Now we can tell the world that he was right!

Sitting in his attic on a sunny day
Mending fifty carpets that had worn,
Humming to himself a song of yesteryear;
His hearing wasn't good but his eyes were clear.

> Everybody knows
> That's the way it goes
> Too bad for Gilbert Green—
> Now we can tell the world that he was right!

Now the house is bent along with Gilbert Green,
Sad to see his sister stand and cry;
And in the basement lies a song that wasn't seen,
Tells the tale of laughing men and yellow beans.

> Everybody knows
> That's the way it goes
> Too bad for Gilbert Green—
> Now we can tell the world that he was right!

—B., R. & M. Gibb

side one

⟦ Gilbert Green, Susan & Fred Meet ⟧

Seriously now I want to start begin and speak of many things and everything as well as ever could or would be in a short form that goes as fast as I can write and wins a prize and loves the worth of women in its time and fights to lose and telephones, a number dialed, the answer humming in my ear, she is not there right now, goodbye . . . in its time and fights a loss against a gain and aspirates and telephones again another time and gets a signal you can hear all the way across the room on account of the way his ear is by the phone part of the phone which means that at this moment she is not alone and there he is across the street, she could see him from the window if she would get off the phone, and telephones and aspirates and gains a loss against a gain, again he dials the magic 8 the requisite amount of times which switches his nickels into dimes, from one hand to the other pocket, a mindless game of numbers that mean something to more than one but no more to one than two or three (it is not yet a bigtime game) and rings and pockets change and knows the answer for one night, one minute, looks and sees her form digressing across the room and down the stairs and out of sight to her lovely lover.

There is a change (it is so cold tonight) and his balls hang down toward the knuckles of his thighs, and ache, a little further back, and up a bit to where it was once when it was there, a thing of dreams, a fabric not too comfortable but perfectly designed, a well worth waiting for, a wish and time and more than just enough. There has to be a change. The phone assumes a steamy look as it stares back from his sweaty palm and gets reflected in his eyes and brings his eyes to earth again. With a sort of elaborate unconcern he quits the place and heads out at the usual speed, which is rather quick, toward an unknown place that seems decided in advance though it could be anyplace, not home, it must be getting closer, and suddenly arrives. Bang! With a sort of elaborate facial gesture he winces at the door that bangs rattling a big plate of glass that does not smash but hangs on ancient hinges polished white and framed in wood and closed by a defective spring thing that no longer works right, except I really want a beer. He coughs awkwardly and takes a sip to calm his throat that really doesn't ache at all and looks around him for the first time, almost. There is only one woman at the bar and it isn't her, the one on the phone, the one in the bed, the one with the hair, this one is entirely different, it would seem to me, it is not the one on the phone nor is it the one under the bed nor does it have the same kind of hair. She does not speak. She does not notice us. She does not dress too well. She smokes. She does not smoke too much. She does not smoke the same brand as I used to. She doesn't dribble her ashes on her dress or on her floor, she isn't messy, she isn't staring but she is the star.

This long look returns his gaze to an empty glass that gets refilled with ale from an empty bottle and floods the room with a great song that has been reproduced for the occasion by a big machine floating loosely in its plastic glass, *Everybody knows, That's the way it goes*, a song appropriated for the space, *His hearing wasn't good but his eyes were clear*, a smile that warms the corners of the ears, *Too bad for Gilbert Green*, a single thought that lights the mind, *Now we can tell the world that he was right!* It isn't much but great, *Everybody knows, That's the way it goes*. In this particular song, as a matter of fact, the romantic version of it is included right within the original recording which makes a scene with a piano and some violins and what not else a sort of a slow thing that plunks a lot as it moves across the rhythms of the song and rises and falls like a violin and fades away just as it is becoming greater.

Bang! In the short silence between two records the surprising door discloses on the outside the figure of the other girl which walks away from it and disappears. There are no women sitting at the bar where the tender rectifies a dainty mess and someone else takes another drop of beer and almost lets his mind reflect a picture of the star as if it was another movie he had already seen. To a different tune that is not distinctly in my mind he is approached by a friendly conversation which may turn either way. At first the side is all on the approach, which represents himself as an admirer of the work of the one who is not getting drunk. He smiles a lot. He is kind of short. He is fashionably dressed. The other one is not offended, indeed he may be pleased. They talk about the music that makes great songs. The one being complimented talks much less and occasionally looks away in a kind of modesty that is assumed and real as style. The one making the compliment turns out to be quite a nice guy although he doesn't know it. The point is that they have a friend or two in common. This leads to common gossip including whereabouts, what they do now, who she married and when he died. The two friends fall silent when the series of records stops playing. The tender serves them each another ale, another taste they share. This lull offers an opportunity for the one who is more famous than the other to abandon his drink and take his leave, or else to make the next remark, or to let the silence lapse off into another song. He is so distracted that it doesn't matter, it slips his mind. He is not thinking of anything in particular but his pleasure in being discreetly recognized is unconcealed from the one who has done so. The encounter is successful and I do know what's next.

The friend of our friend turns on a well-turned heel to confront the porcelain receptacle with a well-earned sigh of relief and excitement at having turned a spade with royalty and, returning to his seat, pauses at the big machine and asks in one direction what songs would be preferred.

"Your, oh, anything." A smile.

The songs that play obligingly reveal a certain taste. The conversation is much easier, it has a lot of lapses, it shifts position very slightly and smokes a cigarette.

"It's kind of scary," says the man.

"What?"

"Meeting you by chance like this."

"I think I would be more scared to meet me by appointment."

A big smile and a little laugh. It may be strange to notice now that there is nobody else at the bar or at the tables except the man behind it. The room is large the men are small the songs are great the beer is tall the mirrors are silver the glass is cut glass the floor is paved in tiny polished stones the wood of the bar shines darkly under the impression of endless coats of oil and the ceiling is the sky.

[[Gilbert Green & Susan Outside]]

Her face is on the grass but it is looking into the sun which makes it squint. The sun is burning a hole in a piece of paper on the grass next to her head, and it does this several different times. These holes do not make any particular pattern on the grass but some of them are bigger than others and all of them are browned. For a second, less, the sun is focussed on her cheek.

"Don't!" she moves a bit away and sits up somewhat.

"What are you going to do?"

"Find another man and do it again, I guess." He kissed her lightly on their lips. Another smile was flashed in each direction not too proudly. There was a large field of undetermined extent with nothing but distance in the distance and more grass and sky. The silence was not illuminated by a bird. The amount of insects was tremendous but only the flies seemed to be a bother. The people were quiet and lightly clad. There was a breeze like the conversation. The people made bright-eyed, langorous gestures. An airplane bit the silence like a saw and the people got up and moved off without holding hands until they came to the slippery rocks obstructing the noisy clear stream in which it looked as if there might be a pool of fish. The water was so cold it hurt. Patches of sand were the best place to stand except the high rocks were warmer. The noise was terrific. The fish were asleep. Right in the middle of this little stream there sits a large flat rock that seems to be made for something that doubtless never was. It is just right for just about anything. Some of it is in the shade of trees and most of it is in the light of day. It is bigger than some tables but it is smaller than others. Its surface is rocky which is somewhat smoothed by the spring floods that yearly erode it but undulating somewhat here and there with one or two small pools of tepid rainwater caught in a pool without fish or recourse. It was there that they rested their feet and warmed up. It was there that he told her his dream.

"It wasn't really like this but it sort of was."

She looked down at her feet which were pointed into a little pool.

"I left the concert before it was over, I just wandered off and there was a big building, you know, right off the stage, like at first it might have been some set for the play they were running later, but it was a real building I don't remember it too well, it is a little sort of red but not brick, I was just looking at it, it was real big and, uh, I don't know, windows, I'm trying to think of a building like it, it was sort of like the Jackson Square Library, but it was really big, but the windows were big like that is and you could see inside, you could see the ceilings and things like you can there and, uh, oh I went in and it was all dark but there was a lot of light from the street, mostly on the ceilings, it wasn't a library though it was a great big room with a stairway going up to the ceiling and I looked around for a while, it was a very nice room, and I was looking at it like I might rent it or something like that, I looked it all over and there were a couple of doors in the walls but they were locked and I thought to myself that *the shelves must be inside there*, I mean I didn't think it was a library at the time but now I'm sure I really thought it was though that didn't occur to me until now, and then different things happened, the telephone was working, I checked that, and I don't know, but then I went up the stairs, they were two stories high and went straight up, at first when I saw them they were against the wall but when I was on them they were somewhat in the middle of the room, not exactly, but they weren't against the wall then, and I remember that they seemed very solid which I liked and they had beautiful railings, I don't remember how they were, but they were straight and had some sort of scroll work, well, I went on up, and this was a funny stairway because it just went up into the roof instead of into a wall and I walked up and opened this trap door, it wasn't heavy but it was locked but I unlocked it, it was just a bolt, and I walked up but it wasn't a building it was like where a building was torn down up there, it was like a parking lot and it wasn't high it was right on the street but it wasn't a parking lot and I just lay down on it it was very hot and it was covered with gravel or cinders but anyway I just lay down on it and I thought, you know, isn't that amazing when you think that this must be a dream while you are having a dream, like sometimes you're afraid you might not wake up or you don't want to wake up or anyway it's really peculiar, but you know you're dreaming at the time which, but I was lying face down on this hot gravel, it wasn't too hot it was sort of like the beach but it wasn't sand and I thought, this is funny, I mean I didn't think it was funny, it seemed you know just ordinary, but when I was lying there I thought that it wasn't a good building after all and uh, you know, I wouldn't be able to rent it or something, well because, you know, there wasn't any building, haha!, so I thought well I guess I'll leave and I stood up but I didn't have any clothes on and then I woke up with a hard-on and that was it.''

"That was the whole dream?''

"I don't know, most of it I guess, it was real clear and I thought about it when I woke up, I really liked it a lot, and I don't know.''

"What does it mean?''

"Oh, nothing, it's just nice the way it is, sort of, but I just thought of it when we got here. I guess the rock is sort of like that or something. I was reminded of it.''

"Was it in color?''

"I don't think it was but it wasn't in black and white, I don't know.''

"I don't usually remember my dreams too well but sometimes I see a color that reminds me of that it was like in a dream I had and I still don't remember what it was about or anything but I remember having the dream by the color.''

"Wow it's really noisy here.''

"Not so many flies though.''

"No cowshit. Oh, uh, let's take off our clothes.'' As he makes this suggestion he follows it out, first pulling his shirt off his head, then disentangling his pants from his ankles.

She doesn't move except to turn her head and give him a smile. "You really like bathing in the nude, don't you?"

"I don't know, I never did it before, I mean outside."

"Okay," she said and she closed her eyes.

⟦ Gilbert Green & Fred at Work ⟧

When they awoke it was eight o'clock and there was a whole lot of sun in through the windows because they were facing in that direction. One got up right away and the other one stayed in bed. One took a shower and one did not. One liked the sunlight and one did not care for it while he was still in bed. They had not slept entwined about each others necks and legs. The place was neither neat nor messy nor rich or poor but it was yellow and it was somewhat blue. It was very large although at first it did not seem to be because the life they led in that huge room was very long indeed and not too wide. When the one who had taken a shower quickly dried himself and put on a shirt, he went into the part of the room where there was some kitchen equipment and took a look in the icebox. For breakfast he chose a glass of milk and a banana and some cookies with nuts in them. When he had finished he took a look at his face in a mirror, arranged his hair with a sweep of his hand and went into another part of the room and sat down and got up and picked a magazine off the floor and sat down and looked at the magazine of many colors. While he was absorbing the news of the day in this way, the one who had stayed in bed got up and put on a shirt and some pants and took a leak and brushed his teeth and shaved his face and combed his hair and answered the telephone. "Call me this afternoon," he said briefly and hung up. He went to the stove and reheated some coffee. He sat down and took a pen and some paper to commit a verse he had memorized during his morning reverie.

Friends no longer young
Delight the face of dreams.

He looked at it a couple of times, put down the pen, checked the coffee, opened and closed the refrigerator, took a cup from the shelf, poured some coffee into it and sat back down at the table, lighting a cigarette first and then adding to his verse.

Wake up and come down
Say hi and take tea
Wash face and brush teeth
Say bye and make bus
Walk quick and don't walk
Save life and buy bonds
Win some and look good
Save time and make bread
Wish well and drop dead
Set screws and lock nuts
Why not and let's do
Set clock and be cool

Anytime she cries it is a tragedy that flies along a line
from her mouth to my ear and leaves pain on my brain. The
well worth what not of our consolation never makes up for
her tears that dry on my ears like snow or
     some ashen likeness.
A lollipop, a candlestick, a perfect flame, an old-time train,
a weather sphere, a window glass, a final lie, a silent pass.

"What shit," he said rising contemptuously from his breakfast and walking proudly to the other end of the room and back, twice passing the one who had not yet dressed without speaking and then turning back to see him looking from the back of the sofa to the ceiling his eyes open as wide as big eyes can be open looking dead.

"You look dead," said the poet.

"I was dead," said the man.

"Dead men don't talk," said the poet.

"I'm not now," said the man, "I'm alive. In what way may I serve your royal majesty?"

"Oh, cut it."

"I had a haircut just last week, mama."

"Oh, do you think we should do the Siegal thing? It seems sort of odd with all those others, but then maybe that's good for a change."

"Why not? Steve's all right. He won't screw us."

"Well, no, but then all those others."

"He's running it, he'll take care of us."

"The way he did before?"

"He wasn't running it, he was just trying to, now he can."

"Do I have to call him, or what?"

"I don't know, yeah, I think so, then he won't be scared."

"All right, well, maybe tomorrow," said the poet, "If anyone calls tell them I'm getting married."

"Haha! Who to?"

"I don't know. I can't live alone anymore."

"You don't live alone."

"Really?"

"Is there anything for video or xerox?"

"Oh there's a whole pile of junk on the table. Sort it out first. It's all shit. It might be all right, I don't know."

"Where are you going?"

"I'm going for a walk."

"There's something going on at four."

"Can't they get along without me?"

"No."

"Well. I ought to sleep more. I'm so tired. Where's my coat? Is it cold? This stuff might be all right but I guess we'll have to work through a new beat or something. It sounds like a waltz to me. Okay—'keys, money, information and rhetoric'—did you get the mail, oh, I guess not, well, good bye."

"Do you have any change?"

"Is that enough?" The poet handed him a bill and said goodbye again and left through the door which shut itself.

⟦ Gilbert Green—Letter ⟧

Dear Charles.

I am not coming this month to see you because I am trying to work on a novel and if I get inspired, some songs. I decided a trip would screw me up. Because it seems like you have done a lot but it is a vacation. I had the money, or almost, but I decided to blow it. We had a big party and I hired a servant. It happened that the twelfth night of Christmas fell on Saturday this year and although I had always hated Saturday night parties, I gave one. I had never hired a servant myself before, and I liked it. I think I will have to have a part-time servant beginning in a year or so. I can get so much more done if I don't have to attend to all the details myself. My philosophical essays are proceeding at the rate of one a month. I just wrote one on the foreign war which is called ''The Outside of a Small Circle'' after Phil Ochs. Stefan is publishing some essays on some plays which are being done by three associated companies and I am doing the pictures for him. They have a playwright, Charles Ludlam, who is quite, quite good, and he also directs one of the companies and acts in his own plays. My plan now is to come and see you when I have done the novel, in two or three months, if you will still be there. A real vacation. After that I'm going to do the Warhol book. Webb's book *The Graduate* made an excellent film by Mike Nichols, which surprised and inspired me to do a novel for film. One of the things I would like to do in England is to meet the Prince of Wales in an informal situation. I don't know if it is out of the question (i.e. that the prince is too young to be allowed to go where he will) but I would very much like to get some personal impression of him if it could be arranged. If the prince himself is any good, it seems to me that I could find somebody who knows somebody who knows him. The world in general has had a hard time recovering from the reign of Queen Victoria, and it would seem to me that the prince is the first member of her family who must be somewhat without her influence. Thus he will be able to undertake the question of what a king should do now in a clearer manner than his predecessors have been able to. Actually it would be better to meet him in this country if he takes an informal tour. It is always assumed that foreigners know nothing. John Willett still has my great book and not a word from him. I assume that other people actually have it and he is awaiting their response. People here have urged me to continue to push the book here, but I am reluctant to do so, I really don't know why. I am willing to let others act for me but I am not willing to sell it myself. Harvey sent his copy to somebody last week. I gave Diana's copy to somebody who is not in the trade, and two more of them are being bound, for Eric and Stefan. Since people are reading it again, I spent most of yesterday reading it myself to see what they may be seeing, and I am again pleased and astonished by it. I found the seeds of most of my philosophical essays in it, and I discovered some continuities in the book itself which I do not remember ever having seen before, things mentioned close together in the text which were written at different times. Now that I am beginning to forget the process that made the book and what I left out of it, I like it better than I used to. I also noticed a date in the beginning of the book which in two months will be five years from now! Let me know what you are doing. Cheers.

G.G.

January 16, 1968.
76 Front Street
New York 4.

⟦ Gilbert Green & Susan Inside ⟧

In this part I was going to talk about this beautiful silvery dream I had in which everything seemed to be silver.
Then why don't you?
I was interrupted by giving a party and a lot of other things.
Well, combine the two.
Okay. I actually did get married. I was tired of living alone. I wasn't alone most of the time, but I was living alone. Everybody only wanted the money or the glamour they could get through me. I like some of them a lot. Instead of waking up in the morning and wondering briefly who I would find in my bed, of course I'd remember quite soon, I wanted something that would always be the same and as soon as I thought so, I got it.

She opened her eyes on a room, painted and plated and silvered, that is, mirrored, and windowed and curtained and carpeted, slipcovered entirely in *silver*. We lay beneath sheets and the heat was terrific. It looked like the moon was not cold after all. It must have been light from the sun, all right, but it was only reflected. She opened her eyes to find me still asleep. She didn't stretch or yawn or make any of those motions or groans that actors give off to indicate that they were not asleep when the camera was turned on. She just opened her eyes on the vast panorama of silvery gray with which my name and my words had invested the room. Her gaze lingered on the plants, which were green. The ceiling was a mirror. The windows seemed to be of ice but it must have been some kind of plastic. The floor was chromed. Stainless steel replaced wood in its myriad household uses and in short there wasn't a thing but ourselves and the plants which didn't share some quality of silver glitter. It looked like a dream.

As she touched the side of my face I awoke. "It looks like a dream," she said. I thought that it did. I got up and took off my clothes and went to the bathroom and brushed my teeth. There is something unpleasant about silver toothpaste, when you spit it out it seems dirty. We sat at the marble table and took our coffee from sterling mugs, admiring our surroundings in silence as we did so. I was given a mound of fresh strawberries with real heavy cream. The silence was so intense that it seemed that the sound of chewing strawberries could be heard by everyone though it was probably completely muffled by my mouth. Except once when I gave her part of a strawberry as part of a kiss. Then she got up and turned down the steam. This made it comparatively noisy because when the steam is on full it makes no noise but when it is on part way it makes a lot of noise, the pipes bang some and they let some of the steam escape into the room through valves. It was much too hot. When you turn the steam off, it becomes silent again. And it gets cold right away. Unless there is too much heat, it always seems cold in a silver environment.

As she was coming back from the other end of the room I intercepted my love and postponed the washing and polishing of dishes and the refrigeration of excessive fruits and cream with a kiss that contained no surprise. We reported gradually toward the bed which in our absence had changed to be an ordinary wood bed of graceful design and ample proportions and considerable softness though not the cloudy feeling of pure eider down. I could almost make out a rhythm in the sound of the heat, or maybe it was just the blood in my ears. The noise seemed to increase and alter by degrees as I grew hotter and the temperature went down. We devoted ourselves to each other during the space of time in which things made their changes. And the heat grew less and the noise encompassed all of the images that we were using and those that we discarded and filled the whole room with a sound that was sound for itself, now with a beat, now without distinction a high sound and a low note sustained in perpetuity and then added to and changed again, now and then seemingly only the pipes, but rising and falling with a blind intelligence that had the effect on our environment of peopling it with dreams, phantoms of our daily life, where bits of it were conducted now and again in corners of our beautiful apartments, with visitors and bill collectors and friends of friends, with lawyers and producers and rich men and agents and old school chums and members of her family, and with musicians and with musical equipment that was of course giving off the sound as it was played. Our dream had become the life we lived. Much less of it was silver than had been before, but there was still a mirror on the ceiling and a lot of other silver stuff. Just then there was a pause of silence in the sound and I asked her, "How do you like being married?" We giggled and took another kiss from which I got up to turn on the telephone which never stopped ringing after that.

It was a very busy day, as usual. The band was playing in the studio, next to mine, partly for rehearsal and partly to sell their sound to visitors. Once in awhile I took the phone myself but mostly other people did that. I didn't write at all but I did some reading but I certainly didn't do much reading either. I had to look at a great many photographs and select some to be used on the cover of the book but I didn't like any of them very much so I took some more since the people who had appeared in the photographs happened to be visiting me too. I had to read a couple of contracts and make the lawyer change one or two things in them which he was willing to do as soon as I explained it to him. I also had to complain to the wholesaler about his prices, which I didn't want to do because it always makes me mad to have to tell somebody off, but I did it because the prices were too high. Somebody was trying to see me about buying something which I didn't even clearly understand what it was, a new kind of food, or something I wasn't interested in. Finally he left after telling me what he thought of me which I didn't hear since the music was so loud and I was doing something else then. I went and talked to the band. They were playing almost in darkness, and I closed the door, and when I came in they stopped playing after awhile, and we just talked about things. Sammy introduced me to his new chick who I hadn't seen before and Danny told a long story about taking his dog for a walk and meeting some people and what they did after that. It was very funny. We smoked a joint or two and they showed me a few new things that would change the music slightly, a way of working with the drums that Danny described as backward and mixing that with Sammy's electric so that you couldn't tell which came from where. A couple of the others had come in behind me and they stood around not making any noise, not even laughing much at the jokes. Then I had to go to the telephone, and then I had to go to the bathroom, and the new pictures were ready although they were still wet and I looked them over and picked out the best ones for the book. Somebody handed me a glass of milk and I put some cognac in it and sat down and talked with Fred about some things he was doing for me in connection with the movies. I don't deal directly with something I don't know very well myself, I get some other people to do my stuff until the thing is more or less settled when I tend to come in and take over, but sometimes I just let Fred do the whole thing for me if it is going along all right and then of course he gets the credit which pleases him. Then there were friends on the telephone asking if it would be all right to bring so and so and so and so to the party, which of course it was, but I told them to cut down on the young married people because they are so dull they just sit on each others' laps and wonder why the party is so bad. By that time it was getting late. Susan reappeared, I think she must have gone shopping because that was what she was talking about and she told me whom she had met and invited to the party at the last minute, they were from California. I put the phone on automatic, which is a device that says I do not want to be disturbed and gives another number that can be called to leave a message. I sat down at the table with Susan and finished the milk. Fred was correcting some proofs, and he came over and had a glass with us after he got rid of the lawyer who didn't seem to want to leave.

Sammy and Judy and Danny came out of the studio and sat around with us, so that even when most of the people had left there were still six of us which is the way it usually is, and I really like it like that. We didn't say much, some of us had something to do and some of us didn't. Judy undertook to wash a few dishes and things without being asked. Susan went away and started to get dressed. Sammy turned on the TV and provided a little commentary on what the various channels were offering at the time. It turned out that on practically all the channels people were either eating or dancing. At least that's what he said. Fred asked if we were going to eat and I said I hadn't thought about it and Danny told us about a restaurant he had found a few days before where there wouldn't be anybody that we knew, except he didn't say that, and I decided that we would go to the Club but eat early upstairs, and Fred called them up and Danny started to leave but I asked him to stay and go to dinner with us and he called up somebody and I went and changed my clothes and while I was away the caterer came and began setting things up and when I came back I introduced myself to the caterer, who was called George, and I told him it would be all right for him to drink if he wanted to and then I introduced him to Susan and Fred and then we went to dinner which was located around the corner.

⟦ Gilbert Green & Susan Talking ⟧

Very soon it will be obvious that this story is not very short, nor is it very long. It is somewhat chilly. I was going to go directly into the party when I started writing about the silver dream and then I thought it was complicated enough to have gone through the beginning of the party. Even after I decided to do the party now, in this section, I was going to do it in the next section. Now I see that all that is changed.

One night I was walking back to the Club with a few other people, but I happened to be walking last. As I was passing a shadow right around the corner, a man stepped out of it and said something to me. I didn't hear what he said and I thought it was a bum or something, so I kept on going, but he came along with me. I was getting ready to be annoyed when I heard what he was saying, he said, "You are a philosopher, Sir." He said he thought I looked like a philosopher. I was ready to see a pitch in his next remark, but it appeared he was really asking me if I thought I was a philosopher. I was interested, and I had half a thought that I would have to get out a bit of change if I had any, and I said that yes, in a way, I was a philosopher. Then he said he thought I would do well as a philosopher, and dropped away into a shadow we were passing. Susan came up and told me something someone had just told her, I think it was a joke, and I thought nothing much of the occurrence, but I kept thinking about it at odd moments at the Club and later but I didn't tell anybody for a long time. When I did I guess I didn't tell it right because nobody but me seemed impressed with this little thing that happened once, but I was, and I just kept it in my mind.

"That's very interesting," she said in a way that I knew that she meant that she thought it might be interesting but that she didn't get it. She was not sarcastic. But although the length of this story encompasses both before and after Susan, and you might say that somewhere at either end were its limits, like a table you can stretch out forever at each side but the middle stays the same, let's go back to the beginning of Susan and rerun that episode, looking out for which way that may go.

The first way I told it was not the way it really happened. Well, in a way that did happen, but it was not the first time I saw Susan. I already knew her. That was the time I met Fred. When I first met Susan I was drunk. When I get drunk, if I am talking well while I am doing it, I don't get sloppy or more vulgar than I usually am, I really get very complicated, and I make little tiny points that I really can never remember, or if I do remember them I know that they don't make any difference. But at the time they seem important. Well, I had been having a long conversation, a long disagreement with Stefan which is why I was getting drunk, I couldn't believe he was not understanding what I was saying so I stayed longer and complicated the issue in ways I do not remember. I enjoyed myself. But when I left, this was before when I didn't usually have so many people around, when I left the house I went to get something to eat because I realized that I was drunk and it was five in the morning and I was hungry. I also wanted to pick up a chick. I couldn't possibly have balled her then, but what happens when I get drunk is that the next day I like a real sexual orgy along with lots of orange juice or ginger ale. I went to a place on the way and sat down at the counter and shortly later a girl in a pink dress and very short hair, a fur coat and a copy of the morning paper came in and sat down next to me. This is an unusual event and it is unknown at five in the morning. I introduced myself and found out her name and that she was a waitress and I asked her if she wanted to come home with me.

"I don't usually just go home with men," was her non-committal answer. She read about the wars in the newspaper and I asked her, pressing her too much, what she was reading. She didn't put me off but she did look around to see if any of her friends were there. She had actually worked in the restaurant where we were eating and so she knew those people but all of them were working. I didn't mention going home with me again. We ate our food and at intervals I made another remark, one of which was that I was really glad that she had come in when she did. Pretty soon one of the waiters grew less busy and sat down and she excused herself and went to sit with him and gossip. But every few seconds she looked around at me, I couldn't just tell why. Then I forgot her name and ordered another cup of coffee to drink while I watched her watching me behind her back. Toward the end of the coffee I remembered her name and went over and said, "Susan" and she looked around as if she was expecting me and said, "Yes."

"I could take you home, if you like."

"Thank you. I have a way of getting home. Thank you very much."

I grimaced and tried to show my disappointment in it and left and went home to sleep.

"That's very interesting," she said in a way that I knew that she meant that she remembered the occasion, but not too clearly, and she was glad to have it described to her in my details. After all, as a waitress, one met so many late at night. . . . She was not too good at remembering every detail, and I was entirely too good at that. But it's hard even for me to remember all the traces of the story that doesn't entirely exist yet. I guess what really happened was that we found we had a friend in common, actually a friend of Fred's. I probably would have thought nothing about her even if I saw her around a few other times, I would only think about her when I was trying to decide what made it happen that she didn't come along, it couldn't just have been because I was drunk because I am almost always drunk when I want to just pick up a chick. She said she saw me at Max's that night when Fred introduced himself. I saw somebody but I wasn't interested in it at the time. I wasn't drunk, I wasn't getting drunk, I was really feeling very sad and it fixed me up to have someone come up and praise me. She said she had gone on a picnic with Fred's friend the next day and found out who I was, but later she said that she remembered me from the restaurant but she probably didn't. Fred's friend was a librarian or something, I had met him a few times at various places and he was always very nice or something but I really didn't know him but I had often been introduced to him and actually this was how Fred had gotten on to me in the beginning and then when he heard my things he knew he wanted to meet me.

"Oh, Harvey isn't that bad," she said. But I hadn't said he was bad I had just said that I didn't really know him.

"That's very interesting," she said, in a way that I knew meant she thought I thought Harvey was as bad as she thought, although she was never sarcastic. I saw her maybe another half a dozen times, but I don't even know if it was her. Once I remember I was walking with a whole crowd of other people and I was sort of walking in front of them because I felt cold and I wanted to get inside and I think I passed her with her friend or someone else in the street. I remember some girl just then smiled at me. I didn't think it was anyone I knew, well, I didn't know her at the time. Then one time, maybe Fred, was talking about her and I asked who she was and I didn't remember the girl in the restaurant but I did remember Fred's friend vaguely when he mentioned him in connection with this girl, if it was Fred's story, I'm not sure. But I remember somebody telling me something about her. And another time, I was walking somewhere with Fred and some other people, it was in the park somewhere, and I asked someone if they knew who a girl was who was staring at me and Fred recalled to me that she was who he had been talking about or he had been there when somebody else was talking about her to me, so at last anyway I made the connection between her name and her face and maybe it was then that I vaguely remembered her as the girl in the restaurant or maybe when I was thinking about that later, about the girl in the park. Anyway by the next time I saw her I really knew which girl it was.

"When was that?" she said, indicating that the story I was trying to tell was a little too long but she wanted to get to the part where she would have a bigger part of the play. It was raining. I was trying to get a taxi for the longest time and I was soaked when I came in. It was cold too. I ran in and took a shower and changed my clothes. I was mad at myself for standing in the rain so long.

Waiting is one of the things I can't take. Even if the weather isn't bad. But after you start waiting you naturally go on waiting and even though usually I can stop waiting very easily, I had kept on waiting, getting madder and madder all the time. When I got dressed again I put on a beautiful thing, these suede pants I used to have before I gave them to somebody, anyway I was still excited from being mad but I was all warmed up and I thought I looked great so instead of writing or something as I had planned to do I guess, I called Fred and told him not to come over and I just went out when I found out the rain had stopped. Actually it had warmed up too, or maybe it was just that I felt so good after the shower. I can still remember I was singing this song, the one that goes, *We live in a world of carnivals and clowns and buildings to the sky that make us want to fly*, that was just going around inside of me all the time then, I didn't even like the song but it was built-in. I was walking someplace, I usually walk if I can, I don't even remember if I was going anyplace or maybe it was one of those times when I just go out and walk east because if I go in that direction there are still a lot of choices left but if I go in the other direction it only means one thing.

If I go east I can go to the Club or to Max's or to Fred's house if I want to, and there are a couple of places I sometimes go to, but not much, places I used to like where they always play the juke box a lot, I wanted to walk so I ended up at the farthest place. I like the place because they keep the door locked and they only let people in after they look them over even though I have never seen anyone refused. I like the thing they do, so I always say thanks to the guy who opens the door to you. Inside it is very ordinary, but the fact that the place outside is sort of dingy and they let you in gives it another feeling than the other places have, I guess it is like a speakeasy must have been. Oh, I remember a lot about that night because I was actually writing the pretty picture song but I was just thinking about it, I didn't write it yet. But I remember my experiences much more when I am writing because I use the experience I have at the time, not all of them, maybe, but a lot, and I notice everything really clear. Like in the song where it says *glasses stacked in sagging lines* it was because of that place where they have glasses stacked on the beer cooler thing in the bar and the metal that's over it sort of sags in the middle because they don't build it to be stacked on but only to be used for part of the bar, but it keeps the glasses a little cold, which is another thing about that place. Oh, actually the pretty picture is in there too, because they have a mirror behind the bar and, you know, I thought it made a pretty picture. I didn't see anybody I knew and it didn't look like anybody was interested in me, and I was just as glad to be alone. I used to want to be alone more. I didn't know how I did things then, I just thought that anything might be happening. So I was staring at myself in the mirror and I felt good. I couldn't think of a tune outside of the one that was playing at any time while I was thinking up this song so that in a way all the lines started out to be suitable to different tunes or schemes, it was very peculiar, it was sort of derivative but then it really wasn't because it was derived from so many things. So I'd get a few lines in my head and then I'd write them down on a napkin or something, I think the bartender gave me a pad. So I got things like *a poet with pad and pen/a very pretty picture song* and *glasses stacked in sagging lines/a very pretty picture song*. I wanted to quote the line "sitting on a cornflake" but it was too long or too short so I thought *sitting on a barstool thinking/a very pretty picture song* which was better than just quoting it anyway. I was looking at the signs in the place and so I got *gentlemen and guests permitted/a very pretty picture song* because they have a sign in front of the back room that says "couples only" and then they have another song that says "quiet performance in progress" because once in a while they have plays in the back room and so I used that too the way it was, *quiet performance in progress/a very pretty picture song*, that was changed, but anyway I got all these things, like *three boys giggle in a corner/a very pretty picture song* and I don't know, but I remember all that so well! Everything I saw fitted in or everything I heard was the right thing and I was getting more and more excited. I'd still have to rough out a scheme and maybe use some regular verses (what I thought then) but I stopped writing it down when I had half a dozen lines or so because you could just go on alternating lines with p in them and lines with g, I could have as many as I wanted and I had an idea for a good song. Oh I also had *pleasant memories of peppermints and innocence* but we cut that out later, except in one version, I still like it but everybody said no, so we used another one, but pleasant memories of peppermints and innocence a pretty picture song was good because it wasn't exactly the same. They said that's why they didn't like it, but it was because they didn't like the group that did the song it came from, sort of. I knew what they meant so I let it go. If we do it again I'll do it that way. I even get excited thinking about all this stuff. That was really a good song. Well, what I'm coming to was that I was hungry and when the hamburg came I found out that this is where Susan was working at the time. I wanted to talk to someone so I said hello! as if I knew her very well which was sort of a surprise but it worked out very well, I mean I was surprised at the way that I came on because she already threw me away and normally then I'd wait for her to make up or ignore her or something, but when I saw her I didn't exactly recognize her at first glance, but I knew I knew her and I wanted to see someone I knew when I was so elated. She sat down and I told her all about my pretty picture song. "That's very interesting," she said, in a way that I knew she was very interested.

How can you remember something that I did? That's amazing, it was almost like that! —G.G.

⟦ Susan & Gilbert Green Dreaming ⟧

She opened the door herself to reveal three policemen wearing hats and ties and things. She said, "I feel a little hung over."

"What?" said the chief inspector.

"I feel as if I had a little too much to drink some time ago, probably gin," she said.

"And you did or you didn't?" said the chief inspector.

"Oh, no, I didn't, but I feel like it." She said, "Would you-all like a drink?"

"No."

"No thanks."

"Not right now," they all said.

"Neither do I," she said.

"When did you find out about this?" said the chief inspector, and as he said so he removed his hat and put it on a table.

"Oh, not very long ago, you mean what time was it? I don't know I guess it was about eight, because when I saw it I just stopped dead in my tracks and I counted the chimes that were sounding the hour. Aren't you going to take any notes?" she asked, changing the subject.

"I might if I hear something that would be hard to remember, but I usually don't," said the chief inspector, taking a chair. "I have to warn you . . . "

"Oh, I know that," she said.

"Do you have a lawyer?" he asked.

"Of course I have a lawyer," she said, "Doesn't everyone?"

"All right," said the chief inspector. "What did you do when you found him?"

"I covered it up. No, first I just stood there and counted the chimes as I said and then I was reassured that things were the same, if you know what I mean, I mean when something happens, when somebody kills themselves, you start thinking that everything has changed but, you know, it isn't really, like I might have gone to the phone to hear the dial tone or I might have turned on the stereo or something like that just to get the idea that things are all right. Well, I was looking at him, it was kind of curled up on the floor, I never saw him like that, he didn't sleep that way or anything, and then I went and got a blanket and covered it up."

"Then what?"

"Then I um, no, then Fred came in, and, of course, well, I had *him* on my hands for the longest time, I guess it wasn't very long but the last thing I needed then was to have somebody fall apart like that. At first I was glad to see him because I just thought for an instant, I mean I really wanted to have a man to call people up and things but I should have known that men are more fragile than we are, but anyway there was Fred, it was terrible, like some sort of jelly or something, really a thing, he couldn't even talk, at first I thought he might die, he wouldn't take a drink or anything. He was just shivering, it unnerved me more than . . . death. I took a look out the window as if I wanted to call out for help as if I didn't want to use the phone to call but I wanted to call someone personally and I almost opened it but then I thought about it, you don't just drag somebody in unless you're really in danger, so I went into the other room and I turned on the TV for some company and I tried to think of what to do. I closed the door."

"What did you think of to do," said the chief inspector.

"Oh at first I thought I was going to die too. It was like a weight on top of my head and I thought, you know, I'm going to die right now but pretty soon I realized I wasn't going to die right then, but the weight was still terrific, it was like, as if, I don't know, as if there was a round clamp on my head like a hat, first of all very tight and then loosening some but still, it was just a feeling, and I couldn't think at all. But I began to get straightened out and the first thing I thought was that I would have to be arrested and all that sort of thing, it was absurd, but I was trying to think of what lawyer would be the best one to call, and then I thought right on top of that about getting a divorce! Well, that really fixed me up. I didn't laugh, or I don't think I did, but I sort of got out from under the pressure and I realized the absurdity of what I had been thinking and uh, I think I'll have a Coke, wow, this really is like a hangover.''

"Would you rather talk to me tomorrow?" asked the chief inspector.

"Oh, no, no, I'd rather talk to you now because I'll forget it all and have to make something up.''

"What?''

"I mean after a while I might not remember what I thought so I would have to say I thought such and such which is like something I might have thought but it wasn't really what I thought or something like that, oh, I'm sorry.''

"Can I have a Coke too?''

"Sure. I don't even know if there is any, there usually is though,'' she said and went into another room.

"What do you think?'' said one of the cops.

"Amazing woman,'' said the chief inspector absent-mindedly.

"Watch out,'' said the other cop, and they all smiled a little. "You don't need us, chief,'' said one, and the two cops actually laughed.

"Shut up,'' said the chief inspector, and at the same time the cops stopped looking foolish and changed their seats and lighted their cigarettes and couldn't find an ashtray and put the matches back in their pockets.

The chief inspector got up and took a look out the window which offered a prospect of the whole length of one street with the river in the background largely covered by a lot of haze into which the sun was settling in a kind of smoky sunset. "Why wouldn't he throw himself out of the window?'' remarked the chief inspector in a general way, not hoping for an answer. Then he went into the hall where he saw a big old-fashioned clock and he called out to her "Susan?'' and he was going to add something else but he noticed that the clock was stopped at eight o'clock or perhaps a minute after.

"I couldn't find any Coke," she said meeting him in the hall and handing him a quart of ginger ale, "And I couldn't find a can opener either. Maybe you could do something about it."

He took the bottle and went into the main room and handed it to one of the cops who opened the bottle and found some glasses on a table and so forth. Nobody said anything for a little while. Susan posted herself where the chief inspector had been overlooking the street, the cops resumed their seats and the chief inspector kept looking at the clock.

"It couldn't have been eight o'clock."

"He would have jumped out the window," they said simultaneously and then they said, "What?" and then the chief inspector said, "What did you say?"

"I was just thinking about it," she said, "I mean I don't think people really shoot themselves . . . "

"Oh they do."

"I guess so, but I mean I don't think he would have done that," she said.

"That's what I thought," he said.

"You did?" There was a note of uncontrol in her voice.

"It occurred to me, but I don't know. . . . "

"What were you going to say before?"

"Oh, nothing, I was just making conversation. What did you do, did you stop the clock?" he said looking at her so as to get her to turn around and show her face.

"No. That would have been beautiful, wouldn't it? No. There's something the matter with the clock, I mean, it keeps time and all, it chimes on time, but the hands don't move except once in a while they start going and but they only go for fifteen minutes or so. There's a part missing or it's broken or something, it's a very old clock so of course it's hard to fix and uh well, you know, oh, but it was always set at eight, I don't know why, but if he noticed that it had moved he would always set it back to about eight. I always tell him to put it at twelve or quarter after three and sometimes he did but usually he put it back to eight. . . . "

"But it was really eleven when you. . . . "

"Oh, hell, I mean, oh," she said turning around to his face.

"Wow. I actually read the time! I probably still thought it was eight when you came in. I mean when you came in I probably would have said it was still eight. That's really what it's like, as if the time stopped. Well, but I did count eight strokes but of course I was probably just counting the last eight strokes, or, I don't know. Does it matter?"

"I don't think so."

"But you do think he was killed."

The chief inspector made no response but sat down at the table with his ginger ale and began looking idly through copies of various magazines that were on the table, some popular magazines, some trade journals and some unknown little magazines. *"And then I woke up!"* she said.

"Did you think you had killed me?" I said.

"I don't know. Wasn't that funny about the clock?"

"I thought it was funny about Fred, I mean I don't know if the clock means anything, or I can't figure it out, but, oh nevermind."

"No, what?" she said, sitting up. "Ugh. Let's turn on some lights. Is anybody coming over now or what? Oh, what time is it anyway?"

"A little after eight," I said with a laugh.

"Uhhh," she said with a shudder and she got up and turned on some lights.

"No, I don't think so," I said.

"You don't think what?"

"I don't think anyone's coming over or anything. I told somebody I might stop in at the theatre but I don't think I will."

"Ugh, oh dear," she said.

"What?"

"I was just thinking about that damn dream. Oh, let's get out of here."

"Go to a movie?" We laughed. "Who played the chief inspector?" I said

"Oh, I forgot, that was really strange. It was somebody I knew I think it was Eric."

"Who?"

"Oh, Eric what's his name, you know, from Cambridge, we met

him, you remember at a party. . . . "

"What a chief inspector! What's he doing, movies or something, why doesn't he ever come around? I like him or, when we met him he seemed . . . "

"He was in love with me and after he met you he told me he was scared of you."

"Oh, dear," I said, "But he'd make a good assassin too, wouldn't he, maybe he killed me."

"I don't think so," she said and then she got up and closed the clock, which, as a matter of fact works perfectly except it doesn't chime at all because I don't wind the chime because I don't like to hear it, it's set to chime every fifteen minutes, and then she said, "Don't joke about it."

"I don't think I would ever kill myself, and I can hardly imagine being murdered, I mean I can imagine murders but I don't think of them as having anything to do with me," I remarked as seriously as possible.

"I can't seem to shake it," she said. "When you were talking just now I almost caught myself thinking that the dream meant that you would be murdered."

"I don't think it does. I think it means that you're bored."

"I told you not to joke about it," she said.

"I wasn't either."

"All right. I'm bored."

"What's next?" I prompted her.

"Then what," she said, seeming to be very bored.

"Then you kill me and run off with the chief inspector . . . "

"Will you stop that?" she shouted.

"Stop shouting." I said.

"I wasn't shouting," she shouted and we lapsed into a silence that eventually put us to sleep.

This is like a movie within a movie. I mean this could be an entire film, you know? It's almost wasted but I love it! —G.G.

Now I just looked ahead at the Club part, and I don't see why it's here, but it's your book, not mine. —G.G.

⟦ Gilbert Green & The Club ⟧

The Club was a mess. The whole upstairs was being re-done. Some
people were doing it, people who you sometimes saw around in
those days, kids who didn't know what to do, and they were
sanding the floor with sanders which made a lot of noise and a
great deal of dust. The walls were all covered with plastic and the
furniture was all pushed into one area sort of haphazzardly but
people were still using it, sort of friends of people who were using
the Club for lack of anything else to do, which is what the Club
was for to begin with, or at least at that time that's what it was for.
You never knew for certain who you would find there, but on the
other hand you were never very surprised. Fred had a joke that it
was the overflow from our place, the sort of outlying hangers-on,
but that wasn't it at all, we often came over ourselves especially
after Mickey put in his restaurant on the ground floor, because it
wasn't a bad place to eat and you were pretty certain not to be
bothered by assholes. The idea was you might get anything you
wanted but nothing was guaranteed. At certain periods, speaking
of the second floor, there was more of a gloss of pool-playing bike
boys although everyone else was there more or less at the same
time, then the fashion would change a little bit and one would
meet lots of artists who had found their way there, at other times
such as right now there would be a lot of really young people who
had been driven out of their homes by the disgusting manners of
their parents but were still too young really to know what was
going on, they were just looking around. Sometimes there would
be these pretty young people around, and they would develop into
something, they would form around somebody and work together

and do something. At the time of this story, that was what was going on.

Quite frequently the Club had to be redecorated. The taste of the people who hung around there had changed, and maybe there was a little more money for one reason or another. At times the Club was very popular, and at other times it sort of sagged. But it really had a history. It had started out late in the nineteenth century as a political club for one of the parties, and they would have meetings there and discuss the candidates and what they wanted to put people up to. The only reason we know this is that one day some real old guy came in and looked around, and he was kind of an interesting looking old guy, very wooly with a big mustache, so we just said hello and so forth, you know, they didn't ask him who he was or anything, and he started talking to somebody all about the old days. He wasn't drunk. People gathered around because something was really happening. He said he heard about the Club somehow and he was amazed to find out that the place still existed. He told us how it had been in the old days with pictures of politicians and a pool table and a little library of different kinds of books mostly about society and things like that but some pornography too, or what they thought of as pornography, probably romantic novels about the dreams of ladies and gentlemen. This was before the First World War, he said, and of course it was a men's club then. But a couple of times a year the women of the men would bring a lot of food and they would have a feast, sitting all around on the floor and they invited some poor people from the neighborhood. Then he said during the war, which was really only a matter of months, the Club turned into a ladies' club because they used it to give their speeches about voting and liquor and they also made their uniforms and bandages and what not for the boys in Europe. He said he didn't know too much about it in the twenties, but that in '27 or '28 he had been passing it by chance, no longer ever finding himself in the neighborhood, and it occurred to him to go and take a look to see if anything was going on, so he walked in and he found that the place was all fixed up, new lights and paint and furniture and they were giving out temperance literature. So one of the ladies asked him if he was interested in temperance, and he said he certainly was not, at which she smiled, which struck him as very peculiar, and he started telling her about the old days at the place, and people gathered around, and pretty soon he noticed that people were going upstairs, so he asked about it and was taken upstairs and given a couple of drinks of real Canadian whiskey. He said he came back once in a while and even for a short time in 1929 he frequented the place because as he put it he had developed a liaison with one of the ladies of the place.

At that point, everybody was really charmed with the old guy, and people lit up a couple of joints and he had some with us, and everybody really felt fine, because it was so peculiar because we didn't have any idea up to that point that there was such a thing as a history that would actually concern us, we just thought, you know, a lot of different things happened at different times. He told us that in the early thirties he had come by again, he wasn't living in town anymore, and the place was all shut down, but he banged on the door and somebody came but they wouldn't let him in or say anything. He said he had a feeling it was some sort of Russian thing. After that he didn't seem to be too interested in the place anymore, once in a while someone would ask him, you know, if he knew any more or try to get him to tell more about the old times he remembered, but all he could talk about was the Second World War, in which he had gotten to be sort of an admiral, kind of a temporary appointment because of the war, anyway he was all over the Pacific Ocean and he saw a lot of strange people and he really liked it a lot but only a few were interested in the war so they stayed and joked with him about it but most of us sort of wandered away and said goodnight. We heard that he came by a couple of other times, one time when some artists were having a huge party upstairs and he came in and some people recognized him from before so they made the band make a huge noise and brought him up and made everybody applaud and cheer, it was sort of a put-on because hardly anybody knew what it was all about, but it was nice for the old guy I guess. Then another time he came and he looked terrible and he didn't talk much and we thought of him once in awhile after that and guessed he died. But the thing is that people began to get the idea that there was more to the Club because it really had a sort of history, although it wasn't written down.

We never did find out what had happened here in the thirties, but we found about 500 pictures of Lenin up underneath one of the ceilings, so the old guy was probably right about that. They were terrible pictures and mice had eaten some of them, but we put one of them up somewhere and one of the kids made a plastic collage of them that was around for awhile but it disappeared, maybe the kid took it back or it got destroyed or something. But it wasn't too long ago when there were mostly artists around, they were sort of the center of the thing, and the place was kind of a shrine for them and they drank a lot and had meetings upstairs which wasn't decorated at all, it was all coming apart, I just saw it once, they had these real serious discussions and there was a whole scene but they mostly just had drunken arguments from what I could tell. They called it The Group or The Movement or something like that. I knew one of the younger guys, he didn't like it very much, he said it was too serious, and of course I was really young at the time and I didn't know a thing, but I went along with him once, and a funny thing happened, some older guy was giving a speech and he was talking about painting with balls, and every time he mentioned it we would have a little giggle, and when we went home, we had this idea to do painting with balls, we got into ballpoint pens and everything, it was very silly, but after that the guy I knew did do some paintings with two round balls attached to them that were called "Painting with Two Balls" and it was funny, but on the whole the scene then was quite a drag.

But even though the artists were breaking up at the time about ten years ago, that was when the Club as we know it today was really beginning to get underway. I was working as an office boy at The New York Times Magazine and I was miserable but I was writing a lot and I had plenty of time to do my writing in because I practically only knew one other person and he was married so I didn't even see too much of him. I mention the Times because that's where I first heard about the Beatles. We had an ambitious correspondent in England who was always sending us the latest stuff, and one day I began to hear about this short about beetles. I thought the magazine was terrible, but I didn't think they would have an article about insects just to fill it up. Then I saw the layout, and then I knew what it was, apparently a group that had got together and sang a lot of dirty songs, they said they could never record them. I looked at the picture of the Beatles that was in the Times Magazine for a long time and I thought that something was happening. Within a few months, of course, they were all over the place, but I remembered where and when I first heard of what was going on.

It was a girls' club from the beginning, I mean it was really a Beatles' fan club, but even then there was a vague idea that it had been something else because how the girls got ahold of it was through the artists, some of whom had very young chicks, and they already had their parties at the Club, sometimes they still do, so it started out that way. But more and more the girls would come around even if nothing was going on and put up pictures all over the walls, and one afternoon somebody brought me down there when I was out on strike. I knew about the place but I didn't know what was going on. She just called it the Club and I didn't know I had been there before until I got there but the place was entirely different. It was all decorated up, although they just used pictures and old rugs and chairs, and there wasn't any drinking much but sometimes they would give you a little Coke or something out of the refrigerator, I mean it was very primitive, but it was nice in there. The lights made pools of yellow light and the corners and the ceiling were very dark and most of the old carpets on the floor were red, and all these pretty pictures of "the boys" and usually several chicks and whoever they brought. The one thing they did have was a great juke box that cost nothing to play you just pushed the buttons. They had the pool table, it was in terrible shape, but once in a while some of the guys would screw around with it, one time I remember I got so mad about something that I broke one of the cues over the edge of the table and after that for a long time there were no cues around at all and the girls used it to stack up their magazines of which they had a really great collection, there was always plenty to read. If they had ever seen you before they would always let you in and let you do anything you wanted to as long as you didn't offend anyone, and even if you did offend anyone you would be given another chance. I was there a lot, I had time on my hands, and I was really interested in chicks at the time and there was quite a selection of them but they were all in love with the Beatles. It was a strange situation, but it was very clever too. What it was was that the chicks were all usually very ambitious and the guys were all so young that they weren't permitted to do anything much and we didn't exactly know what we wanted, but they did, so they ran the scene. Of course we became more and more like the Beatles, which they dug, and we didn't have to get married which before was the trouble with screwing around with chicks because they only wanted to get married. This way both sides had it made. It couldn't last but it was good while it did.

The first time that the Beatles came to New York, we were all ready for them. The girls had infiltrated Capitol Records very thoroughly and somebody had even talked to Brian Epstein when he came over to arrange the concert. They got a lot of money from somewhere, probably their fathers, and they fixed up the Club some more and had some of us build them a hi-fi discotheque machine that couldn't be beat, two turntables, a tape deck and fifty watts of power from four different speakers. They got it around that the Club was the most *in* place in New York which I guess it was in a way except that there weren't any stars around in those days it was sort of an amorphous group of ambitious little girls and their so-called men, it was our gang. By the time the Beatles arrived we were having trouble keeping strangers out of the Club because the girls had done too good a job. People would hear about it and they thought it was a nightclub. It almost was but they still didn't charge anything; if any rich people came in they asked for donations and gave them a Coke and they usually didn't come back but they did give some money, so it was changing quite a bit already.

The night the Beatles came to our club I didn't go to see them. I just went home alone. I thought I was going to go, actually I was very excited about it, but at the last minute I decided that I was just going to go home. I was told all about it, however, for two weeks after it happened. I'm sorry now I didn't go. There might be more to say here if I had. But I doubt I missed much. Since then I have seen so many stars of different kinds and the ruckus that surrounds them that I know how it is, and it isn't too bad, but it is a big crowd of people you don't know all over a small group of people who like the crowd but who are trying to behave as if they are people which they really aren't, they are objects, but they are objects that do things, they are automated to entertain the crowd, and it's saddening. Later on, of course, there were so many, many pop stars that they didn't get the type of adulation that the Beatles got at first and of course too the Beatles themselves changed their style and never went around together much after they got married so of course if you only had George Harrison around, who I met at the Club a couple of years ago, there wasn't all that kind of crap because they put it down themselves in the movie. But the point about the Beatles and the Club is that when the girls saw A) that they could get the Beatles to come to their club and B) that they probably wouldn't be in love with one of the Beatles who all had their own chicks and things like that, then they got kind of straightened out. At the same time they realized their power and they got a slight chill from seeing that their ambitions weren't unlimited after all, they didn't really think the Beatles were as great in person as they had thought that they would be.

Fred calls the Club "the brothel" which he pronounces like brother. This is a great dream, and even if it isn't entirely a reality, and there are so many different aspects to the Club that it never gets to be very clearly defined and different people use it for different purposes, it is something which nevertheless is a legend in its own time, it makes up for what we missed in other parts of life, it is a fantasy that is also true, it fills out the space of dreams with lifelike anecdotes and a history of usage and abuse, and fulfills the function here that its existence at the moment is a few words of homage to my beloved Susan who built the Club herself.

⟦ Gilbert Green—Crit ⟧

PROBLEMS WITH THE NOVEL.

It is too unrealistic, i.e. there are no bad guys.
It is too vague, i.e. you can't always tell what's going on.
It is too clever, i.e. half the time you find out it was a dream.
It is confusing to follow.
There are no characters.
The real people who are mentioned will sue us.
It does not denounce middle class society.
It does not tell people how the business really works.
It does not tell people what it is like to be a poet.
It makes no distinction between hetero- & homosexuality.
The early chapters are too short & do not lead to what follows.
It does not help people to deal with the problems of daily life.
It is too abstract, i.e. it is pretentious and arty.
It cannot be made into a film because the story is not succinct.
The writing is too much like common speech.
It is trivial, i.e. it does not deal with great people or questions.
There is too little dialogue.
It does not disguise the fact that it is composed of fantasy.

It's hard to tell that most of this side is from my point of view, not yours.
Are some of these things true? It certainly could be filmed and I doubt
that the real people will sue.—G.G.

⟦ Gilbert Green's Song ⟧

The real and only real right way, like a cloth or counter pane,
I make a fight to win the day, with words serving life
  or double blame,
Fortunately no more to say, than morning proceeds,
  evening succeeds same,
Easily the flowers in May (no more to say) will come
  to welcome rain.
She brought me the thought of a double sensation,
  It broke in a stream that became adulation,
    I used up the joke like a decoration;
      And, finally winning, I spoke to the nation: Friends, said I,
    When I was a young man less than twenty-five
    It gave me great pleasure to know I was alive
    My ideas raced like a certain kind of horse
    Until I found out that my life then was worse
    Than a sentence in jail or a tour in a war
    So I got married young to make it better far
    I retired from society and put myself to graze
    Along time of my morning and my nighttime haze
    Making up a dream of life that was and what might be
    I thought a lot and as I thought I would I'd see
    Visions of the finest hair and wine and no mistakes
    That showed me to myself as being great.
    When I was a young man less than twenty-five
    It gave me great pleasure to know I was alive.
The real and only real right way is what I do and what I say and
what you do and what you know and how you look and how you

go and what I see you do and say and wear, so pretty is your hair, and better still the clouds ring out free fruit and love, the real and only real right way will content yourself at every moment, making sure that you have made it, singing to yourself and me that this is it and this is as I am the way I like it, now and then, the forty windows looking out on boats and fish and ice and ordinary things, to look, for example, at any fearful thing and notice smiling in its eye and forget to fear the thing you see, which is called acceptation: All this and more—I count the lines on finger nails accustomed to disgusting habits that I do not feel the force of much disgust that my habit has accepted me and others will the same—think not what you should do but only what you would and you can and the real right way to dress is right for you and for none other, it suits the dress, the suite, that becomes the you I know or not depending on a lot of chances, it need not be expensive and even not long-lasting nor too washable, and why do you make mistakes? Because you are wrong, because you are too long in certain measurements, because the colors of the year are not those of the apple of your eye, because of shoes and on account of coats already sold, because of being in the wrong places at the wrong times of day, because of chills that alternate with fevers that alterate your head? Nonsense! You never make mistakes which are impossible to make, you only break the lines between the you that would be you and the you that is the you you are, you cannot even choose the wrong perfume though I shan't like you if you do, but someone may or no one might, and if so that's the way you are tonight. Could it be my hair? It was and will be and forever should, a certain line that can't be fixed in many ways, a drop of length split into many parts, a transformation that belies the lie I make, but wait, and take a look and shave your face according to your face, or let it grow to points that it would indicate by roughness or a curl, or hollows here and dimples there, even begrimed it may look lovely, you are your own pornography, be it brushed or loose or sinecured and sutured up, the hair of men and women is their most expressive feature. All fashions are alluring, every dress can suit some one, the pretty pants that he wears now may not look so good on her, the life of the mind expressed in dress, "Oh Roy! you are so beautiful," and it befits her that the least something may be wrong with that hat or with her nose or with her toes, that are *too long*, but then that's that, a very pretty picture song I sing from the ins and outs of courts and things right into the fabric of daily life where it must blossom if it will, a very devil of a load of platitudes and fancy cakes that are no longer dressed to kill. The real right way to dress for spring is in a flower of your friendship for yourself and I shall take a favor from the weather too, it is so fair and fresh and free, and do as I would do on me.

〚 Fred's Story 〛

Gilbert Green was already dead by the time I began writing this story, some of which was actually written by him in fragments we thought he intended as a novel about his wife, though nobody remembers ever hearing him speak of such a thing. But there are a lot of signs in the stuff that point in that direction. Maybe he just sometimes wrote things down with no special intention. Barry got it very well in the song the way it goes, *Every day I go away and get ideas. . . . Couldn't I write a song about a man who's dead?* So Gilbert Green doesn't exist, of course, but the story of him does. And we take his point of view, because that's what he always wanted us to do. He said, "Now that I have made this name for us, why can't anybody use it, why can't you, Fred?" We explained it over and over to him, but he always came back to the same point, that he wanted everyone to use his name, but he meant, really, to be him, and take over, if only for a minute, and do things. Once in awhile some of us did do things in his name but it was always himself who had to come in and take over and re-do them. He was the man who could do things, even if the only thing he ever did was to make his name work wonders. Gerry always liked to pretend to be him, and even now there may be a few people who if they saw Gerry would think that they had seen a ghost, but Gilbert Green didn't actually like the fact that Gerry liked to play G.G., and I suppose that's what their quarrel was all about. But he went on insisting that he wanted everyone who would to share his name and enjoy, as much as he did, the great way that name worked. He never understood why that couldn't be.

In a way, Gilbert Green was still a child when he died. He had no children and he didn't seem to want any, although he liked children well enough, I mean little children, he always looked at them a great deal when he saw them and he once said something about how sad it was that you couldn't really talk to them, they would always just play a game with you. Susan didn't like children, but he did, although he didn't live with them. But he seemed to understand children and he talked to them directly, he never played games with them and he always told them what he thought of what they were doing or anything that came to him to say when he was interested in them. He never told them lies or played silly games with them, he talked to them in a plain way, I doubt if he ever considered whether they would understand what he was saying or not, he just went ahead with it, whatever he was thinking about at the time and talked with them about it straight. They usually liked this, but they didn't express their enjoyment of him by jumping around and smiling when they saw him they just said hello or something. I thought that if they could have said so they would have said that he was like a strange child, who wouldn't play the games that children condemn themselves to play.

Like children, Gilbert Green never stopped looking around him at everything and everyone, not looking for something in particular, the way people always do, but he kept an eye out all the time and he was always interested in what there was to see, and often it was a very little thing, the way somebody looked at him, the way paving stones were arranged in different places, a certain light, or a tone of voice. He was especially good at remembering people's voices and one of the ways that he would use to flatter people a little, which really wasn't flattery on his part, was when they would call up he would remember their voices and mention their name before they did. Sometimes this didn't entirely work, for example, one time shortly after I met him I called him up and he thought it was Andy, but of course I was a little flattered by that mistake anyway. There was a sense in which his ear was his best sense. It was true that he had a great ability to notice and distinguish between sounds. Sometimes he would stop and say what's that, and cock his ear, and half the time the other people couldn't hear a thing, and he was never satisfied until he figured out what the sound exactly was and where it came from, which he was usually able to do right away. He was also good at imitating other people's ways of speaking but he didn't use this for entertainment, the way some people do, he very rarely did that, but he was very sensitive to all kinds of different accents and he mainly used his ability to imitate them when he wanted to ingratiate people without their being particularly aware of it. He had two or three different English accents and a New England one, a Southern one, and a couple of New York ones, and some very flat American tones, and he could actually read aloud in German although he didn't speak it, and he could speak French quite well but he didn't understand much of it. Anyway when he wanted to get people to do things, he would subtly color his own voice with a trace of their accent, he didn't just imitate them outright, although once I did see him screw up an Englishman that way, but usually he just made them feel more at home, so to speak, by himself sounding more like them.

Maybe it's odd to think of speech in the same way as hearing but that's one of the things he taught me; it was like his lesson that reading and writing were the same thing too, "In a way," he would add, with a smile. Of course sometimes people would challenge these things he said, his messages. They would be belligerent for some reason or, sometimes they were just assholes who he somehow got to talk to. Whenever he was challenged he said something, he usually repeated what he had said maybe in a slightly different form, but if people pestered him he would completely dismiss them with a glance that was like an animal's, not that it was fierce, it was just blank, or you had a feeling that although he was still there, he was absolutely somewhere else. Sometimes he had been having quite a good time talking with some people at his house or somewhere else and then one of them would annoy him in some way and he would simply leave. He was rarely rude, but he would turn with a remark to someone and go out the door leaving everybody wondering what ever had happened to him so suddenly. This was a good technique since it deprived him of the company of all the people he didn't want to see. It also gave him occasional unexpected moments to walk around and do something he had not intended to be doing at the time, which was one of the things he loved to do. Even when he was incredibly famous he would sometimes just show up alone and sit and talk at my house. He did it with other people too, some of whom were quite surprised at first because they would have thought that he wouldn't even remember their name, but there he would be on their doorstep starting a conversation.

One thing he couldn't bear was what he called alcoholics, by which he meant sloppy drunks, people who slurred their speech or didn't walk right or said things they would be sorry for when they drank. He got drunk from time to time himself, but only people who knew him very well or, strangely enough, people who didn't like him, could tell that he was drunk. Anyone could tell that he was hung over the next day and actually I think what he liked best about drinking was his hangover, not his high. In a good hangover, which meant usually that he had had only Scotch whiskey the night before, he was very whimsical and he would do funny things and things would appear entirely different to him and he got some good ideas that way. Those were the days when he would do things that were not expected. Maybe a contract he hadn't signed for a week would get torn up or he would think of a completely different backing for one of the songs or it would come to him exactly how some furniture should be arranged that he had never liked before. And although drinking made him impotent, his hangover often produced the conditions he called "a real good orgy" and sometimes, if it looked like that's what it was going to turn into, we just locked the door and turned off the phones and to hell with strangers for that day. Sometimes it never developed into anything much, but at other times everyone he saw that day would become indicative for him of an insatiable lust that expired only at the end of the day, unless he had been drinking gin the night before, when usually he disappeared into nobody knew quite what abyss of licence for the next day and night.

People have said that as a young man he was practically sexless, I think they meant when he was in high school, because I once met a cousin of his, a woman, who somehow or other decided she wanted to talk to me about Gilbert Green's sex life as a child and she said that there had been some episodes when they were both about seven after which she said she later thought of herself as having lost her virginity at the time although she added she actually hadn't, but she said that both she and her brother had gotten quite an education from him. It's fairly well documented that in high school he only had dates on the most ceremonial occasions although he had a number of friends who usually speculated that he was still sexually inexperienced until after they no longer knew him very well. From his writings and occasional remarks, he indicated that he rarely met any desirable women. Also I think that maybe he was in the habit as a teenager of falling in love with rather older women of thirty-five or so, friends of his parents, he used to mention some of them, and he used to go and talk to them until they threw him out, for hours and hours about everything and anything. He probably didn't have it in mind to actually fuck them or have an affair but he mentioned to me once a few years ago that he was so disappointed in women of thirty-five who were then a little younger than he was because he had been looking forward to that situation for a long time and when it came about he found he didn't like women of thirty five any more than anybody else. In other words, I think he was chronically dissatisfied, and if we can believe what people who study these things say, that was one of the sources of his genius.

But again, like a child, he never quite stopped looking for the source of satisfaction which I suppose he always thought was right around the corner. He liked sexual pleasure a great deal although he was never completely satisfied with it in any form. He had a great message on this, which he only started saying after he was about forty, which was "exercise your prick." He said he had had some kind of an orgasm practically every day since he had been ten and while most of his contemporaries were complaining of their impotence he said they really liked it because they evidently hadn't exercised their pricks before they found that they didn't want to do it any more. I don't know if I quite took his advice, but under his influence I became sort of more profligate or whatever the word might be, I mean I took it where I found it and I lost no opportunities, and I sort of felt more alive being sexual than I had before, and I still do. What I want to try and say is that there is something to the way in which they say that sex destroys creativity, but I mean if it does then that's fine, you get your satisfaction one way or the other, and the greatest souls, in my experience, can be completely profligate and still not lose a single poem because no sexual experience could ever satisfy their craving.

One time we were talking, or, he was talking about various friends of his whom he knew as a young man, I suppose one of them had come to visit or something, and he would always receive them pleasantly but he would actually be suffering the whole time because he thought they had become so dull, it was practically unbearable to him in terms of what he remembered them as being. Anyway this time he wanted me to assure him that it wasn't him that had changed so drastically, and I didn't know but I said I thought so, and he went on with it awhile and then it occurred to him that when these old friends straightened out their frustrations, when they said what they wanted, they like died, usually in their late twenties, he said, but sometimes later, and then they didn't notice things and didn't laugh at funny things but only at things that were supposed to be. That was one of the ways he liked to judge people, by what they laughed at and at what they didn't. He didn't insist that everyone think funny what he thought funny, but he could tell a lot about a person by when and how they laughed. He himself had more of a wry smile which told you that he really liked a joke, he rarely laughed out loud but when he did the thing was really funny and his laughter was very infectious and everybody would be laughing with him. Even when he was much older than they were he always kept young people with him and they always liked his way of doing things and I would say as well that we kept him young.

⟦ Gilbert Green ⟧

Did I make a clear mistake? Did I take a fine advantage that was not mine to have? Did I live in such a way as would offend her sense of time? Had I dined too early or too late one night? Could I fight on and never win? Was there a sin that my awareness of it had discounted? It all amounted, figured up, to a fine essay in crime. I don't know how to make head nor tail of this and that is something that a Master never can admit to friends for that is just what they admire in him. I confess it only to myself in place of them, a substitute that may define at least the walls between my speeches, and entertain a while away.

" . . . and the beautiful Mrs. Green . . . " It was a fragment that impressed me at the time and kept on going through my head, I even thought of making a song around it but I never got around to that. We had met some famous old literary coot at a party and he was *fascinated* with us, which always amuses me, but not long afterwards the guy who gave the party showed me the manuscript of the old fellow's memoirs on the last page of which he mentioned his encounter with us, trying with his last breath, as it happened, to put down Andy Warhol whose film I had highly praised to him. " . . . and the beautiful Mrs. Green . . . "* I had never seen it that way before. Nobody is called *the beautiful* any more, and to see it like that gave me a pause and a thought. *I thought I was becoming historical.* I suppose it led to all these notes in a way because I was sure that if I didn't tell what I knew of the matter then there would

* In fact, you know, this was said by John Ashbery at Tom Hess's house in Beekman Place the first time we went there for dinner. —G.G.

be no other authority though it occurred to me that Fred would do his best. So one day I just began writing up what I knew and by now I am getting into what I don't know, which is interesting, but I don't think it has much to do with history. How could anybody, outside of a small circle of friends, be interested in a list of the information that I lack? Or the institutions concerning which I am unable to close the synaptic gap? Or the feelings that I don't remember taking place within me at the certain times to which they would have been appropriate? It is all the sheerest gas like ether. It is oriented to sleep and it produces dreams whose characters are instantly forgotten, like in obscure periods of one's life, one can't remember what one did from day to day. Once in awhile there is a song I wrote that tells me what I did that day or a letter I come across that reminds me of something that I thought. When I think of the one that goes *Did I make a clear mistake* . . . etc., I remember how I felt one day but I really don't know what it was about. However, I do remember one thing.

I was taking people to see Charles Ludlam's plays almost every weekend (they only played them on the weekend) and I guess it was kind of a test to see what my friends would say in such a circumstance. I found that most people were very affected by it but what they said was that they didn't like it. This irritated me. They showed that they didn't like to be aroused. They behaved the same after the theatre as they had before it. I have never understood the way people can come out of a great film and go ahead and tell their usual bad jokes or make a stupid remark. An experience like that always turns me in on myself and I prefer to be alone, but if I am not alone, I certainly don't want to talk. For a certain time I become the actor that I saw. Nervousness is disgusting, and I am liable to be nervous, so I really know what I mean. Many of my friends would be very unhappy with me if they knew that I am liable to be nervous because one of the things that they admire about me is that I never express that kind of noise. When I am uncomfortable I become quiet, or sometimes I leave the place I'm in, but I don't begin to jabber the way most people do. Occasionally I insult people when I feel uncomfortable, which is all right because it changes the situation right away without my having to leave the party, but sometimes I insult people I don't wish to hurt, which is a mistake and I have to watch out for it. In an old book I once saw they said, Somebody was the kind of person who would sooner lose a friend than forgo a jest. I have lost some friends that way myself and I know what they meant.

The people I despise are those concerning whom there is no secret and no surprise. When I know someone inside and out, which occasionally can happen ten minutes after I meet them for the third time, I just lose interest in them. Once in awhile it is amazing, even to me, to see the way aversion can develop. Usually it happens suddenly, taking a single remark as a pretext. One time I was writing away like I am today and some guy came in and bothered me about it, he asked me if it was going to be a real novel. I knew him for years but as soon as he made that remark I threw him out of the house on a pile of insults. I realized that I had never liked him, which is to say that I knew all there was to know about him. It can happen very quickly after I meet someone, particularly the type who wants to pick a fight all the time. They can start picking a fight with me, and I will say what I think and if they persist I will tell them politely that I don't like to just argue. If they keep it up they will never see me again.

I don't know if I ever found out all there was to know about "the beautiful Mrs. Green." That literary fragment, among other things I noticed people saying at the time, led me to believe that I had no idea what other people thought of her, which after all is a large part of what people are made of.

⟦ Susan's Turn ⟧

I don't know if you don't like me anymore or what, she wrote him in the only letter that she ever wrote to him, but I thought of trying to write you a letter and see if that makes any difference. I guess I don't understand things very well. I never seem to know why anybody does what they do. I don't understand why you do what you do and I have been with you for three years. I don't understand why I do what I do, even. The other afternoon I caught myself being jealous of Fred and I thought there really must be something wrong with me. Of course my mother doesn't understand a thing anymore, and I think that was her idea. She made some remarks the other day when I went to see her, and though she didn't say so, she gave me that idea. I got mad and walked out on her, but later then I thought of it myself, sort of, and then I got mad at myself, and here we are, involved in correspondence.

I think if I told you all this you would probably smile a little and not really listen so I thought I would write it to you. I know you're very busy with the movies and everything, but maybe if you get a letter from me right in the middle of it all, the thing will make some sense. I always try to do the best I can for you. I'm sorry that I'm not a man. They always talk so well and you enjoy their talk so much . . . I wish I understood things better, but I don't. When we had the Club things were so different than they are now, it was really wonderful then and I think you liked it too, you must have or you wouldn't have stayed with me. And I really had something to do even if I didn't have much money. I was trying to find a man and I did better than I thought I ever would. That's why it was so good. Things used to happen very quickly—now it seems they take so long to change.

I guess we're older. May God preserve me from being like my mother! But more and more I find myself saying the things she says and practically thinking the way she does. It makes me so mad! I don't think I'm making very much sense, but I'm trying to sort things out.

Neither of us is the same as four years ago, that's obvious. For one thing, I don't have anything to do except be your wife sometimes, but Fred does a lot of what I might do if he wasn't there. I want to make it very clear that I don't think it's right to be jealous of Fred, and I really like him very much, but all the same he tends to take care of things for you. I don't know if you want me around or not, but I'm pretty sure you don't need me, at least you don't seem to. I like to buy things we don't need, but it isn't a way of life, it isn't work. Every once in awhile I meet somebody at a party or somewhere and I think I'll go off with him but of course I never do and I guess I don't want to or else I would. I'm not making a threat, I'm just trying to tell you what I'm thinking. It isn't easy. Don't fly back right now or do anything unusual except just try to read this letter and think about it.

You're always saying that I'm bored. It's true I've read eight mystery stories since you've been gone. I don't even remember offhand what they were about. George and Ruth took me out to dinner and we had a good time but I missed you very much. People were saying such stupid things and I had nobody to say that to because everybody was being stupid. I can't tell people that they're stupid and get away with it, at least I don't think I can. Viva was there and she seemed to be twice as bored as I was but she really wasn't bored at all, or I mean she doesn't mind being bored, she likes it or something. She's in George's new play so of course she isn't really bored because she has a lot of work. I could never be an actress.

I just thought that people who are satisfied with their lives or who are really excited or something are just good actors, I mean they convince themselves that this is all worth it or it makes it or something. It's the same thing if you feel depressed you can go and put on a beautiful dress or something and the fact that you know you *look great* changes the scene. Of course there have to be people to look at you but that can always be arranged. I'm not very expressive.

I did a strange thing that night. I wasn't saying anything, as usual. We were downstairs at the Club and we were standing in the middle of the room and everybody was talking in French because there was somebody there from France and he couldn't speak English too well, anyhow I was listening to them. After awhile I sort of lost interest and I was looking around and I noticed somebody at the bar and he was staring at us and pretty soon he started taunting people for speaking in French and for living in New York, he must have been brought there by somebody who later got fed up with him and left. He noticed that I noticed him and he came nearer and started shouting all kinds of insults at us. We didn't pay him any attention, and pretty soon he came up closer and called us a bunch of fucking frogs. I went over and hit him. He was really amazed and shut up completely. I was amazed myself. Then I turned around back to the group, and Tom Hess came over and kissed me on the cheek. Pretty soon we left and went home. I felt like I had been hit. It was really something.

I feel a lot better writing this all down, but I don't think I am saying what I mean. I'm very proud of you and I'm mad at myself, but that isn't what I wanted to say either.

I don't mean you should get rid of Fred, but there has to be some change of some kind. Maybe you should get rid of me instead. I have thought of leaving you just to see what it's like, but I decided not to because I love you very much. But if you want me to go you ought to say so and get it over with. Do something for Christ's sake, do something! I can go on this way for a long time, but something has to happen, sort of like the way I hit that guy. You will probably do something unexpected. I don't mean you ought to do one thing rather than another, I don't know what you ought to do. I thought of leaving on a trip or something, go to Florida with Mary and the kids next month, but I don't think you'd even notice that I'd left. You'd be glad to see me when I came back and that would be that. I'm going to stick but I want to tell you what I think.

Things have changed so much! When we ran the Club, you didn't have to do anything, it was all on our side. I liked what you did a lot. But you didn't have to do it. All this doesn't make one bit of sense. Maybe I'll throw it away. It does make me feel better. Mary just called and I'm going over there. Well, we had a nice time, but I didn't tell her anything. I read this all over and I'm going to send it to you just so that you know where I stand. Don't think I'm trying to tell you what to do because I'm not. I'm trying to get your attention—it used to be so easy and now I don't even know if this will do it. I am very sad tonight but I feel like sleeping now. Video called today and I told them what to do with the other five reels. I love you.

This is too near to the bone. Do we need this? Authenticity and verisimilitude are not exactly the same! I can't tell what effect this letter would have on the readers. Would it frighten them? I ask because it scared me, then and now. —G.G.

⟦ Gilbert Green & Susan Talking ⟧

"What does that mean?" she asked.

"I don't know," he replied, "probably something about trees."

"I mean what does combustible mean? Does something have to be able to blow up in order to be combustible or could it be a piece of wood?"

"I don't know. It sounds dangerous, doesn't it. Combustible." He chewed the word and sucked on it a minute. "Combustible."

"It sounds like something that might blow up if you ask me."

"I wasn't. You could look it up."

"You're the word expert."

"I know, but that's Latin. I don't know much Latin. With the ability to bust, no, it couldn't be that."

"Maybe it is," she sighed, "but bust doesn't sound like Latin does it."

"Nope."

"Sometimes if you change a *b* to a *v* you get a better idea," she said, "vust doesn't help either."

"Dust."

"Is there any more wood? The fire is going out."

"Out in the hall," he said, staring down at the dying embers. She said nothing for a while.

"I can still feel it, though," he said.

"I can't," she said, "Are you sure those glasses haven't weakened your eyeballs?"

"Wow, you really don't like them do you."

"No, I really don't."

"I'm not even wearing them."

"Of course you aren't. That's why it's so nice."

"No, it's not, it's because of the fire."

"I guess you're right," she said.

"Why do you do that?" he said.

"What?"

"Stop talking like that."

"I don't know. I don't feel like talking."

"You know what that guy from Video said to me the other day?"

"What?"

"He said I'm always right."

"He's right, you are."

"We're both right, right?"

"All right," she sighed.

"How nice it seems to be always right," he said, reflectively.

"It must be."

"Maybe it would make a good song or . . . " his voice trailed off into his thoughts.

"We really need another piece of wood."

"How nice it seems to be always right," he quoted, "By the flames of reality burning bright."

"The flames of reality?"

"Yeah, the flames of reality, real flames."

"There aren't any flames any more."

"That's a good last line," he said. "Is there any more wine?"

"I don't think so."

"And you wouldn't have to rhyme that one."

"What?"

"The last line, you wouldn't have to rhyme."

"Oh." she said.

"On a damask couch by the light of the moon . . . "

"By the light of the fire."

"But there isn't any fire."

"Right again but there isn't any moon either."

"Laid on the couch by the light of the moon," he said, "Placed right in front of the art of the tune . . . it's too complex, too many syllables."

"How many?" she asked.

"There aren't any flames any more, There aren't any flames any more, There aren't any flames anymore," he sang to a tune of his own invention.

"That's nice."

"Left with its mouth in a strange position . . . "

"Oh dear."

"Their rightness assumed a jaunty air, assum-ed . . . "

"Left with its mouth in a strange position, their rightness?"

"That's good. Yeah. Repeat *left with their mouth* and then . . . With a right hand thrust and a left hand snare."

"What are you talking about?"

"One guess," he said with a smile.

"Oh dear, she said with a laugh," she said with a laugh.

"Oh yes! he cried with a shout," he said. "I don't want to forget it."

"I'll get something to write with."

Nevermind, I've got it. How—nice—it—seems—to—be—always—right, By—the—light—of—the—real—flames—burning—bright, or flames—of—reality . . . "

"Real Flames."

"I don't know. How nice it seems, let's see . . . On a Damascus . . . no . . . Laid—on—damask—by—the—light—of—the moon . . . "

"What's damask?"

"Cloth. . . . by the light of the moon, Placed—at—right—angles—in—front—of—the—tune, refrain three times. O.K. now the bullshit."

> *Placed with its mouth in a strange position*
> *Their rightness assum-ed a jaunty air*
> *Left with their mouths in a strange position*
> *For a right hand thrust and a left hand snare.*

"Let me see," she said.

"O.K., but it doesn't read," he said handing her the paper.

"I think it's sad, she said," she said.

"Cut it out."

"No, I really do," she said.

"Maybe it is. No, I don't think so. The verse is bawdy and the refrain is sad, that's what it is."

"What's bawdy?"

"The verse."

"No. What *is* bawdy?"

"Old-fashion for dirty."

"Is that the whole thing?"

"I don't know. It could be, but it could go on and on, one verse of one kind, the refrain and one verse of the other kind and the refrain."

"Why don't you call the refrain the tag?" she said.

"I like to say refrain."

"I guess it's more romantic."

He said nothing for a while.

"Do you want another fire?" she asked him.

"No, do you?"

"Not particularly."

"I think I will lie down on the floor," he said.

"It's so dark."

"It's not even cold."

"Because of the fire."

"There aren't any flames."

"It might be good."

"You look like wood."

"You have a one-track mind," he said.

"No, that's you."

"How could it be," he said absent-mindedly. "It's so dark I can't even make out the pattern on the ceiling."

"I'm cold."

"I'm not, I'm hot," he said.

He looked up and felt the chilly stubble of her legs which warmed his hands and melted her eyes and removed his glasses and blew through the room like a heating appliance to arrest the conflagration of their minds and attest to the configuration of their souls. It wasn't especially hot or cold or dry, and neither one of them said anything for all the time they took.

⟦ Gilbert Green—PLINYSA ⟧

"It was a cold and bright and cheery pleasant day in Pleasant-ville and Long Island and New York and South Amboy and all around when we received word on the wireless receiver that the government of our lives had fallen from its power. PLINYSA, the metropolitan district of our souls, was safe again at last. Jubilation surged through the taxed wires of the consciences of millions stranded in their homes. We all strained our ears and opened our eyes. Money was meaningless and the police were stripped of rank. The electricity went out at noon and stayed that way until power was restored at the same time on another day. This meant that for the time being there was no time at all. To find a heated house in those days then was rather rare. Later we found out that the automobile industry had collapsed due to the strain of the war effort, which was draining away its last resources, all of which were urgently needed just to fill ever-increasing growth-rate demands, which first fell short and then piled up like a garbage dump. It was a real emergency, the first one we had experienced in all history except for the Civil War which nobody remembered. In order to keep warm, people put on all their clothes and went for long walks everywhere, and those who were not yet love-worn and impotent copulated freely in every nook and cranny of the city and the country, chiefly, I noticed, in stalled autos. Fifteen million salesmen committed dishonorable suicide by eating rancid cottage cheese for lunch. Two hundred thousand housewives dined on capitol hill, gnawing at the statuary, which had been cleaned beforehand, and tearing up the grass with their time honored laments. We were really free.

"Something had to be done because the situation was intolerable. We hastily improvised a cabinet out of shoeboxes stolen from a local outlet which held secret meetings under cover of every public fountain because, strange to tell, the water was the only utility that did not fail or freeze that day. Drenched to the skin and crying real tears to boot, we decided the obvious, viz. that power had to be restored. We communicated with the other agents of delivery by walking on the water pipes which responded with an overwhelming vote of confidence. As long as the water was on we had nothing much to fear. Still there was a great deal to be done. We divvied up the shares, which were provided from the flooded vaults of banks. As long as we were restoring power ourselves, we thought, we had better do a good job of it. Every man who responded to the call was temporarily drowned in a fountain that we called a fountain of pure blood, but as a matter of fact it was only city water. Everyone who survived this ordeal was placed in charge of an entire field of action. The most urgent problem was the restoration of power and this was delegated to George Washington because of his impassivity under duress. He was not named king, we thought his name was good enough as it was, but the fact that he had the name of a king to begin with did not escape our attention. George Washington's first act was to open all the larger houses and manage to feed the hungry housewives who, he said with some justice, were the source of the nation's strength.

"The second most important problem was to get rid of the debris left from the collapse of the automobile industry. Henry Ford requested this assignment and after deliberations lasting over a long period of time his petition was granted with the condition that all this material must somehow be used to solve the housing problem, so as to kill two birds with one stone, as he said in his picturesque acceptance speech. The avoirdupois system of weights and measures proved entirely unequal to the task of estimating the weight of the job Henry Ford had shouldered, so it was forthwith abolished with the provision that a new system would be oriented when anyone invented it. This hasty decision had the unexpected effect of making everything weightless for the time being, fortunately for the fortunate Ford.

"The third measure of the extraordinary government by fountains was to send an envoy throughout the world to check on conditions everywhere and report back. At the time we had no way of knowing if this was an isolated situation or whether it was universal or at least worldwide. With everybody running to and fro the way they were we had a clear picture of everything in Megalopolis, but for all we knew, life might be proceeding just as if nothing had happened elsewhere. We wasted some time trying to decide who to send on this hopeless mission, as a matter of fact nobody wanted to go anywhere, so we fell to drawing lots. Everybody at the fountain was entitled to make one nomination, and everybody thought of somebody they wanted to get rid of for a while. The hat was passed and all the nominations were read into the minutes of the meeting. This was an interminable process, because every time a deputy was bathed in blood it was subsequently his right to select an enemy. This went on at the rate of seven every minute or so it seemed, it was done as quickly as was commensurate with the dignity of the occasion. A totally endless process! In the midst of all this paperwork, we began to lose sight of our objective. It looked for awhile as if there was going to have to be a war, a situation which we all sincerely wanted to avert. So we just kept on working with the list as best we could.

"In the midst of all this confusion, George Washington's second act took place. He managed to speak a few sentences in this new language which became the law of syntax. He said he didn't yet figure out how to hook up all the lights and stuff but maybe that was all right too since life would get too complex if everything went too fast and some people need their sleep. He said the housewives were pretty happy under his command and not to worry. He said do anything you want. He said that ennervated metals are fit for food if they are first burned in ashes. He said Henry Ford is a good guy after all, don't bug him. He said the constituent assembly are wasting their time with paperwork but it is just as well because otherwise there would be war, which cannot be done at this time. He said again, don't worry. He said forget your Latin as I have. He said every man has a duty to produce language and stop screwing around so much. He said there is no contracts of any kind left over from the past. He said I may not speak good but believe me. Finally he said the secret of fire is in the fountains and then he shut his trap.

"We received this intelligence with amazement and gratitude, and to express it a moment of silence and inaction was declared and processed at the fountains. Since there was then no time, this moment lasted hours or maybe days. All work was suspended except on the part of Henry Ford's emergency crews who worked continuously without much sleep or thought of the comfort they were missing in the paid vacation line. Everybody else thought about themselves in the light of George Washington's remarks for the first time. Some wept silently, some began to write, some prayed to the sun for good luck. On the morning of the third day of the 'vacation' we awoke from restful slumbers full of food and drink. The first thing we found out was that George Washington had fixed the telegraph over the weekend, and we immediately wired our gratitude to the ends of the earth which responded with heartwarming encouragement. Then we realized that we didn't have to send out a special envoy so we burned the lists of enemies and cooked a good breakfast for ourselves. Since we were not hungry anymore, we arranged all this food artistically on the fountains and then washed it down the drain. As soon as we noticed what we were doing we declared that art was possible. Everyone felt a little troubled by such precipitate action but at the same time we got a favourable report from Henry Ford who said the houses would be ready ahead of schedule. Accordingly we organized a street dance. As a matter of fact this was already taking place when we passed the resolution, so in effect what we did was to ratify what was already happening. We also decided that since we hadn't bathed any more deputies during the vacation we probably had enough already. And so we danced the night away.

"Then George Washington did the greatest thing he ever did. He turned off the water. The telegraph was working fine and houses were going up all over the place but there was no water. He didn't admit at first that he had done it but we didn't ask him if he did because such a thing was unthinkable and, hence, we didn't think to ask him whose fault it was. Our thought was, more or less, something is trying to destroy this seedling democracy at its roots.

We felt a little depressed, or sobered up. This was essential since we were lucky to have survived this far. We got a shot of our own medicine right where it hurt. Of course nobody knew exactly what to do, but we started thinking right away and stopped the production of art for the time being (as usual, it had already stopped of its own accord). Don't forget that at this period there was no time at all. Therefore there was no rush. Still the fact remained that we had to have some water. We didn't have to have it at any particular time or anything, we absolutely had to have it. We were face to face with death.

"At this point the author of our misfortunes came to our rescue. Without consulting or even bypassing the assembly at the empty fountains, Frederick Ted Castle began issuing orders. Firstly he researched if there was a substitute for water as readily available. And what did he find? That there might be but we don't yet know what it is. Secondly he dug all the dirt from around the pipes in which the water used to come and took a look at them. What did he see? He concluded that they were very rusty but not too leaky. Thirdly, the author put all the dirt back in place. Why did he do that? So it wouldn't be such a mess when it rained. Fourthly, he called for funds and assistants. What did he get? Paid disciples. Fifthly, he held a meeting of all his assistants and told them that they were his friends. How come? So they wouldn't be disloyal later. Sixthly, he reserved the right to select all the enemies he wanted to. Whom or what did he select? Nobody. Seventhly, he retired into the inner sanctum to debate with his conscience. What was the upshot of this dialogue? His soul was refreshed and his mind was rehearsed. Eighthly, he denounced George Washington in front of the empty fountains, falsely accusing him of treason. What did George Washington say to that? He smiled for the first time, sort of a grin. Ninthly, the author turned the water back on at its source and life came to life again.

"This series of events had many results, not all of which have yet been determined by any means. The first thing was that there was time again, which had been stopped dead since the electricity went off. As soon as he was reinstated, George Washington fixed the electricity which came on again at noon the next day. The clocks still told the same time, but the sense of time of the people was now regulated from the interior of each soul in accordance with the pace of the breathless anticipation with which every pair of eyes had watched the nine acts of Frederick Castle unfold. Although each of the nine acts were comparable, since each was one of nine, each of them was of a different character, so that the nine parts of the day, the nine parts of each season, the nine types of souls, the nine major rivers, the nine television channels, the nine best dressed women, the nine signs of birth, the nine races of man, and the nine flowing fountains all took on certain characteristics which have been variously described and endlessly elaborated with a view to the continuous entertainment of all the time in the world, but in general the nine characters can be roughly derived from one word descriptions of the nine acts of the author as follows:

> one equals substitution
> two equals examination
> three equals restitution
> four equals multiplication
> five equals consultation
> six equals reservation
> seven equals objectification
> eight equals obfuscation
> nine equals respiration

"Then a funny thing happened. Everybody adopted the nine slogans and at the same time their author declared in no uncertain terms that they were all lies. This created confusion again, whereas everything had been quite clear for some time. When people asked George Washington what he would do in their place he said, First of all I am in your place and second of all take it easy. Then the people pressed George Washington to issue nine decrees, but he said I have done that before. Finally the people decided that they knew as much as anybody else seemed to know which had a good effect. Anxiety was abolished from the land and from the people and from the language that they were beginning to invent. Everything had come out in the wash. What happened to the author? He went right on dreaming up something else to do."

This is still funny. —G.G.

⟦ Gilbert Green & Susan Talking ⟧

"And then what?" she asked.

"Oh, I don't know, there was some other stuff, and then, I don't know it wasn't exactly like that but it sort of was," he said, putting down the papers from which he had been reading to her. "I really like what George Washington said."

"Yeah, I did too. Was it just like that?"

"No, I made it up," he said.

"You're really hung-up on Fred aren't you?" she said.

"What's that supposed to mean?"

"Like you're jealous of him or something."

"I thought it was you."

"What?"

"That was jealous of him."

She did not reply.

"Did you see that thing in the paper? It was funny."

"What thing, no, I didn't read the paper," she said.

"A lawyer got married out in Jersey and he had these pictures taken of the wedding and when he got them back he sued the photographer because the pictures of her were ugly and grotesque and got him in trouble with her family. I mean she was probably ugly and grotesque to begin with."

"What's so funny about that?" she said.

"I don't know, I thought it was funny."

"Who was ugly?"

"His wife in the wedding pictures."

"Oh. I don't even have any."

"Why not, I mean, I saw some someplace," he said.

"Oh those were the ones Fred took, they were all of you and

that chick he had then, what was her name?, oh Ernestine.''

"They were not all of me, they were of both of us."

"One!"

"What?"

"One of them was of both of us and I wasn't even looking at the camera."

"It's true they weren't any good but there must have been more of you."

"Just one."

"What a shame," he exclaimed with a smile. "Subsequent photographs by another artist have proved that she was not ugly and grotesque at all."

"Oh shut up," she said, suppressing a smile.

"What's for dinner?" he said.

"Oh, I don't know," she said, "Canned pork and beans, I guess."

"Again!"

"Again."

"I want a Porter House steak."

"So do I," she said, with real interest. "Let's check the freezer."

"I already looked. There's just a ton of french fries."

"Let's throw them out."

"Okay, but let's eat first. Seriously."

"We'll stop smiling."

"Must you be facetious at a time like this?" he said.

"I don't know," she said, "I wouldn't have to, I guess, if . . . "

"If what?"

"If. . . . I don't know, if you, oh nevermind."

"What," he said.

"If you don't know I can't tell you," she said.

"I want to hear some music. Let's go to Max's"

"Oh," she said, "All right. Do I have to change?"

"Well maybe a different color on top, I mean if you want to."

"I don't but I will," she said.

"No, nevermind, I don't care."

"You don't care!"

"Stop it."

"Okay."

[Gilbert Green—14 Women]

There have been fourteen women in my life
And, Baby, that's a lot of strife
Now it's you that wants to change my time
To make the preternat'ral climb
  Okay, Okay, I say, but watch out!
My mama was the first to go
As soon as I was old enough to know
Then little sis performed the magic rites
When ma and pa thought we had fights
  Okay, Okay, I say, but don't shout!
Then there was the little girls at school
They lined up like barflies at a pool
They called it practice when I thought it was love
Five girls left first a kiss and then a shove
  Okay, Okay, I say, you'll find out!
Suzanne the eighth was my first real girl
We made it like the movies in a heady swirl
Of hair and thighs and kisses much too sweet
And little talks that we did not repeat.
  Okay, Okay, I say, she's not stout!
Upon a time when I was still too young
There came a woman whose name was sung
Into my pillow with my daily bread—
For all she knew I might as well be dead.
  Okay, Okay, I say, that was doubt!
The five great girls of my teen age
Left each her mark upon its page

A certain laugh, a little bit of a smile
And more than that I got a practiced style.
  Okay, Okay, I say, Making out!
Now it's you that wants to change my time
And I'm giving you my straightest line
I've made the mistakes that I could choose
From now I'll always win and never lose
  Okay, Okay, I say, and don't shout!
There have been fourteen women in my life
And, Baby, that's a lot of strife
If you let me go we'll make it quit
I don't even know if this will fit
  Okay, Okay, I say, it's your move.

It's too bad we can't put music in a book. This will be great in the movie.
—G.G.

⟦ Fred's Serve ⟧

It was decided to call the band *Oscillations*. It didn't have to have a
name at all until it got out onto the market. Then it needed one
very much, and the name had to be right for the product and for
the band and for the ears of the public. Everybody rushed around
for a couple of weeks. Finally Sammy and Danny spent three days
at the studio on Eighth Street and made a record of their
oscillations, using the twelve track machine for all it was worth.
The microphones for the vocal track had to be changed three times
before they gave the right effect and a lot of things went wrong
from time to time. The guy who was pasting up the jacket liner
even went on strike because he was only getting five dollars an
hour and the strike worked because he had all the proofs and the
originals so he was given half a point on net. Everything else was
sort of shut down for about a week while everybody was trying to
figure how to produce a record. It was a madhouse but everybody
learned.

It was kind of like putting on a play and just before it opens
everything goes wrong. Even after the sound was all in final takes
there was trouble with the copyright and we had to set up a new
corporation under B.M.I. to take the blame. But first of all there
was the question if it was to be recorded straight or if it was to be
mixed after it was recorded and as it turned out they did a little of
both but it was more or less straight so that if the band played live
it would sound more like the record. Everything was rewritten at
the last minute. Even the notes on the liner. Some of the tracks
were placed in different positions after they were made so that the
band had to try to play them that way in order to reproduce it for

the audience the next night at the club. They never made that scene, they slept through it, on account of having been up for three days but we played the tape and it was really great.

The effect was that it made a scene for *yellowrock*. Before the record there were, of course, the Mothers and the Velvet Underground but they were isolated and the stations wouldn't touch them even though they advertised. And there were bits of the Beatles, the Doors, the Cream, the Fudge, the Stones and maybe Spirit and a few others that didn't really fit in anywhere, but after Oscillations all of these different pieces came together and made a scene for *yellowrock*, which was the name of the album. First of all it was handled right commercially in that we recorded without A & R getting in the way and then worked through a nominal producer who got the credit but didn't really have a thing to do except sell the thing and even that was mostly programmed before. In other words we did what Zappa and Reed and Lennon did to begin with, but then we said to hell with Verve-Folkways, and sold it off at the top. In the second place, everybody was really working full time and we had good people to push it. It's just like in the theatre, everybody has to be doing it completely or it falls. And in the movies too. Whenever there's a lot of people, they all have to be on at every point so that no detail is worse than the rest. Of course a record is a good way to find out how to do this sort of thing because it doesn't cost as much as some things do, it's sort of small scale, but that's temptation too because you think you can get away with things but you really have to spend a lot for anything that's any good.

The big danger in all this is that people start putting each other on trying to convince themselves that something is great, and maybe it is or maybe it isn't, but sometimes the thing gets out of hand because everybody wants a great success so much that they start saying that everything and anything that the group does is great. You have to have this to some extent. You can't have people feeling that nothing is any good, they have to feel that everything is basically great and you take care of this by making sure to begin with that everything is basically great by what you know yourself of the scene. But when you get this going well, it may happen that people get carried away and they think that anybody who says that anything is wrong is like a traitor to the cause. This is the dangerous point and it can lead to fights and people quitting and everything. The thing is that everybody has to be able to do their best and it is surefire if everybody knows that they are on, completely on. As soon as for any reason somebody's thing has to be even slightly underrated, then that person will probably try to pick a fight or undermine some other part of the process, maybe by just tripping over a mike wire but also maybe by trying to convince somebody else that things are basically not great. Like you cannot have two women who are trying to make it with the same man working on the same project, it will inevitably fail or at least be screwed up by it.

The other thing you can't have is anybody who's doing nothing. They make it like a joke for all the others. They may not feel it like that but they really despise the whole thing. If they won't work, you have to throw them out. The only time when people who do nothing and know nothing are any good is when you do nothing too, for example when you are very young or very, very old. Then it always seems like they have done something or that like you they will probably do something when the time comes. You find out if they will or not if they are still around when the time comes. Liars and fakers are the plague of good works. Fortunately we were not plagued with them in those days.

The real right way to do anything is to just go ahead with it and do not be afraid to show your ignorance or to make a mistake. If you are really doing it, it is likely that the mistake will turn to an advantage and a bit of ignorance is a sign of health. People who know everything really know nothing and they don't know that for sure. Beware of jargon but don't be frightened of it. Some people talk well but if you break their jargon you find out that they don't understand a thing. That is what is called having no sense of humor. Sammy used to work for this cat who does movies, they said with a helpful air. A cat? asked Dave White. Yeah, a gray cat, they said, and we had a good giggle. You have to break the tension in the air and sometimes late at night everybody just falls down laughing and everything stops being done but at night that's great because it's endless and the whole thing will fit together in the day after the great event when everything went wrong.

Sensitivity is the key thing, and it is the opposite of compulsion, so what I mean is you have to have a bit of both but too much of either one will bring it down around your ears. Like you might seem to be hard but that is all right if you're really listening to everything at the same time and when something comes up that is something, you know it right away. Otherwise you might miss it. *Yellowrock* was one such thing. At first we didn't know anything about it, we just liked it very much. We liked a lot of other things. We liked everything that was any good and at that time there was a lot of that. We dug Gerry's thing, even though it didn't work too well at first, we even liked Brian Wilson's stuff sometimes, we thought Phil Ochs was great and just then Donovan cut out of the Dylan stuff and made his own great sound, we really loved Cass Elliot who never went out of style at all, Lou Reed was great, and Dylan-Zimmerman was a god. Practically every day there was a new record that had something great about it, sometimes it was only the cover, but usually it was more than that. We picked up on everything. If we had been just compulsive, we would have been discouraged by all this proliferation of great sounds, but, no, we really liked the others heart and soul, and right in the middle of it we rediscovered Cole Porter thanks to Mama Cass and then there was a little history too. But all the same, if we had just been sensitive we would have just dug all these sounds and never done the thing we finally did which was not like any one of them but it was related to everyone that we liked and even to some we didn't like. Nobody would be able to remember all the great stars we idolized now, but it doesn't matter, because we turned our lights inside our own brains and it came out like *yellowrock*.

After it was done we were almost screwed by a comparison. Somebody wrote it up and in that they said that it was just Chinese music put through oscillators with a jazz beat behind it. That just about turned us off. If they get a way to put you down before you're off the ground, you've already had it before you begin. The thing was it wasn't true, first of all, and the thing that really saved us was that the comparison wasn't a cliché itself. Nobody knew any Chinese music so that they didn't and couldn't say, "Oh yeah it is like that" and drop it cold. They did know jazz though.

It was handled perfectly, as it turned out. When we heard about the Chinese thing we simply laughed because we knew they might have pegged us to almost anything that was being heard at the time, but Chinese? Ha-ha! Then we turned around and said *all modern music is jazz.* We stuck in Stravinsky and Ives and Gershwin and Cole Porter and Mae West, for luck. It was done with aplomb. It amazed the pedants and flattered the musicians and just pleased the run of the millions of the viewers and ourselves. Then we pushed *yellowrock* for all its salt and that paid off in actual dollars so that really everything was set. There was a new TV with lots of gadgets, we all had our hair re-done, and some people bought a car with what was left, a very beautiful car called *You guessed it.* It was supposed to be called *Yellowrock* but that was too straight.

Maybe this doesn't make any sense. If so, just take it as it is. Maybe you're confused by all this noise, but that's life, one can't remember everything. Maybe we didn't do things just this way, but we did do it enough like this to show that we knew what we were doing and how to do it now for all. Maybe this account is biassed, dividing things that were the same to others, and putting some things first that people thought were later. You've got to remember, girl, to make your life worthwhile, you've got to be wanted, you've got to be loved. And this is how we did it more or less. It wasn't easy but it wasn't hard to do. Every hour, every day. We did it continuously all the time and made a set that couldn't make it but it did and played a game that wasn't standard but it was and answered a question that wasn't asked, but we did.

There was a thing afterwards. What to do now. That's a big hang-up for most groups. Sometimes you can do more of the same, or you can do anything you want, but you have to want it. *Yellowrock* was great and we kept it up, every day in every way, but at the same time Gilbert Green said let's turn our thoughts to movies now and so we did and that story will be both longer and shorter than this one has been but it wants a fine development, so as to begin. The story was much longer than the book of it will be.

You do not stop and admire yourself for longer than the second that it takes to brush back your hair from out of your eyes and take a short nap of dreams that are entirely different so as to see the way you will be when the changes have been rung again from a vision planted in my brain.

⟦ Gilbert Green—Valentine ⟧

The frosting on a lovely cake is cold and dreams will make it yellow for the Valentine that has no shape especial and things move so slowly now that we are almost old! I didn't do so much last year as I had thought I might. I feel a little depressed tonight with melancholy that poets always know. There is no snow. But there is light and heat and food and entertainment for our time enough. Another Valentine, another lonely kiss.

I learned a lot, for example how to say no while saying yes and meaning both of them to that extent, how to eat less and what to do in crowds of fairly famous people, how to dress and how to speak in vague and common terms so as not to give advantage or offence. You have been my Master and I think it will continue. I am a little sad tonight with the sadness that any poets who know it know from the experience of many mistresses who love and then retreat toward wordless masters where they live away. I am tired too from giving great performances among my friends. I am almost rested now and ready for real dreams, to eat less, to dress, and to say yes. . . .

We haven't seen each other much again since late one night and after then in a dark and noisy restaurant nearby when you proceeded from the rear in company with all the glory you have made to give yourself the aspect of a king, modestly to walk between the hairdos and the costumes of your fame, and I crossed your path and walked with you a few feet on the other side of the recessional procession, and asked a question and received polite replies and shut the glass doors against the noise outside. We are not ourselves, or any other. Avarice is deadening. Life is going on.

Our winter is a sad time full of memories of past success and future dreams, or so it seems to me. My mistresses, bless their well-shaped heart, have fled me to other hearths where nothing stirs, and I in turn have turned to wars of words. I have found out that we have our enemies who despise success and innocence with all the force of ignorance they can contrive, piling false starts upon mistakes to make a void of what is really great. I was all set to jump to your defense, but I had also learned to lay low and let this pass, or I found out again that my own life was the one I had to save. I will come back to you when my book is more than done and offer what I have to give once more, a changed man from your influence to change in my turn what you gave back to the source, and to show that great arts in equal channels flow.

February 14, 1968.

I had completely forgotten about this valentine to Andy Warhol. I used to write one every year around this time, because I first met him, you know, on St. Valentine's eve when "Chelsea Girls" was playing at that theater he rented for it on Broadway. —G.G.

side two

Waring's Turn with Fred

Waring & Fred & Gilbert Green

Gilbert Green in the City

Wary & Fickle

Fred & The Golden Girl

Fred's Dream

Fred & The Girl

Wary's Poem

Fred & Wary

Fred Afraid

Fred & Wary with Friends

Fred in Love

Fred's Song

Susan Herself with Fred

Susan Late at Night

Susan's Party

Susan on Gilbert Green & Childhood

⟦ Waring's Turn with Fred ⟧

The story is much longer than the book of it will be.

The facts are very simple. A series of chance meetings over time by people who craved the same desires. Everything was going marvelously. But it was not permitted to them to reformulate the design together until such a time as that when this book will become the film. The period was characterized for the principal character by (A) void in the mistress column and (B) renewed interest in daily life. Here you will see the exact point at which the old gods had lost their wonder and a new star was not yet born. Exprimetime.

The first meeting was an argument a long time ago. Each denounced the other's joy in intellectual terms. They realized no traction or attraction. One put his feet up in the great winged chair. The other remained resolutely on the floor and tried without success to talk to someone else. It was a draw that gained respect from both sides. It was an argument about modern music. One took refuge in the freedom of expression the other languished in the sacristy of seriousness. The effect was that they saw each other often at different kinds of musical events. This was not expected and it was not unwelcome.

For who, on entering a room full of strangers, has not occasionally been quite overjoyed to meet there by chance someone whom one has met before, if not in the best possible light, because is it not so that on those rare occasions one feels one knows that one's world is larger than one thought!

The meetings were respectful. One was small and tight. The other was kind of big and loose. Nobody who knew the one well knew the other very well, though they had many mutual acquaintances. This went on for a long time too and they really wanted it that way.

There can be too much love at once.

At first it was mostly just a nod and a salutation. As they began to run into each other more often they would perhaps pass the time of a coffee break with a remark or two, continuing their abortive conversation. These were respectful silences, as I have said before, and they were more and more frequent and less and less silent. Each quietly admired the other's dress and address. There began to be excitement in the air.

The break, there is always a break.

Disciples love their master right away and masters are immediately flattered and pleased by their attentions. This is a kind of love of course, but it is filial. True love is usually not as hot. But then too it is as hot as you know. And as you do.

The break came on a winter afternoon.

At that period the Club was brightly lit. Each of them was accompanied by habitual companions and no women at the moment. These companions were old friends who were gradually taking other paths. This meant that both the characters of my play then felt rather alone although they were surrounded by expiring friendships. One was seated having a strained conversation with the disciple of an old friend. The other was eating a roast beef sandwich at the bar. They noticed each other right away and nodded to each other dourly. That is a word that has been out of use and deserves much more attention. They acknowledged each other's presence without haste and without visible affectation.

The break must happen almost simultaneously on both sides but someone has to start it. From the bar, the one who had been eating eventually passed near the one who had been talking, who saluted him in an offhand way. There being an extra seat there, they both sat down and exchanged a compliment on each other's taste. Over this long time before, they were becoming more conformable to each other in point of taste, but their works still did not so much resemble each other as draw strength from their mutual opposition which was now so clear cut that it could turn, in the space of one remark, into a strong attraction.

They were still awfully wary.

The lighting of the Club was strong but not theatrical. A somewhat yellow light played about the bright colors of their faces and hands and the muted colors of their costumes as they sat and talked to several people. They both spoke with intelligence in a mannered way. Most people do not speak with much mannerism in their voices, but what I mean by this sort of mannerism is the way that it is quite possible to tell who is singing a song. It is not the tone, it is the manner. Most people answer the telephone in a mannered way so as to identify themselves immediately to the caller. Then they lapse into something more nondescript. Not so with these two characters. They kept up a manner all the time. The light departed from their hair in a variety of different colors, and that was one thing more in which they were alike, viz: that their hair when newly washed exhibited more than one shade of color and in each case though the main color differed, there was a little bit of early white.

At that time too, the Club was not too popular. A few weeks later it would be jammed with costumed, perfumed exhibitions, but just at that time the crowds were still outside. Later on the two were left to their conversation which consisted now of an exchange of observations rather than a contention of different points of view. Nobody bothered them. Nobody thought it odd. Nobody thought a thing about it except the two of them. At one point, on the way to their still separated paths, they congratulated each other on having lived through the years.

"I'm glad we aren't shouting at each other anymore," said one with a rather rare and helpful smile.

"Oh, shouting?" said the other gently as his disposition was. When that was done a thoughtful silence resumed the encounter and covered it with a thin layer of something much like dust. Dust is not much admired today but I must say that I sort of like it.

Let Bruce rearrange the order of this side. —G.G.

⟦ Waring & Fred & Gilbert Green ⟧

A rather distracting and a somewhat shattering experience.

The music plays, friends come and go and Fred writes as fast as he can go, with intervals and with delays. He lives on charity throughout the larger part of the war. He does not yet know how he is going to do it, but now that the war is over, he determines to make it in a big way. The weather improves occasionally, subject still to considerable relapse effect because although the war is over, the winter still has its force to spend. Fred listens to the music, he doesn't write it down. Over a huge Italian dinner at a little restaurant with friends he contemplates the future of a dream. The past is not yet moving fast enough.

They exchange notes on their families whose members have recently come to their attention once again. Wary becomes a little sentimental about Fred's sister, never having had a sister for himself. Fred declares that he doesn't know his sister and Wary thinks that that must be a shame. They generally serve each other bits of food with lots of sauce. They discuss the costumes of the other customers, some of whom they almost know. They conjure images of Italy itself, each of them travelling alone and separated much in time, moving up and down its coast and inland with the strange foliage of the olives and the peaks of little hills achieved on unmapped paths.

"Your reflections on editors have always made sense to me," Gilbert Green wrote as the scenery of far-off lands went past the sky. *"What you suggest, for us to create frankly raw material for use by editors is really a fine suggestion. I always work on getting out material for people, never leaving off the possibility that they*

may want to make their own. And the editor, not the audience, is actually the audience. I wrote a very long piece with many parts and aspects. I told them that I doubted that they would want to print it. They responded that they would like to use it but it was too long. I said, Well cut it down for me. I read the new version which was half the length of mine. It didn't make much sense to me but they left in the parts that I liked best. I asked them if they liked it this way and they said that they were pleased."

Wary warns me about the people of his entourage to whom, at his suggestion, we make an unexpected visit in the middle of a rainstory that never stops but drips. We view some art work and talk of politics and school. His disciple offers him a job which he declines, politely. When we speak of words they are at first incredulous but then they get my meaning and they are relieved. I only feel good when the opposition falters slightly. We stay away from touchy subjects altogether and make polite agreements on subjects of no interest. But I still insist that it is a shame to burn the flag in public. The news of the election has been somewhat encouraging. They do not understand why I am not militant and monolithic but they do not object to it too much. It's hard for me at first to talk to people who are not used to me because I have to fill them in on everything.

"I went home and wrote a new beginning and a new end to the article, which, from my point of view, made it so that the piece was a collage of different pieces, and I thought it was improved."

The music from four speakers at the corners of the room fills our ears with sounds that are never written down. The conductor stands before his dials in the company of educated engineers. They make a hundred tapes at his command and then they re-record them for the broadcast. The floor is painted white, the walls are painted paintings and there are hardly any chairs. The air is bright. The size of the music increases with every setback of the building. It is a disappointment for which we are prepared that some people aren't so bright. It don't disturb us much. The whiteness of the room contains a smile for each of us.

"I had taken the precaution of having the whole thing re-typed. When the proofs were sent to me, I found half a dozen words had

been changed in my absence. I objected violently to this. I didn't weep or make idle threats. I stated very carefully that all these word changes were wrong even though what was wrong with them might never be apparent to the editors or to the readers of the book. I expressed a very tolerant attitude toward the situation and the function of editors, but an absolutely intolerant attitude toward word changes. All my text was restored and the work was printed without a single error."

They viewed each other from every angle in concert with the music and the room. The conversation kept on going but it was not of too much interest. They conscientiously avoided asking any favors of each other. The atmosphere was easy. To some extent they showed each other things but in a desultory way. They were not fearful of a silence. Fred notices that Wary's voice sounds very good on tape. He walks around looking at unfinished paintings from every other angle. This one goes with this music very well and there is no other painting like it, there can be no comparison.

"We decided to write letters to the editor pointing out certain mistakes. My letter was amusing. I saw the editor soon afterward and he smilingly complained to me about having called his editing a garble in transmission. In this case I did not give in to the temptation to assume that they were actively trying to screw me, I just said there are some things that editors naturally do not care about that writers do, and I told them what they were."

In company, Wary was likely at first to make one or two too many jokes while Fred inclined to silence or simple little questions, but he took care to laugh at some of Wary's jokes, the ones that were a little bit obscene. He even made one joke himself. He was not too pleased with his appearance, but there were so many people there that it was impossible to have a conversation.

"I felt glad that I did not have acquiescent editors."

There was a different scene in every room. The little crowd moved from one room to the next to change the character of the conversation. They did not laugh too much at anything. Wary was showing Fred his friends. In one room that was quite chilly we were shown models of mechanical dolls that could be made to jump around and kiss each other awkwardly and noisily. We were told how these dolls had been invented and what they would be used for. Certain machinery was displayed that made a noise and sprayed paint with a hiss. In the next room, we talked a little bit about the country. Some of the people had thought they might move to there and there was a slight discussion of different advantages. Stefan had just showed me that differences are not important, which I always knew, and I had insisted that they were still interesting, but I noticed that it wasn't always true. Wary made some jokes about the hazards of the country and everybody laughed again.

"Selling something is breaking down resistance to it. People do not want to part with money and they also have a powerful desire to be convinced to do so. There is really no telling how this may be done. It is a process of give and take. A professional buyer has to be the one who does not want to spend the money regardless of its availability. But most people are very willingly sold. In my opinion, the call to revise the first third of your book is nothing more than an opportunity to sell it. They are saying that the author must concern himself with our problems, or else we will not bite."

In the kitchen, everybody took on a different function and regrouped for different orders. Wary was not affected by the performance of his friend whose object was to move him to the country for the summer. He had just visited a different city and although he admired the plants he did not see what good a change would do him, although he didn't object one bit to a change of scene for other people. Drinks were made and served in perfect little cylinders of blue which Wary joked about with Fred.

"You shouldn't throw their request in their face by demanding what they meant about the first third of your book, but ignore that until or unless they mention it again. You should walk in and say, Well, what can I do for you, and the first demand they make, such as take off your coat or sit down or have lunch or change the title, should be immediately agreed to. Don't forget that people do not mean what they say. They practically always mean something else even when they themselves are under the impression that they always mean what they say."

Upstairs, they laid themselves about the floor and listened to the music of the rain. The roof was vastly spreading over the floor on which they lay and it only leaked a little bit. The television provided material for the decoration of their conversation. Everyone felt fairly much at ease although the encounter was a little pointless. Wary told his disciple that he would not go with him. Fred walked around in a circle half the time, not fast or anything like that. The conversation that developed out of the efforts of the TV producers was not too interesting, but it was effortless and extraordinarily conventional. There was a brief flurry about what could be considered to be *perfect* because Fred said it meant that what was perfect was all over and quite dead. After that they kept off interesting subjects and stuck to topics of the day. At one point Fred and Wary congratulated each other that they were both living at a time when so much of interest chanced to pass.

"Mechanistic logic ignores that in everyone there is a center, what I want, wherefore people cannot be defined as products of a situation. Situations affect subjects, they do not create them. I have been much affected by your attitude, expressed to me but not used by you last summer, of being kind to editors. As my long anecdotes go to show, I do behave that way, but I do not seem to be too kind. Everything is very delicate and in the end there is no real right way to do it."

At dinner, Wary had said to Fred, "Which do you like, accomplishments or situations?"

"Situations, naturally," said Fred, sharing another piece of toast.

"It's not where you stand but how you sit," laughed Wary, warily.

⟦ Gilbert Green in the City ⟧

But in my new-found innocence I never noticed.

Clad for a rare and ceremonial occasion in which his family name must be invoked once more, the combination of the ancestral gowns and the flowing, curling hairs of my real life attract more stares than smiles as he passes his servants in the street. The garb is ancient and slightly holy, he notices, tugging at a button that is secure but loose. The servants all step aside in almost military order. Most of them are unknown but now and then he sees a friendly face that may be nodded to or not, depending on the situation. My hands are clasped behind my back as I stride along in my black and subtle English greatcoat, gloved and clasped and buttoned to make me seem as tall or taller as I am. The day is great with music from the sun. He hums an ancient processional as he paces up the street. That day a thousand servants had a view of a beautiful young man in the royal clothes of obsolescent power and rather than bowing down or making way any more than need be they stared at a memory they did not exactly have of a young king strolling in the sun alone.

His heels made a sharp and perfect noise as they quickly struck the pavements, his coat was slightly linty but of an exactly perfect length now long out of style, his colors were muted but of the best materials. It is a strange procession. Everyone behaves in ordinary fashion, but they stare despite themselves. His head is high, his gaze direct, the points of his not too pointed shoes point exactly in the right direction. Just then a beautiful and famous woman slightly known to him, turns back in my direction which she has been following to say, "Do you ride horses?"

My mouth turns up a little bit in gratitude and I say, "Why yes." "I thought you did," was her reply. I felt like that that day.

He goes by a way that is familiar and one that is not as direct as other ways might be. There are three errands that must be accomplished with this costume. At first, two lawyers who do not fawn too much must be intimidated into carrying out my wishes as I wish them. The news that our cousin has had her orders countermanded in Africa that day is in my ears as I confront them and they pretend not to be surprised. They lightly compliment my costume and my rings. I speak very clearly and reach into an unfamiliar pocket as if I were searching for a coin. At last I find and make the seal and bargain which is entirely in my favor because it does not prejudice my servants. I leave them with a remark which from any other mouth would be ridiculous but they are so overcome with gratitude towards me that it strikes them as the voice of god, I say, May you live fully and work wonders today. I omit the extraordinary and the ordinary signs but I take my leave with leisure, pretending to admire their pictures which nobody else has ever noticed, but without a further word. The door closes just as the second button of my gloves is fast.

The auguries were right. He piles success upon success. The second stop will flatter a minor functionary who may be useful to the young man later. This is accomplished without much ceremony, for the two of them are of equal age, or almost, the functionary is slightly older. The visitor walks into the office unannounced and immediately takes the only chair so that the visited does not feel he has to rise to the occasion. He is discovered as he is eating a cupcake, part of which is refused as soon as it is offered. The office is crowded with a book or two and papers are neatly strewn about. They make fast and common gossip, and exchange a note or two which touch acquaintances. The conversation is so directed that the functionary, should he ever think back on it, will be certain that his visitor had no especial purpose in his visit but that he just enjoys his company. This is the greatest kind of flattery that peers can make to peers and it makes the functionaries so treated into lifelong worshipers. The boss is out and the functionary feels his oats. He realizes that the visitor has no power over him, but still his being is suffused with the greatest willingness to help the non-power that he faces. He makes a mental note to do everything he can for him. Then he becomes amazed as the young visitor remembers a detail from the life that is so unremarkable, and with that final compliment, the prince of the lost realm takes his leave again, unexpectedly thanking others for their kindness as he goes.

The third point is a simple purchase from a salesman. For ten years he has worn a certain kind of spectacles, and now he desires to change his style. The doctor was familiar and polite, assuring him that his eyes are not much weaker than they ever were, taking great care with bits of glass and spots of lights. It might seem odd that this errand should be accomplished with such grace, after all, everybody is always getting glasses fixed and they usually do not dress for it. But the point that goes unrevealed in the performance is that the customer is superstitious about his eyes. Everybody is quite polite and he handles them, after his successes, a bit high handedly. After all it is his looks and the way he sees that will be changed. He does not give his name at first. The salesman is a snob. Gilbert Green finds this irritating, but he determines not to give his name. The salesman is evidently of the persuasion that if you give them too much choice they will not be able to make up their minds. Therefore he pretends that he can offer a very limited selection. Gilbert Green has not exactly forseen this eventuality, but he has had a chance to notice an attractive style before the salesman got around to him. He has a habit of choosing things to buy on the instant and then looking at other things that he might buy very thoroughly and always ending up with his first choice. The pattern is repeated on this occasion. He requests his choice and it is judiciously brought to him. He shilly-shallys to the point where the salesman loses interest in the sale and turns to more pressing business. This gives him an opportunity to look at himself in the new glasses from every point of view and in different colored mirrors. It is exactly what he wanted. "How are you doing?" inquires the salesman on his return to the indecisive-appearing king. "I shall order these." When the name is dictated into the ear that writes out the form it is first mistaken and then recognized, and then it is acknowledged that the business and home addresses must be the same. The clerk is a little uncomfortable at taking the phone number of a king, but he doesn't show it much although his friendliness improves. He takes a final bow by saying that the preparation of the glasses will take several days longer than one might think they would, and the young man in turn annoys the clerk by pretending to consider other styles of glasses after he has made up his mind. Suddenly I turned on heels and left without a word, the shop.

In the flick of a shutter with two frames between, Everything changed his clothes and his scene. He is outside another shop, having just purchased and worn his modern robes which look more natural on him. He doesn't wear his glasses when he doesn't have to drive. He doesn't walk either, he sees himself in attitudes and all kinds of different dress, none of them too funny. He is going to find out if anybody has gotten sick in a few days because it says that around the ninth of March "the one you love most" will have an expensive disease and he would like to find out which one he most loves. He has a thought to pray for peace. There is no interesting disease. He tries out different cars. What a shame the British folded; the new Bentley is too low for cowpaths, nice in green, a problematical expense. Would the peasants stone me on my rounds?

A waking glimpse catches sight of yellow sunny curtains and music in the background, the police must be singing in their cage again. He almost smiles and tells the world.

Cigarettes are extinguished painstakingly, so as not to spoil the ashes. Our manager arrives with a host of propositions, all of them horrifying, but we accept the both of them and go on to sign our fame-card smiling. This will be a big mistake that makes a lot of money. Let us mis-take our mis-trust and turn it to contempt for everything like that. Okay, all right, accord. Gilbert Green feels comfortable in his native dress although suddenly he has no pants on anymore, but it's just a brief chill that comes on stronger later—black underwear is thrilling too. Donovan approaches, praying softly on the wind. His robes aren't any color but they are changing colors mighty quick. It's so hard to concentrate it's not even worth the effort. The tennis shoes are shorn of grace and silently they pinch the toes. Do you remember how we used to walk the path with trees uprooted by disease and talk our dreams in little visions that rather sang than muted out concerns for children that came barefoot and all booted up for snow and every other way with cuts and bruises and with momentary passions and with high times, you can get anything you want, and the next question is, what will you have?

Some pillows are harder. The magazine is black, and white. The boss tells a little joke that is much funnier than it is. We are exhausted by the effort. Well write a letter. Good-bye. The parts of the brain that deal with abstract thought as a rule are separated from the rest of the brain by a tiny vessel that might atrophy at any time and then where would be we? Back with the grass and the carrots and the sea, it is not a particular color really it is just around, and swing the camera there to get a view of that sunset. They are always perfect. You kill it with words, not with love. For what cliché is the cliché *interesting disease* a cliché?

⟦ Wary & Fickle ⟧

The music was no better right at first.

They found each other strangely agreeable. One would mount
an argument and the other would disagree with it by casting it in
other terms. They often smiled. There were numerous tests of
authenticity, and of tastes. They were stalling for the right
moment to begin. The one who never stayed up late stayed up
until after dawn without complaining. They talked all the time.
The one who did not take the question of what was art too
seriously did not smile too much when it was seriously and
repeatedly proposed. One admired women and one did not admire
them. The one who admired women did not love them and the one
who did not admire women loved them. Both of them found them
quite amusing.

"The thing about women," said the former, "Is that they go
right to the point, if they want something they let you know."

"But men are interested in a lot of different things," said the
latter, "So it seems to be more complicated. A lot of women
pretend that they are interested in many things, but they really only
want one thing, and, of course there are a few women who really
are interested in all different things."

They mixed their agreements with the pleasures of some
glances and each one bought the other something, to show there
were hard feelings. They did not discuss the other people with
whom they found themselves. Instead they discussed the business
to which they were both passionately committed from different
points of view. One found it such a laugh that the other was not
sure if the commitment was really passionate. This was the subject
of considerable interrogation.

"Would you give up everything for your art?" said the one who was engaged in doubt.

"Well," said the other, "Do you mean if my mother asked me to give up what I'm doing, would I give it up?" They shared a laugh.

"How old are you, almost thirty?"

"I'm twenty-five at the moment," and the question was not returned.

They took long walks in the neighborhood owing to an unseasonable thaw during which one could still see one's breath but one didn't feel too cold. They exchanged visits at each other's houses, and they admired in more detail each other's work. As they walked they told each other of the details of buildings that they noticed, passing them. And they exchanged notes on each other's characters.

They were the same age and they both had the same amount of fame at that time which was actually not nearly enough. But one had steeled himself to live without much love while the other more openly required an inordinate amount and got it, but still it was not enough. They both detested and solicited flattery from others. Thus their friends were always changing sin e as soon as anyone flattered them, they could no longer be a friend. They put words on each other's characters, *Fickle* for the one and *Wary* for the other. This made them smile again.

They told each other stories about when they had not known each other, stories that were very valued because they gave them each an impression of what somebody who saw them from afar might think of them. One of them, namely Wary, was probably more interested in what other people thought of him but they both had an interest in it. They did not discuss clothes much, except to make a remark on various extremes of costume that they encountered. The process was a slow one.

"I'm constantly amazed by how long everything takes," said Fickle to his friend. "I mean we've been talking a lot recently and we're doing all right, you know, but we haven't really understood each other yet at all. If we really had a language, everything would be as clear as, May I have a piece of pie, is."

"It's all right," said the other, "Come and see me."

"All right, I will," he said and then they parted.

Their encounters were looked for on both sides, perhaps more on one than on the other, because it could be that one was in greater need of a new friend than the other would ever be. But there was no doubt that their meeting had taken place at a convenient time for both of them, perhaps at a somewhat less convenient time for the one who wanted a new friend more. It was evident that they respected each other, because neither brought an entourage when they "chanced" to meet, and besides they were both respectful to each other. It was an even standoff and they both liked each other more for that.

⟦ Fred & The Golden Girl ⟧

And is the lie then disappeared?

The Leap Year leapt on a certain day noted. "Hi," she sailed, coming up and sitting down. "Do you mind if I ask you a personal question?"

He smiled at her.

"Where did you get that shirt? It's beautiful."

"There's a long story behind this shirt."

"I don't mean to be nosy. Somebody made it for you?"

"Not exactly," he said, "Are you interested in it?"

"Not exactly," she said with a laugh, "Does it matter much?"

"No it doesn't. Do you want a drink?"

"I don't know if I do or not, maybe I will."

"What. Some wine? It isn't too bad."

"I'll give you some money," she said reaching into her book.

"Look," he said pointing to the floor.

"Wow!"

"It'll buy us a drink," he said, picking up a number of coins off the floor, not counting them but sort of weighing them in exchange for a damp little bottle of green glass.

"I'm not propositioning you or anything, but would you like to come up to my place for a drink?"

"Sure," he said.

"I work for the government, and you have to be awfully careful when you're exempt and everything. When I first started working there I was investigated from the time I was born up to two years ago and they didn't find a damn thing, I saw the report after I was hired, everything was covered up."

"Oh," he said.

"I control six million dollars and it's kind of fun spending all that money for other people, I like it a lot. I buy advertising art. Anything to do with advertising I know all about. I've lived in the building for three years and I don't know a soul in the place. That's the way you have to live in my position. I'm not drunk, or stoned, or anything. Do you want to know something? I've had an ounce of Mexican Gold in my place for a year and I haven't touched it. It just sits there in the ice bucket. Do you want to turn on? I really don't, but you could if you wanted. I mean no strings attached. Are you scared of me?"

"No," he said with a smile.

"Oh, that's good. Sometimes I think that people are scared of me. You know why? Because I'm scared of them. I figured it out about two years ago. I was fooling around in a printing plant with the inks and I was making some paintings with the inks they had with the knife they use to get out the ink, it's sort of like a palette knife too, and it was so funny, I was just doing these little things and all of a sudden I figured it out that I'm scary. I have a beautiful cat, you see these scratches? That's where she scratched me. But I love my cat, I think she's the only one in the world that isn't scared of me a little bit. Maybe it's not true, I don't know. Isn't life wonderful?" She sipped her drink. "I never get drunk, I think there's nothing worse in the world than a woman who's drunk, don't you think so? I mean that's what my mother always says. You really ought to meet my grandmother. She's a real bitch. She used to be a designer and she still does some things, and every once in a while I go up there and she says to me, you know, like, well, if you're a good girl I will leave you all my money, and I say to hell with that my father will take care of me and she carries on about ingratitude and things. She's the only woman I've ever met who talks more than I do."

"You take after your grandmother," he said.

"How did you know? In some ways yes and some ways no. Like I have very good legs. She's seventy-three and she still has legs, no varicose veins and she uses a depilatory, she's really beautiful. I'm gaining weight now and I may look a little too plump in the face, but I'll never be fat, nobody in my whole family on both sides is at all fat. We come from everywhere, Sweden, Spain, Germany, France, and my mother's father is Irish, so I'm a mutt. I mean, really, no strings at all, but would you like to come up? It's just around the corner. I never do this. But tonight I thought I will just go in and pick somebody up and bring them up and show them my things, do you want to?"

"Sure," he said, packing himself up.

"I have to be awfully careful. You'll see I have a jail lock on my door and five other locks too. But don't be scared. I'm really harmless."

"I'm not scared."

"You must have something to do with the arts. I can just tell. You have a sort of intellectual look. I don't mean bad intellectual, I just mean intellectual. You certainly don't talk much. Are you nearsighted or farsighted?"

"Nearsighted, I guess."

"So am I. Would you believe it? I've had contact lenses for seven years. I lose them all the time but I've never had any trouble with them. These glasses are just for the street so people won't see me, they're just glass. Can I try your glasses? Oh! They're so strong! You must have really bad eyes, do you?"

"I'm not as blind as James Joyce."

"Oh, I didn't know he was blind. I love Aldous Huxley. When he died, he died on the same day as President Kennedy, and I really felt that loss so much more than I did about the assassination, I just couldn't feel anything about the president but I cried for Aldous Huxley. He was like a god. I'm not religious, but I had a strict Catholic education and everything so I sort of am even though I'm not, if you know what I mean. Huxley was blind too toward the end. I have an I.Q. of 182. You remind me of my brother. You don't look like him or anything, he's seventeen, and white-blond, not pretty but beautiful, and I told him to go to college out of town, just to get away from the family. He got four scholarships but I told him to go to Harvard or someplace and make Father pay for it. Well, this is it, chez-moi. Brrrr. I'm cold. I have a twenty-four hour doorman but I guess he's asleep. It's not an old building. It's tremendously expensive. I make sixteen thousand dollars a year tax free. Isn't it amazing? I still never have any money. I just waste it. Right now I have thirty-five dollars to last until payday in a week and then I'll have over a thousand dollars. Then pretty soon I won't have a cent again. My father helps me out sometimes, one time he just gave me ten thousand dollars and you know what I did? I gave it away!"

"Great!" he said laughing.

"I'd give you some money, but I don't have any right now. This is the lobby. See that picture there? When I first moved in someone I knew came into the building and picked it up off the lobby wall and brought it to me as a present. It was a new building and they had just put the paintings up that day. So to please him I hung the ugly thing in my place, I never even knew he stole it off the wall in my own hall! So then they sent everybody in the building a notice describing the thing and I snuck out one night and re-installed it. Isn't that funny? I think if you can just laugh at life everything is fine. See? I have six keys for the place. Nobody else even has one, I had the original locks changed."

"Nice place," he said.

"You have to excuse the mess. I don't have a cleaning woman because I don't trust anybody with my things. Where is Sebastian? I call her Sebastian, which is a man's name, so that she really isn't anything. She's three years old and she's never had sex. She's a virgin! That amounts to twenty-one years of our life. And then I think, well I was twenty-two before I had sex so I guess it's all right. You don't know any horny male cats do you? I didn't think you would. She must have locked herself in the closet. Sebastian? There she is, isn't she beautiful?"

"A pretty kitty," he said stroking the cat.

"Be careful, she doesn't trust people either. It takes a while. We're very much alike. We're very wary of strangers. I haven't a damn bit of cat food, you'll just have to drink milk. Would you like some Scotch? I don't have anything else. My father came down from Westchester last weekend and drank all the Bourbon."

"Do you have any beer?"

"Tons. Have a Scotch. I don't drink much, but once in a

while. . . . Look at this. I got it for three dollars and made some poor guy carry it up three flights of stairs, that was before I got this job, and last month I was offered two-hundred and fifty dollars for it. It's calibrated in kilograms so when you weigh yourself you have to do a lot of multiplication to figure out how much you really weigh. I gold-leafed it myself. I also did that, over there on the piano, see?'' She picked up a print from the music stand of the upright player piano. "That was my Christmas card this year. It's a woodcut. I control five million dollars but I love the arts. Ever since I was tiny I had the most expensive art school, and music school and everything. I played at Carnegie Recital Hall five years ago but I didn't think I was really great. I love to play though. Isn't this beautiful?''

"I love those pianos,'' he said.

"I got it at an auction. Seventy-five dollars. The mechanism is still being fixed and there are a couple of keys that stick a little, but I had it entirely rebuilt. I have this marvelous old piano tuner, Mr. Kertiss, and he's about eighty and he comes and spends a whole day here working on it about once a month. He's the only person I've ever trusted with my keys. He comes in while I'm at work and works on the piano and feeds the cat and stays here until I come home. He's marvelous! Now I'll get you a drink. How do you like it?''

"Just some beer, I don't think with the wine . . . ''

"I always keep beer. I don't like beer. I think we're going to be friends because all the people I like like beer, even though I don't like it myself. Would you like to see my books? That lamp's broken but I guess you can see them. Some of them are really good. Here I was in Catholic girls' school, practically a convent up in the Bronx, and I discovered Huxley all by myself. That was when I really learned to read, at the age of thirteen. I'd had the best education my father could buy but I had never seen a good book before, and suddenly I found this old paperback and started reading Huxley. I wore out all the paperbacks and then I bought new ones, and then a few years ago I went down to Fourth Avenue and bought some real books, all first editions, and I read all of Huxley all over again. See? There they are. In some cases I've got both the English and the American first editions, but I have all the American ones. Scotch?''

"Beer.''

"Okay, Okay. As I said, no strings attached. If you can just see life as a joke everything is okay. You know what I mean? I mean that's what he did. I'm not really messy but sometimes I'm not prepared to have visitors. I like to keep everything neat but sometimes I don't have the time.''

"Your place isn't messy at all.''

"No it isn't is it? I'm not a nut about cleanliness or anything but I do like to keep everything neat. I've got such a collection of things, I'll show you everything. Okay, here's your beer, and here's my drink, and turn out the lights in the kitchen, I don't like it really dark, but I don't like to waste light, and I think I'll just go and powder my nose. Sit down. I'll be right back.''

Wait until the war is over, and we are both a little older.

"Ready or not,'' she called from the boudoir, appearing. "Did you think I was going to change?''

"I don't know,'' he said, "I guess I thought you might.''

"Surprise. Come here. Look at this. It's real. I framed it myself, as you can certainly tell but it is beautiful.''

"It is,'' he said, "It really is. I always loved Klee. . . . ''

"Who? Oh that's not Klee, it's by a friend of mine, I mean if you want to see some originals!''

"It doesn't matter. I love that red. I always love the colors. There are great paintings I could never like just because I don't like the colors.''

"How strange! Have you got your drink? I want to show you everything. This one is original, so is that. I picked them up for nothing in Paris because they aren't signed but I know, I had them appraised by the appraiser for the Met and he said they might be worth over a thousand apiece although as he said they'd be hard to sell, but he said after they die everything will go up immensely.''

"You seem so different, although you didn't change.''

"What? Are you putting me on? What do you mean?''

"I just mean that I'd almost forgotten what you were like before, I remembered you differently."

"Oh. Oh dear. Don't push it."

"Don't push what?" he said in some dismay.

"Nevermind, you know what I mean. Let's see your teeth. Not bad, a little yellow, that's all. When's the last time you went to the dentist? Must have been two years. Smoking does that. See mine? That is thousands of dollars! I mean it."

"They're very good."

"They better be! I don't even know how much my father has spent on them (he still pays my dentist bills) but it's a fortune. You see I have weak teeth, essentially weak, they're always falling apart."

"I can't get over it."

"You can't get over what?"

"I mean in the little time you were gone I completely forgot you, or I invented what I thought you were like and now here you are again and I keep thinking that the one who went to the bathroom was not the same one as I see here now, I can't figure it out." He sat down.

"Okay. I'll go back in, flush the toilet and come out again," she said.

"No, no. . . . "

"Here I go!" She went into the bathroom and came out again. "Oops, I forgot." She went back in and flushed the toilet and came out again. "Is that better?"

"It must be, thank you very much."

"Do you want to see my silver? It's very, very old. It's right here, somewhere. I don't use it, I just hang on to it. The drawers aren't messy, they're just crowded. I'm going to have to get a bigger place. The things I have won't fit in here anymore, it's terrible. Here it is. 1841, solid."

"It's beautiful. Sit down."

"Where's my drink? Oh, there it is. Oh, thank you," she said, sitting.

"Why don't you use it?"

"Does it matter?"

"No it doesn't."

"Because I don't like to clean it, that's all, you see how black it is."

"Yes. Are you afraid?"

"I suppose so. Aren't you? No, I suppose you aren't. I think life is a joke on everybody. I guess that sounds bitter, but I'm not bitter. I just really feel that things aren't the way I thought they would be. I'm a little scared, but really I'm horrified. That's why I take chances like this. I figure I might as well get right into things. It's like committing suicide a little bit at a time . . . "

"Or all the time."

"That's what I mean, all the time. Aren't you smart."

"Do you want to go to bed with me?" he said.

"I don't know," she said, "And I can't talk about it or think about it or anything. If it happens okay, if not not. Don't push it. That's all I have to say. I was twenty-two before I had sex and then it was, well it really wasn't, I mean I just didn't, so I thought maybe next time, you know, or, something like that, but it really never was exactly, well, I mean what I said, I didn't just ask you up here to seduce you."

"Okay."

"Isn't Sebastian beautiful?"

"Pretty kitty."

"I can tell you like cats, because she likes you. I think you've passed the test. Everybody who comes in gets the once-over from Sebastian."

"I used to like cats . . . "

"I've had her for three years. My god three years. That's a long time. If I didn't laugh so much I'd cry. My god three years. How old are you? Twenty-three? Twenty-four?"

"I'm twenty-five."

"Oh, I'm older than you are."

"That's all right," he said.

"I don't think age makes a bit of difference. My brother is only seventeen, but we get along so well, you'd hardly believe it, I mean that we were so far apart in age. When I'm rested I look younger than you do. Isn't that funny? I'm going to live to be very old,

- 106 -

everyone in the family always has, isn't that funny? I mean it's funny for people our age to be thinking about being old, really old."

"It's normal I guess. I think about it sometimes. When I was very young I thought I might die any time but now that I'm older I think I will live to be very old."

"That's beautiful," she said.

"I really have to go," he said.

"Why? You have another drink," she said. "Do you want to hear a beautiful record? I guarantee you've never heard it before, nobody else has it. Fix yourself another drink and I'll put the record on. One of my record players is broken but somebody gave me this one to use in the meantime, it isn't a very good one but it works. Let's see. Oh, here it is. It'll just take a minute. D'you want to hear it?"

"Okay," he said, sitting down again.

She fiddled with the dials and produced a military band playing *Hail Britannia!* "Isn't that funny! What did I tell you! Listen to that! Do you know what it is? That's the British National Anthem being played by the Coldstream Guards! I think it's the funniest record I've ever heard. And listen they march around, there, now they're marching around. I think it's beautiful, don't you? And there's a lot of other ones. I think the next one is Scotch, but the German one is beautiful." She scraped the needle across the record to another point. "There."

"It's usually sung," he said.

"I can't carry a tune worth a damn," she said, "I can play beautifully, when I get the piano fixed I'll play it for you, but I really can't sing at all. I really liked the Nazis. I mean I didn't like what they did to the Jews, I'm part Jewish myself, but I really did like them. I work for a part of the government that was infiltrated by the Nazis and they still have a lot of Germans working for them right now, isn't that funny, but I actually like them, they're so well-organized and so careful, just like me. You may not think I'm well organized, but you should see me at work. Everybody says I'm so cold! I'm not cold, I'm just well-organized."

"Maybe I'll call you up sometime," he said, rising.

"It is late. I get up at six thirty," she said, rising.

"Whose national anthem is that?" he said, listening.

"Yugoslavia's, I think," she said, listening, "Yes."

"Do you have a number or something?" he said.

"You may call me if you wish, I'll give you the number."

"Thanks," he said, smiling as she handed him her card.

"Goodbye."

They touched their tongues and felt each other's lips in a brief embrace that hurried out the door and waited for the elevator with considerable impatience.

⟦ Fred's Dream ⟧

The past was contained in ever present dreams.

It is time to sort out the story a bit. I am speaking of the time which was the first time that Fred ever heard of Gilbert Green. At that time, Wary and Fred were constantly in each other's company. It was an interesting time in both their lives. It was a time when they already shared every experience with each other but they did not yet abuse their friendship by remarking its shortcomings. The time was encased in music, and they often talked about it. One night they were talking much of the time with Dennis Oppenheim who had just met Gilbert Green at a big party to which a lot of beautiful people, including himself, had been invited quite by chance. After Dennis met Gilbert Green, somebody told Dennis a story about him which indicated that Gilbert Green might in time be great.

Dennis, having just met Gilbert Green, wanted to find out who he was because he sensed that he must be somebody. Dennis happened to be standing next to Ted Castle, whom he had met several times before. Dennis asked Ted who Gilbert Green was. Ted told Dennis that he had been standing in a group of people at another party about a week before. One of the group was a good friend of Gilbert Green's, so that it happened that Gilbert Green came up and began talking to them. It readily became apparent from the conversation which was punctuated with talk of Andy that Gilbert Green had been working with Andy Warhol. At that time this was a very exciting thing to do and not very many people had the opportunity. And so Ted said to Gilbert Green, "I understand that you are the brains behind Andy Warhol." "Not exactly," replied Gilbert Green, "I am Andy's representative on earth." Dennis was not exactly sure that he liked this anecdote but he was very glad to be able to repeat it to all his acquaintances. Wary did not like the story very much and Fred was very pleased by it. But he did not press Dennis for further details from the life of Gilbert Green, which probably would have annoyed Wary very much or somewhat, he just kept the name of Gilbert Green in mind, who wrote all of Andy Warhol's songs for him. This is not true, it is just real.

That night, sleeping in his bed alone, Fred had a real big dream. It showed him through a cave that was in part a club, a restaurant, and Andy Warhol's studios, which Fred imagined to be very vast and have a lot to do with things that Andy Warhol actually had no connection with. Gilbert Green did not appear in Fred's dream and neither did Andy Warhol, though it seemed to Fred that Andy Warhol was holding forth in the restaurant part of this vast fantasy. Fred was sitting at a little shabby table with some scripts because he had just been given this new job. An amalgam of various women came in who Fred thought was Cass Elliot though she looked like Bunny Eisenhower and talked a lot like Brigid Berlin. They started to do something that had to do with singing, and suddenly Cass Elliot burst into a torrent of abuse that was directed specifically at Fred. Fred didn't like this at all, but he was confident that Andy Warhol had definitely given him the job, and he had the vague thought of saying so if he got the chance. He endured all abuse. It occurred to him that he had taken Gilbert Green's production job, and maybe Cass Elliot's abuse was only due to the way women never like any unexpected changes though they soon get used to them. The light was very theatrical and so were the performances.

Bob Dylan was playing the guitar. When Cass Elliot stopped shouting, Bob Dylan undertook to explain it all to Fred. He said he had no personal objections to Fred at all, in fact he rather liked him. Since it seemed to Fred that Bob Dylan was much more important to Andy Warhol than Cass Elliot or whoever she was would ever be, Fred was suffused with the warm glow of comraderie. But, Bob Dylan continued, the position of *reader*, which was the name of Fred's ill-defined position in the company, was a very special position in the whole set-up, and Bob Dylan said he couldn't understand why Fred had been appointed to it. "We'll just have to go through everything again and waste a lot of time," he said. Fred's heart sank. Bob Dylan said that he had no objection to the way Fred was doing it, but as far as Bob Dylan was concerned it was all right for Fred to be a reader, but they couldn't have him there as *the new reader*. It was a very subtle point and Fred sort of understood it. He certainly appreciated how nice Bob Dylan was trying to be. He thought of trying to find Andy Warhol and have him settle it but the next scene was entirely something else.

They were all seated at a rather elegant outdoor lunch at a large round glass table with a central umbrella over it, being Fred and his father and two rather fat old English people who looked as if they had been dead for some time. Although he was much too warmly dressed for the weather which was fine, the Englishman's white beard was at least two days long. The English woman was dressed about the same, and she wore a hat, and her hands seemed to have been bitten by a blight. These old fogies, who were friends of Fred's father, were politely congratulating young Fred on having sold his interest in Andy Warhol for $40,000. Fred was enduring the luncheon with some grace, although he did not like it, because the wine and the food was excellent and he was glad to have his father pleased with him, though he regretted severing his connection with Andy Warhol, but he was pleased to have the money which, Fred slyly thought, was much more than $40,000, it was really more like $80,000 because of some vague other thing which was going to be sold also, so that Fred was rapidly consoling himself with the thought of practically $100,000, which he thought that the English people would never have believed.

The house stood on a hill surrounded by two square miles of rolling wheatfields reduced to stubble for the treeless winter. Or, more accurately as a matter of fact, 3000 *square chains* of land. It was not delapidated, it was a stone house with all the stones in place. The great green Bentley stole carefully up the rough dirt drive that was so seldom used now and then by reapers and combined machines. They entered by the back way, full of cobwebs and rotted plaster falling down through leaks, and moved through two dingy rooms that had once been beautiful in their simple crudity toward the front door which could be opened only and then with difficulty from the inside bolt. It gave upon no steps but a view from the top of this small hill of a small steel mill, with its eight high chimneys and its walls of corrugated metal situated down below the hill, across the crossings of the two highways that formed half the boundaries of Fred's landed land.

They—it was not clear just who—moved about the house in a desultory way remarking old stuff left by kids trespassing on the fantasy of a city squire who had newly bought his life's desire. The attic was brilliant with sunlight from a row of dormers, the cellar was murky in uncanned jam and undried figs that smelt of lye. From the outside, each of the four flues of all of the four chimneys of the house puffed experimentally a little smoke for the first time since 1912. The air was fairly clear that day since the mill was situated leeward of the house. The airplanes made more noise than melting alloyed metals and even automated rolling stampers. It was a summer's day in the middle of the winter. The whole thing was reminiscent of 1841 and a number of subsequent years when black slaves were smuggled faithfully behind the chimneys of the house towards Canada, now not two hours away by foot, where they would be given sanctuary and not have to fight a war in Southeast Asia later. The green porcelain French coal stove was not hooked up but it fitted perfectly into a tiny bedroom upstairs. The great stars of the nineteen sixties are still hiding underground, but they are no longer waiting. The authentic experiences of the nineteen sixties will all be composed of memories that will be a little bit mistaken. Some day there may be a little life in politics. A long brown curl gently encompasses the right frame of his old brown glasses and a single silver hair. The roy of his pants' cord clasps and unclasps rythmically against a somewhat deformed pair of eyes and he awakes to a host of petty recriminations, clothed in tongue mud and some soot.

⟦ Fred & The Girl ⟧

And the clouds will cry.

"You're late," she said, after she had re-locked the several locks that locked her door. Then she indicated that the costume he was wearing made her costume look incongruous. He said he thought that she looked fine. She started babbling right away. As her evening wore on, his interest in it declined. She challenged something he had written. But he had not even written it. Thus the whole thing was a ruse, and that too was bothersome. Her only interest in his conversation was when he mentioned something that he owned.

"Can I see it?" was her reply and his was an indefinite delay. At her suggestion, they tried to read the poems of Rimbaud. Her accent was hideous and she mistook most words. How can you pretend to understand the poem, he thought, as she massacred the verse and he tried to improve her understanding by telling her in no uncertain terms that each syllable must be savored. He read some poems and she corrected his pronunciation, wrongly. As he read aloud, she read too in an undertone that overbore his every pause.

"I think we could do great things together, with no strings attached," she said and it occurred to him for the first time that she really was a whore. In the meanwhile, at her suggestion they were getting slightly drunk. He proposed a dinner which she referred to as a bite to eat. Finally she did not like the only poem that he really liked and she didn't understand a word of it. Since they were French poems, she only liked the ones that were translated with a dirty word.

"You better watch your language," she said when he used the same good words, and he laughed at her and she swallowed hard on his insult although she had not heard the words she had been directing at him in a steady stream since he arrived twenty minutes late. One time he put his hand across her mouth in a playful way and she wriggled free without stopping talking once to think.

"Oh well if you want to go to Max's, I'll have to change my clothes." She objected incisively to three restaurants that he proposed and while she powdered her nose again he made up his mind and told her his decision. She did not like the food, the other people, or the service, and she abused a busboy who was admiring her so much that he spilled some grease on purpose on the lining of her coat.

"To hell with Andy Warhol," she said between avid bites of disliked food, while he expressed his admiration of the man. Then she pointed out another man who was dressed to resemble a movie star, and who she said had been flirting with her all evening. He replied, to her annoyance, that it was apparent that the man had been flirting with none other than himself. She then expressed her dislike of the possibilities of eye contact while I said I thought that it was fun.

"Let's get out of here," she said and closed the door on hateful images. She rejected other opportunities for diversions, preferring to get down to business right away. They felt each other up. She had another drink, and he made her make some coffee which involved washing the coffeepot in a very special way of which he had no knowledge or interest. They disagreed about what music was best. She talked of sex, just like that. Just like her little cat would if possible.

"My father says this place is just like a Japanese whorehouse," she screamed more than once and he thought that the thought would never have occurred to him but it was right as rain would be right now for his confused emotions. "The thing is not the screens but the fact that you cannot get out of a Japanese whorehouse unless they let you out because of the complex locks." This is not true, it is just real.

"Oh, oh!" she moaned immediately as he touched her and she

proceeded to direct his touches and turn out the lights and close the window screens and open up the bed, moaning lightly all the time. By now she had stopped talking altogether and the blackness of her whiteness was intense. Everything was uncomfortable, as when one is engaged in swimming. He was disgusted with himself, and it was evident.

"What's the matter," she said at length, opening her eyes and mouth.

"I think you frightened me," he said.

Don't be so messy.

Don't talk like that.

Don't lace your shoes upon my bed.

But what he told himself was *just don't apologize*, and his last words to her were, "How do you get out of here?"

⟦ Wary's Poem ⟧

The dominant perversion.
    My wife is extremely unhappy.
    I didn't know that you were married.
    I'm not married.
    Oh, what is she unhappy about.
    I don't really know.
    She doesn't like the way you wear your hair, or what.
    No, I don't think it's that.
    Do you want to talk about it.
    I think that would be a good idea.
    What do you want to talk about.
    There never seems to be enough money.
    You mean your wife thinks you are a failure.
    I don't think she thinks that either.
    Why doesn't she go out and get a job.
    Because she has to give all her attention to the baby.
    Do you mean to say that you are jealous of the baby.
    I don't know, I might be. It certainly is expensive.
    Aren't you expensive too? I bet you're more expensive than the
baby.
    What's that supposed to mean.
    Just that.
    I suppose I could stop smoking.
    You could eat nothing but spaghetti which is very cheap.
    I gave up getting haircuts but that doesn't save too much.
Besides, pretty soon I'm going to go and really have my hair done.
It has to be really, really long first and then I'm going to go to this

place I know about and have it cut in such a way that I can part it in the middle or on either side or not at all if I want to. Won't that be beautiful?

It probably will be quite expensive.

Can't you think of anything else to say.

You brought it up in the first place.

All right I did. Would you like a cup of coffee?

Maybe I will. Do you have any milk.

There probably is some, but don't use it all up or my wife will kill me.

Then where would she be.

Right back where she started from.

Where does she come from anyway.

Alaska.

Isn't it very expensive there? It seems to me I heard they don't have any food or eggs or something.

That was during the Gold Rush. I've never been there myself. I understand that it is very expensive and there are hardly any roads.

Then you wouldn't have to keep a car.

No, the only way to get over the glaciers is by airplane.

Does your wife wish she was back in Alaska.

No, but she might wish that she had never left. Actually it was her mother who left in the first place, my wife didn't have much to say about it at the time.

Has she ever revisited her homeland?

She was going to go to her father's funeral but the car wouldn't start and so she didn't go. She was glad she couldn't make it.

What sex is the infant.

Female.

Is your wife's mother rich.

She never made it.

Then the three of them all rely on you, is that it.

Not exactly.

What do you mean.

Does it really matter.

Of course not to me. I thought maybe you would think it was important.

Not now.

Why not?

I used to think it was important, but now I don't think so anymore.

That's really very funny.

I don't see what's so funny about it, but I'll share a laugh with you if you like. It feels good to giggle, don't it.

Doesn't it.

It certainly do.

Many's the time, oh dear.

Oh my goodness!

What is the world coming to.

Let me out of here.

Get down on the floor.

What's that supposed to do.

I don't know. That's what you do when you've had too much to laugh.

Nobody ever laughs in dreams.

I know, isn't it peculiar.

I guess it is, I never thought about it. I mean I knew it because I read it in a magazine but I didn't have any reaction to the information, I just accepted it.

Just like that, huh?

More or less.

Do you feel better now.

I have a headache. Let's do something.

Okay, what shall we do?

We could watch television.

It doesn't work very well in this part of town.

Why is that.

The steel buildings cause a lot of ghosts.

I saw a movie with Marlene Dietrich last night. She looked old. Maybe she was old. She's certainly old now.

But Jane Wyman looked very young, younger than I've ever seen her look.

I don't think I've ever seen Jane Wyman.

She's not very good-looking, she's sort of plain like a housewife.

I don't have a favourite movie star, do you?

I used to like Audrey Hepburn but now I like Donovan. They both speak French.

What does that have to do with it.

I don't know, I just thought of it this minute.

You think of the strangest things.

Do I? I never used to think I thought of anything and then one day I started noticing what I was thinking and I thought it was sort of strange but then I thought that everybody's thoughts are really sort of strange.

You had an awakening.

No. I went to sleep. I decided I was an intellectual after all.

I'm an intellectual too, but I work with my hands.

Of course you are. That's why you're not fat.

You're not too fat.

I'm not too fat but I am fat.

Maybe that's what your wife doesn't like.

That's right, she probably doesn't. How did we get back on that.

I don't know, isn't it funny?

The last time you said, Isn't it peculiar.

So what.

The whole conversation seems to be repeating itself.

But it's not is it.

I don't know. It might be. I feel I've said that before too.

And you did or you didn't.

I can't remember exactly what I said.

Neither can I.

Maybe we should just go ahead and repeat the whole thing.

We won't be able to remember it all.

I guess you're right. Still, we have to do something.

We are doing something. Would you rather do something else?

Not particularly.

⟦ Fred & Wary ⟧

And is the lie then disappeared?

The question for awhile was who was going to be in whose entourage. It was delicately handled on both sides and it was not discussed. Wary had nothing but the remains of an outworn entourage which he could not recommend to friends. Fred was building a new grouping upon the ashes of the old. They sat in two white chairs with footstools, opposite each other and side by side by legs and talked about the question of loneliness and the question of insanity.

The world continued to revolve, so slowly at its center and so madly at its outskirts, while Wary and Fred brought each other up to date about each other's lives. They were exactly the same age, which pleased them quite a bit, and they had both decided independently that they were very lucky. Good things always happened to them just when they needed it. They were quite glad to be so lucky and glad besides to find someone in whom they could confide this fact. They also confessed to a profound sense of doubt and they quickly congratulated each other that this doubt was indispensable if they were to be great men. All great men are also somewhat hated and despised while also being greatly loved. They greatly love themselves and hate it on occasion. These things they had learned through endless observation and a great deal of introspection.

More than once, said Wary, he had felt the cold wind of insanity brush his ears. Fred took a somewhat different view. He said, All artists are already insane. That would depend on what you meant by insanity, which they did not discuss. Not medical insanity, but the insanity that says, *I refuse to be a slave.* Many artists do not escape slavery at all, but that isn't the point. The point is that they might be able to. It was sort of a nobility that they did not discuss because Wary had just about decided that he didn't think much of nobility because he had known somebody who had thought much of nobility and he didn't think too much of him. The grand manner has fallen on evil days, said Fred, and they agreed.

Thus, although he was inclined to dress up fine and fancy, Wary hid himself in clothes that were just as carefully chosen as they would be if he wanted to show himself. He was a worker, after all, and he liked their simple kind of clothes. Although he didn't say so, Wary was just on the point of adopting finer dress, he was looking around at all the different costumes and imagining them on him. He would never simply have adopted a facile passing fashion. Some time before he had shaved his head which meant that when his hair grew out again he would have changed his style, and this moment was approaching fast. It worried him a little bit. He had rented his beautiful house and moved downstairs to a very plain place. Then he got rid of his friends and lived completely alone. He worked like hell to the accompaniment of very good music. I have wasted my life, he thought as he worked. But he saw that he was still lucky.

As he masturbated more he was reminded of his extreme youth and as he worked he thought it over making no decisions but just fondly freshening his memories and dreams. Among other things, a big white house and a small white cat. His life hadn't been wasted as long as he was now at work. His life was a strangely solitary process with which nobody else could help him. It was so slow and still it was fast. Among other things, two or three teachers who had almost seen what he held within him, waiting for the time. The time was now and he knew it well. He had had a whole lot of experience.

Suddenly he had accumulated quite a bit of perfect work. First, he arranged to show it to the public. Then he bought a new music system which was something that he really wanted and almost thought he needed. Then he turned up the volume and invited everyone he had ever met, which was a lot of people, to a grand ball in his own honor. This epiphany complete, he kept on working steadily. Wary did not quite trust his luck.

His sense of time went off in two or three directions. His great show, after so much preparation, was somewhat of an anti-climax. Other things seemed to happen fast. He declined one job and took another, very highly paid. He kept his dress discreet and only celebrated at home in private. He saw his work dismissed briefly in the press. He spent a week in Miami with his mother. And he met Fred who loved him and his work.

"What everybody wants is always to be loved," said Wary, completely certain, "And anybody who doesn't know so must by lying as they go."

Just a couple of guys out on the town.

First they dressed for dinner. Then they went and ate. While they were eating they admired the chicks that other men were eating with. They lingered over coffee at the Club, where such dress was rarely seen, and all their acquaintances paid them a little homage. Then they went to a huge party at the Metropolitan Museum and had a drink. Somebody came over to them and dragged them off to meet ex-Queen Jacqueline who, as it happened, was talking to the Mayor, and so they met him too. Nobody said much though everybody seemed to be polite. Then, feeling rather high or something, they made another circuit of the galleries, nodding to a few acquaintances, and walked out into the not too cold spring night and kept on walking. They walked a long, long ways, their heels vivid against the sidewalk, their shoes sparkling in the lamplight. They didn't say much of anything at all.

They felt sort of on top of the world and each understood the other's sense of it. They walked very fast but they did not get out of breath. It was a leisurely fast walk. At one point they made a detour so as to pass through the concourse of The Grand Central Terminal, and on the way out they stopped in the men's room to take a leak. Then they decided not to go to the movies. Instead they just kept on walking, talking occasionally now, but just making remarks, not having any conversation.

The elevator took them to the sixteenth floor and they walked the last flight to the penthouse where they could hear percussive electric music blasting out of the music room, whose windows were wide open to the rooftops. Somebody gave them a joint of grass which they smoked with pleasure. The lights of the Empire State Building cast an appreciative glow over the vacant terrace where the wind blew lightly. They had an opportunity to admire some photographs that had been taken in the same place in daylight by a famous heiress. One or two were really great. The music was so loud that nobody could talk much. They sat on a low stone wall and looked at the buildings and the moon. After awhile the players decided to take a rest and the two friends exchanged a few remarks with them, laughing quietly. After a while like this, they decided to go to the theatre.

They were half an hour late for the midnight performance by Charles Ludlam at the Gate. It didn't bother them at all. They went right in and sat right down just in time to see Charles Ludlam make his entrance playing Norma Desmond and himself. They laughed and clapped and loved the scene. The incense was almost suffocating. During the fight between the actors they were hit with a banana peel and half an orange which they threw back on the stage. They had seen the play fives times before but once again it was completely new and utterly exhausting. By the time it was over, nobody had the energy to clap or bravo very much. As they left, they repeated a few choice lines to each other as they walked along.

"The throw of the dice will never abolish luck."

"Never ask a soldier about his wounds."

"Of human sufferage, of common aspirings. . . . "

"We have never been so insulted in our lives."

"Okay C. B., I'm ready for that close-up."

"We all suffer from the infirmities of impure blood."

"I feel a little depressed."

"You take the cake."

"No more nookie for you until Tamberlaine is slain or overcome."

"And may the god of dramatic art have mercy on my soul."

They felt weak with laughter and drained by fantastic visions of the past and of the future. They had had a great time on the town and then they fell asleep.

⟦ Fred Afraid ⟧

The opposite of viciousness is tenderness.

Fred was in a sorry state of mind. He realized for the first time that he was afraid of something. He could have given it a name, but as far as he could see he only knew a little bit of what it was. This realization was brought about by the fact that he was in love, for the first time in some time, apart from passing infatuations and more legitimate associations. His fantasies when the loved one was not there grew tremendously upon their subject, and whenever he saw the one he loved, his fears were immediately put to rest. By that time he had had enough experience to realize that fear is something, and to recognize its presence. Before this, he had felt fear but he had never realized that it was fear, he just felt something strong, and he almost always responded to it by embracing the situation that created it. This was an extremely successful technique for destroying fears. Now that he thought back about it, he knew that that was how he had happened to do much of what he had so far done. It was his special vice. He could even recall the time when he had climbed numerous rickety ladders in the theatre, although he could have told others to do that work, just because he loved the fearful toppling situation.

One time he went to a dark part of town in search of some excitement. It was a trucking depot, and the long rows of empty vans backed up against the riverbank made cover for various intrigues. He smoked a cigarette in the slight chill and looked out across the river. It was so dark he could hardly see his hands. His hands did not shake but he was so afraid that he had left his glasses and his wallet home, changed his clothes and wore very little money. The place was desolate but it was fairly noisy due to the elevated highway running overhead. He threw his cigarette into the water and walked along between the trailers, slowly. Suddenly he encountered another solitary young man who just said "Hello" in passing. He sensed that some of the trailers might be occupied by other people and he did not peer too deeply into them, and then he did peer deeply into one of them and saw nothing but the blackness of closed black tubes when they are examined closely. Looking ahead along the river bank he saw someone light a match in the far distance up ahead. At one point he had to scramble over large concrete debris that was quite a bit like rocks. When he had achieved near where he had seen the light there was no one in sight. He lighted a cigarette in turn as if he were involved in an intrigue which required that signal. The river was extremely calm that night and he didn't feel one bit cold because there was no wind and there was maybe lots of danger.

Having smoked half the cigarette, he came out of the shadows and walked in front of the line of vans in full view of nobody he could see by street light. The place was deserted. Suddenly, nearby, he heard the sound of several feet running nearer toward the rocks. He ducked into the next shadow and walked along its truck. The disturbance stopped within ten feet of him. A man with a flashlight, a long flashlight with a larger lens, was holding another man on the ground by the throat, shining the big light in his eyes. The downed man cringed as the light man threatened him. "I've been looking for you," said the top man in a fairly ordinary voice. Just then three men hopped across the rocks and clattered to a stop around the couple on the ground. The light flashed instantly across their faces and returned to its main target. The downed man said, "Let go." One of the newcomers, after a second's pause, said, "Are you going to let him go or not?" With a little shove toward his quarry's throat, the man with the light ran out like mad, waving his light all around him as he left. The downed man got up, clapped the shoulder of one of his friends and walked away with him. The other two men separated, one of them happening to pass by Fred as he left saying, "It's all right now," and then disappearing around the corner of a truck. The silence was again complete. Fred took another cigarette and stood in a vacant area between two trailers at the edge of a huge puddle looking out upon the slow, flat water. In about two minutes his revery was interrupted by car lights that drew quickly toward him through the puddle and almost ran him into the barrier at the river's edge. He stepped aside, looked with annoyance at the headlights of the police car, and walked slowly past as four policemen emerged from it. In the street he found four more police cars unloading. The cops said nothing to him as he passed them, but one of them looked as if he would like to spit on Fred. He thought that the madman with the light had probably called the cops in the hope of screwing up his friends. The cops searched the insides of the vans in vain. Fred walked slowly away from the place, thinking that if he had been questioned he would have insisted that he had a right to walk there, and stopped to have a cup of coffee at a diner he was passing where the only other customer almost said "Hello" to him, probably mistaking him for some other man.

⟦ Fred & Wary with Friends ⟧

A night of debauchery is followed by a brief spell of good luck.

Wary and Fred developed the custom that on one night of the week they would meet at the club for a drink without making any special date. Usually it was fairly late by the time one or the other of them showed up, and the one who was waiting commonly entertained doubts about the arrival of the other until it happened. Then they usually chatted comfortably with each other and with friends. One time Wary had told Fred that he probably wouldn't make it because he wasn't feeling well, and as a matter of fact he never showed. But always otherwise they met each other casually enough.

There was a very light fear connected with the Club, which was that Fred never knew in advance who he would meet there, and their custom relieved that fear somewhat. At the time of their acquaintance, as I have said before, they were both broadening their circles. At the same time they were introducing each other into them. This is not real, it is just true.

On the night in question, Fred arrived very late with a very young disciple because they had been detained at a dinner party for some potential customers. Wary was there with an old friend of his who he wanted Fred to meet. The old friend had a very bright gaze, a ready nervous laugh and a brief beard. The very young disciple had a hunger for experience and a tendency not to talk. In a way then, the conversation was composed of three instead of four. It was so late that they were all quite familiar right at first. Wary announced that he wanted to find out if his old friend and Fred would get along. They developed an instant superficial friendship. The kind that usually has no consequence although both of them remember it with a little fondness.

After joking avidly for not so very long, they decided to go to Max's and look at all the people posing there. They went in and sat down and posed with the others at the counters. They laughed and exchanged some observations and they hardly noticed that no waitress had come to notice them until pretty soon the bar closed for the night. On the way out they pretended that they had felt very hot inside and they took off all their coats, and since Wary was not wearing any coats, he took off his shirt. That made it even funnier.

Wary's old friend asked where they proposed to go. The question had not occurred to anyone else, but Fred immediately volunteered his house. The old friend wanted to stop by his house to get some grass, and the very young disciple drove them, chatting happily among themselves. When they got there there was some ribald confusion while the guests and the hosts were settled with their drinks and smokes. All this was actually recorded by the very young disciple who wrote very fast in snatches at the conversation on a handy typewriter for about fifteen minutes as fast as he could type without trying not to make mistakes and eliminating capitals a lot. It was a good transcript and they thought that it too was funny. The situation was very peculiar and it made Wary and Fred feel young again.

After they had had a few tokes of his grass, Wary's old friend quieted down although he was still liable to laugh. For a time they were alone although they were together. The old friend stretched on the couch. The very young disciple curled in a chair. Wary took a turn at the typewriter and produced half a page of symbols and numbers that looked like writing. Although it was good they did not laugh much more. Fred turned out the lights and dug the radio. It wasn't very dark because of street lights on the outside. It was dusky. The radio was fairly quiet. The music, though, was popular and not too romantic. Wary joined his old friend on the couch. There was a place left which the old friend invited Fred to fill. They sat there very quietly firmly ensconced against each other's thighs digging the strange remoteness of the light and of the music. The very young disciple was invited by the old friend to join them on the couch but this was not done. It occurred to Fred and Wary simultaneously that the old friend might become impolite, but he kept his cool instead and pushed himself down so that he was sitting on the floor between the feet of his companions. As the dawn arose behind them and among them, Wary and Fred joined hands behind the curly head of the old friend below them, and one of the old friend's hands was clasped to one of Wary's legs. They sat there very quietly with the very young disciple looking carefully at everything until the dawn increased from a glow into a glare when the party dispersed by mutual agreement. As Wary and his old friend left, Fred kissed them both good-bye and the old friend made another joke as an apology.

"That was a very repressive-expressive situation," said Wary some days later.

"I wouldn't have liked it if it had gone any further," Fred replied. "But as it was I found it beautiful."

What are you afraid of? What am I afraid of. Many things, not everything.

A certain kind of tree bends pretty in the wind. I bid fair to imitate that character. His conversation is strangely awkward, somewhat overheard and not laughing very much. They separately confess that they have lately become somewhat fearful of something and the conversation veers about without much of a direction. One of them resorts to gentle bragging, the other to mild confessions. The youth in which the other people did the talking makes an inconclusive end.

"You seem to be quite uncomfortable."

"Not any more uncomfortable than usual."

⟦ Fred in Love ⟧

I can't do what ten people tell me to, so I'll remain the same.

Fred was being torn limb from synapse by the winds of many controversies some of which he wasn't even sure of.

First he rushed to declare his love for Wary so as to secure at least one point at first.

He suddenly found himself being courted in different ways by various people that he didn't know very well.

He noticed that he was pleased by all this attention but he couldn't decide what it all meant.

After years of being a complete unknown he had suddenly become beautiful and attracted all kinds of attentions.

Some of his court seemed slightly envious of his situation, and everybody smiled a lot whenever he was present.

There was a bit of a contest to see who would get the credit for having discovered his existence, but nobody was able to win.

In a short time he was quietly offered several opportunities to indulge in sexual orgies, and one very young girl demurely threw herself at him.

Surrounded by so much choice, he was forced into the position of having to decide what he really wanted.

He took the precaution of indulging in a sexual orgy with people he did not know in a fearful situation surrounded by water and cops.

In such a strange and physical situation, he was not the star of the show but only one of several players who was well treated by the star.

He fell out of the trailer considerably exorcised and then stared down a cop who was coming to investigate with a light smile of exultation.

The next night he was driving along a road and he was so busy thinking that he almost killed himself by ramming the back of a stalled Mustang.

He was amazed that his last thought before the accident was the name of the car that he ran into.

But just then the accident was averted by the purest luck, there weren't even any scratches or police inquiries, except those that Fred made up himself.

He looked at his naked body in a lengthy mirror and considered it for the first time as a sort of public love object, and decided to exercise a bit.

The next night he was surrounded at the Club by people who half suspected that he would be able to help them out professionally at some time.

He accepted their praises gracefully, indeed he was very pleased to have these people on his side for whatever reason.

It was an extremely eventful season just at the beginning of the spring you remember when the President of all the people pretended to resign and the King was shot to death in Memphis.

Some of the people courting him were younger than he was and others of them were just a little older.

He still encountered a certain amount of indifference, wherever he found himself, but he hardly noticed it because he was so busy.

One night he unexpectedly found himself in the Flavin room at the back of Max's talking with Stefan Brecht.

They were surrounded there by almost all of Andy Warhol's entourage, and Fred had the experience of being nodded to by the hero of this book.

The light in that room is extremely red and it has the effect of making people look different and on the whole rather better than they do.

Viva was looking better than Marlene Dietrich ever looked as she posed with her eyes, her nose and her chin pointing straight ahead.

Suddenly she was no longer looking in that way, she was standing next to Fred pointing herself straight into the face of Stefan Brecht where she spat a load of insults and departed before they could unstun themselves.

"You shit," she spattered loudly, "Thanks for writing that asshole review."

Then Viva got another star to go over and complain to Stefan Brecht about his having said she was a "pig" but as it happened she didn't really care.

It occurred to the two friends simultaneously that Viva might fall in love with Stefan Brecht if he gave her the least opportunity.

The conversation turned directly toward the nature of power and the question of intimidations which involved some small confessions on Fred's part.

He said that he desired most of all to triumph over fear in the midst of fairly famous people.

Stefan Brecht was of the opinion that it was Fred's destiny to be successful in whatever he really undertook to do.

They stood their ground and sipped their beers and listened to Andy Warhol's music until many had left to prove that they were not easily intimidated.

On the way out Fred performed an obscure threat by means of bowing low to Andy Warhol who smiled a little bit and nodded three times to acknowledge it.

One day in the middle of this process of events Fred took two baths although as a rule he rarely bathed until he itched.

He lay in the warm clear water with the ends of his long tousled hair getting wet and reflected on all his past successes and his future projects.

He put his feet against the wall above the faucets and pushed his shoulders against the rim of the tub and admired his prick as it grew firmer.

He was suddenly filled with inchoate poetry which did not include a word that he had ever heard before.

He decided with the directness of a great desire to do something definite to attract attention to himself as a work of art would do.

He had a vision during a momentary nap of all the players in the world as midgets as ridiculous as foreshortened limbs could make them.

He found himself in the audience laughing and applauding heartily but without his own reward.

He nudged his companion who did not return his smile but rather turned away so as not to be bothered with it.

He awoke with the tension draining from the top of his spine into his shoulder blades and he stretched and massaged his neck and dried himself.

A great feeling of power and well-being spread itself beneath his new clean clothes and as he brushed his hair around his ears he smiled at himself.

In a brief moment he had turned himself from being an object back into the subject he had always been and would remain.

He noticed it was getting late but he was so pleased it didn't matter and with a final self-same wink he realized that he had changed his schedule.

The experiences of many days came together and released their lessons upon his brain where they flowered and got picked.

He turned on the radio and danced a lively jig alone until he was somewhat exhausted and lay upon the floor and felt its texture and the heavy cloth.

As the light descended outside he took a little wine and thought of Wary, and Nancy and Robert, and all three Davids in a row, and Ernestine, and Stefan Brecht, and Viva, and everybody else who was called Fred.

When the darkness was complete he wept to a sad song that happened to him.

⟦ Fred's Song ⟧

Write a song. "The Real Right Way"

A chill wind at the last of winter
pierces the body to my soul
gently warning us for warmer times
too far away to know.

My life as I can see it now
passes by the other side
of something like a window
made true & square & clear.

    The words may cast along the types
    each to each an integer of time
    the factors that I pray for
    the formations I must know.

        Friends recruit the rights of loves
        keeping back a hundred dreams
        that can recome when time requires
        to marry indigence and spleen.

The real and only real right way
will live toward making up a scene
in which the sharer knows no shame
by which the bearer casts no blame.

    Abstract lines retrace the space
    where childish passions played
    and broke the time in parts of nine
    that should undo the test of grace.

Thought as a question could be sought
near trees of every type and rocks
or out of sight beneath the sheet
and in the middle of a traffic jam.

The lillies of the valley weak and droop
from the edge of a single glass carafe
reminding me my time is free
to do what I may wish to see.

Our history lies abandoned toys
a mess upon the rug of days
to be repiled and stored away
to gather dust & rot & rust.

The only real right way to dress
declares you as you are at best
at which the swearer knows no shame
by which the bearer casts no blame.

Ever so never may I fill like gas
the emptyness that guilt employs
but may inspire their rhymes with mine
and games and lusts and chests of air.

Love is also like a tear
to try the soul against its pain
and fail to win and sue to lose
crying silently without regret.

So much eloquence leaves me blind
to the changing subject here
then what is the question there
and when may we reply.

The now that time makes great for men
whose hour shall quickly live
must last the season of their fame
as a well worth weighted test.

The real and only real right way
will word its line toward a day
on which the swearer knows no shame
by which the bearer casts no blame.

    Right now the leg will be disguised
    in gentle lines that show the toes
    with heels that click to send a glance
    toward a single lonely man.

        Colors loved for eyes or pose
        will wave a tasteless match of rays
        to raise the wrong against the strong
        and correct the sight of queens.

            The hair will fly as free as hair
            without a hate to cover or adorn
            the light expression of a look
            that custom-crowns each crown.

                The final touch will be a touch
                to kiss a bird or change a friend
                the voice we can command to show
                fine men to grow from none.

    By which the bearer casts no blame
    in which the wearer knows no shame
    and time will make a sign to something
    The Real Right Way To Dress For Spring.

This verse is confused. On the one hand it starts out as a description and then it ends up as a dream. Or maybe it's all a dream. But I agree it has to be here, or near here. It's good cinematically, too. —G.G.

⟦ Susan Herself with Fred ⟧

Reality on tape.

Is it on, oh I can see the little thing. This really might be boring you know? *You mean boring to do or to listen to.* I don't know both I guess. I don't know what to say. *Okay, just talk.* Well I was not born on a farm. I think I'll say what we're doing first. I'm going to talk into this microphone for hours and hours whenever I have a spare minute or something, if only they'd stop these investigations I could really devote myself to it, but anyway I'm going to try to say everything I know maybe not about everything, do you want everything or not. *You can just talk.* All right I'm just going to talk and see what comes of it. Then I think they're going to edit it and write it up for this book. I'd write it myself but I always get carried away when I try to write and it makes everything I think sound so peculiar that I, besides I don't like to write. Especially not about myself. It's going to look like a lie because, well, it will be a lie, the situation will be utterly falsified, but the idea is, I don't know whose idea it is, but the idea is that I will get used to talking and since I won't be able to remember everything I've said after awhile I'd better stick to what I really know even if I don't really know it, like things I've heard, because that's the only way it will make any kind of sense. This really ought to be one of those talking books. Put it on a cassette and play it in your car or something. Why don't you do that? *Maybe we will.*

Gilbert Green was my husband, briefly, oh god that sounds terrible. It's true though I married him when I was nineteen and now I'm twenty-five and it's all over. It was practically my whole life up to now. I met him when I was a waitress and he was a nobody. He didn't look like a nobody he looked like he was somebody and he knew it too and even when he was nobody he'd go around in crowds of people and take a look at people looking at him to figure out who he was which they never could really do until later and by that time they had forgotten where they first saw him, but anyway as soon as I laid eyes on him I knew that he was going to be somebody and I asked everybody about him after I met him and one or two of my friends already knew about him and one boy even told me that he was great. I mean he already had admirers before he really was great. I was always sure that I would marry a great man. That's not true, I half the time I was quite sure I never would get married at all because the men were so, well they weren't men, I don't mean they weren't good in bed or anything like that, but they agreed with everything I said and that I didn't like, I still don't like it, I guess I never will. I had this idea of a Spanish man with a little moustache and this would be a great man and he would slam the door in my face and go out by himself, I really had a lot of visions of what it would be like to be married to a great man and I must say it was not at all like that with Gilbert Green.

He was sentimental about women. He hated himself for his sentimentality about women. He had the worst time with them because he said he could never judge them. I guess he meant he couldn't understand them but who wants to understand their lover? Horrors. Anyway when I met him he was really frightened of me I guess, or I don't know, but I knew he liked me but then he never called me up and I certainly never called him up but we would see each other around, maybe at the Apex, no, that was later, well, at Max's or the Club, I used to see him once in awhile at the Club or even on the street and it was a funny thing but we never really talked much at all that whole time—it was about six weeks but it was really about a lifetime in my life—but the funny thing was that after awhile we were like old friends I mean we knew each other even though we really didn't know each other one bit. We noticed each other immediately if he would walk into the room or I would walk into the room even if it was very crowded I would just know that he was there if he was there and later on one time he told me that he used to have the same sensation. He said he felt good as soon as he saw me. By the way, I think that was the only time he ever really said he loved me. I certainly learned something about that. My dreams had been full of these Spanish lovers who were always slobbering all over me with compliments and here I was in love with a man who didn't even speak to me. I thought it was kind of great. I wasn't happy but there was a lot to do because I had to try to figure out where he would be all the time and just be around in case he was looking for me or even if he just happened to see me. But the thing was I knew it wouldn't work if I just threw myself at him I could tell he would just leave me on the floor. It was delicate.

I'm sort of hot, I'm going to take off this, I guess I don't have to say that do I, I mean it isn't television, but they'll take all that out anyway so it will make more sense. Are you going to rearrange everything too or do I have to try to be coherent? *Just talk, Susan.* All right, I am talking, but are you going to change it or just take out things? *I don't know.* You see all these Nazi pictures where they fix up tape recordings so people say things they never meant to say but by the time they hear the record they're so exhausted by all the brainwashing that they sign it anyway. Wow! I'm being brainwashed. I'm glad I thought of that, that's exactly what it is too. At least I'm not a criminal. "Just tell everything you know" that's all they tell me to do. Talking is so much better than crying all the time. Some of you sentimental bastards in the audience are probably putting me down already because I'm not in mourning, actually I am wearing black underwear but you wouldn't dig that either, god I hate sentimental men like Gilbert Green. Isn't it funny I always say the whole thing, I mean the whole name, Gilbert Green just like that. Actually I never used to call him anything at all, I never used his name I don't remember a single occasion when I called him by his name. I must have called him Gilbert once in awhile, but I can't recall it. He had lots of names for me and they changed all the time but I never called him anything at all, except you or him. I didn't think it was strange at the time. Once in a while when Fred was drunk he called him G.G., I don't know why or anything but he didn't like it at all because I guess it seemed to him that Fred was laughing at him when he said it and one time I saw him almost hit him, I mean Gilbert Green never hit a single person in his life but he came close to hitting Fred once and then a long time later we were having this terrible argument about nothing as usual and I called him G.G. and he just slammed the door in my face and went out all by himself. If I was a writer, I used to be a writer, I'd say that he wept when I did that but as a matter of fact I didn't see him again for more than a day so I don't know what he did then and I certainly never asked him about it. When he came back he was in the midst of another huge project and we just forgot about the whole thing right away because there was so much to do and this was still when he wasn't making any money so we had to do everything ourselves. It seems to me that was when we reorganized the Club but maybe it was something else.

Oh, I was going to say though that he did weep sometimes. I mean he did weep a little bit at funerals, even funerals on television, but he wasn't ashamed of it I think he enjoyed a good cry once in a while. I never saw him weep at movies though the way I did. It made him really sad when things were over, when something was all done. He hated to finish doing things, I mean he enjoyed the sadness but if he really finished something he just wasted all his time for a long time afterwards, and he hated that, so after awhile he would protect himself. I mean he would make the projects so huge that they could never be all done and anything like a book or a picture that came out of these huge projects were more like a by-product than an end. That way he kind of suffered more all the time because stuff wasn't getting done instead of in these orgies of self-pity that he used to go through, I gather they were even worse before he knew me because he didn't have anybody to take it out on. He had his friends but he always had to be nice to them or they might leave him, I really think that's why he decided to get married so that he would have somebody to try stuff out on who wouldn't be threatening to leave. I used to tell him to leave me when we were fighting but I never left myself or said I would. I wish I had thought of this when he was alive I would have had a secret weapon. I don't really wish I had had a secret weapon. I really didn't need one.

Is there any Pepsi or anything? I'm not used to this. *That's not it.* Of course I'm not used to talking all the time like this but what it really is is that I am used to having a Pepsi once in a while and I was sure you would have some for me. What? *Of course you can.* No, I like a glass. What's the matter with you anyway? I think you're rattled. I've never said that before. That's the trouble with you Fred, you're rattled. Oh, that's funny! Thanks. The thing is that the whole thing, I mean all this recording was really my idea, that was a super lie what I said before about not knowing what to say it was just like when people get up before a microphone they horse around to get over their embarrassment and tell a lot of bad jokes and things and everybody laughs a lot although they aren't amused by the jokes they are really laughing at the speaker's nervousness or something. I'm certainly never going to listen to this tape. It would probably stretch me out for days. I'll read the transcript if they ever finish it. If you want to go back far enough, the whole idea for talking away like this is really Andy's and I don't know who suggested it to him, probably Brigid, but it might have been anybody and what I mean is when you try to figure out where something started you can just forget about it because nobody will ever know where the original idea came from, it seems that it was just suddenly everywhere. Somebody gets credit for it, like I just gave Andy credit or something like that, but really it's just nowhere and it doesn't matter. The only reason I know this is because we used to be so stupid, we used not to do this at all because it was too much like the things they did at the Factory. But after awhile it didn't matter. It never did matter, except we thought it did. So many people died all of a sudden that it seems to be a new age already. And we're coming into this new age with a permanent hang-up and that is, well, the Estate of Gilbert Green. E.G.G. That's not bad. *It's very good.* I know it's good, why do you think I said it? *I'm sorry I'm sort of on edge, what do you like or not like.*

Well, one thing I really don't like is breaking laws. It always seems stupid to me when people break laws. I would never get caught doing something wrong. I mean against the law. I might do something unfortunate, like breaking something I didn't want to break by mistake, but even little regulations. One time we were five minutes late with our tax returns and I really thought that something terrible would happen but of course nothing did.

Another thing is I really don't like things to change too much. I mean of course I like pleasant surprises, but not sudden changes. If I have decided to do something I want to go ahead and do it. If I suddenly can't do it or the people I'm with decide to do something else, it really bothers me for a while. If you invite people to come and see you and then they don't come I think it's always really bad even if they have a good excuse.

They say most women don't like fighting but I'm a little different about that, I really sort of like a fight, I mean not to be in one but to see two or three men fighting. I'm not talking about wars but just personal fights. I always think they must feel so good afterwards assuming they aren't hurt. But wars, of course, well I guess everyone agrees on that by now, there's not too much to say about it, obviously modern wars are really horrible.

I really don't like women very much, isn't that funny? I mean after all! I like a few women but even there the women I like are always changing and most women I never get to like a little bit even. I think most women are phony, I mean never in a million years would they ever tell anyone what they think, they just say everything for effect, and so you can never figure out who they are, they're just playing a game with everyone they know.

I also don't like certain kinds of food, of course, well I think I really probably like all kinds of food but there are ways of preparing it that I don't like, for example, very rare meat, I don't really like that although I can eat it, and runny eggs, I suppose that's the same thing, and I don't like fake food what I call fake food like frozen cakes or instant coffee or frozen dinners or breakfast cereal or any but the very best candy.

I hate alcoholics, and what I mean is people who get terrible when they drink, or people who drink liquor while they are eating or people who drink so much they get sick or pass out, sometimes I don't even like people who drink all the time although they don't get obnoxious you can always tell they are always drunk because their responses aren't quick and their eyes have a cast to them but most of all I hate lecherous drunks most of all.

I don't like people that I understand too well. For example I don't get along too well with my mother because I know her and we are very much alike. Maybe it's because I don't like people to be like me around me or something. I would never fall in love with a man I understood, I mean I might like him a lot but I wouldn't even want to go to bed with him. I don't like the feeling that I know exactly what's going on all the time.

I don't enjoy going to the theatre, but that's a special thing, I mean I used to think that I would be involved in the theatre and of course I'm not and when I was I didn't like the actors I thought they were all sort of awful because they were always trying to be charming, they really didn't have any idea what they were doing they were just taking directions like slaves, it wasn't life and it wasn't art, of course I suppose a great actor is different.

I guess I really don't like weak men, they're often very pretty but I don't like the feeling I get that I could really hurt them just by saying something a little tough or, well, I mean the men I like must be very tender or something like that but I don't like the feeling that they're going to disappear or weep or collapse at any moment. I think people have to be a little tough inside which is what I guess strength is all about anyway.

I can't stand really cheap clothes or stuff that is coming apart in a cheap way, like the seams are breaking. I think you can wear really good clothes for maybe ten years and of course they get a little bit worn out but they still look great even if they are somewhat out of style because they were so good to begin with. There is nothing worse than having something you hate to wear the next year or so, and that just means it wasn't good.

I don't like modern furniture, especially a whole house full of it. It is uncomfortable to be in a place that is jammed with modern furniture, because there isn't anything that is really beautiful it is just showy and hard, there's no decoration. It's like in clothes, I like really good old furniture, it can even be quite dirty or a little lumpy or something but the whole design of it is delightful and you feel much better using it.

As a matter of fact I find that I don't like to be interviewed, I mean you know I don't hate it so much I can't do it or anything, but people usually ask such idiotic questions like when did you meet Gilbert Green, I mean, it's an interesting question but not from a stranger, you would have to know somebody pretty well before you would really be interested in how you met your husband, but now that I think about it I guess most women would like to know.

I hate dirty windows and full ashtrays and overflowing garbage cans and accumulations of dirty dishes and very dusty things and clothes that have something spilled on them and dirty toilets and bathtubs, but the funny thing is that I don't rush around cleaning them up, I'm not at all compulsive about it, but I really don't like them and I try to avoid slummy situations although I'm not too neat and I don't like housecleaning one bit.

I don't like loud noises either, I don't like the taste of Scotch, I would never use an addictive drug, I hate bitter cold weather, I feel uncomfortable wearing brown, I don't like figs or dates, I, let's see, I don't like imported beer, I don't enjoy shopping, it always wears me out, I don't like to be kissed in public, and, oh, I don't care for most jewelry, I hate mink coats and Cadillacs, I don't like to fall down and is that enough?

Yes, plenty. We never really talked about his stuff too much. He used to talk about it with oh, you, Fred and later George and Andy in the old days, but it wasn't like conferences, he would just ask people questions or make a suggestion as to what to do, his mind was always full of ideas, most of which he really never used, because the thing was that he always wanted the people around him to do what they wanted to do and not necessarily to do what he wanted them to do. And the thing was his suggestions were almost always good so that if he made a suggestion it would almost automatically be carried out by whoever he was talking to and as he grew older his whole thing, almost, was to avoid making suggestions as much as possible. He realized that his suggestions were a form of showing off or searching for flattery or affection and after awhile he was so successful that he really didn't need any more flattery or affection, he really had to protect himself from admirers he didn't like for one reason or another, and as I say he really wanted the other people to get in on all this that he had built up, kind of a success machine, but of course the trouble was well it was very complicated. I was going to say the trouble was that since the success machine was really just his life it required a terrific effort for other people to use it without ruining themselves as individuals. After awhile he gave up the effort to cooperate with people sincerely and he used to go around sort of ordering people to do things he had no desire for them to do, I mean it was like a parody of somebody like him, and so he would give all these useless orders sometimes to give the people a laugh and to just point out that he understood the situation and that it was very difficult. In other words, his whole life was a power struggle but when he had more power than he ever needed he would waste it a lot in order to make his subjects feel less impotent themselves. He had had the experience of working for Andy so that he knew what the situation was and he also knew what the possibilities were for other people to influence him, in other words to take control of his life. That was one reason that he was always getting new friends, people that nobody around him knew to come and help him with his stuff or just be around to talk, because he knew if he always listened to the same people he would get into a rut, or he would start doing the same stuff over and over. He avoided conventions and formulas like the plague. He hated slaves. He hated contracts. He always stood by his friends no matter what they did to him. He was very lucky. He courted danger in order not to be a slave. He hated the idea of accidental death, and he was never careless about physically dangerous situations but he would even take real risks in order to do what he wanted. He never went skiing or completely lost his temper or drove badly, but he was willing to stand up to anybody from whom he wanted something. If there was a bad situation he would start to bark, I mean it sounded like a bark when he spoke. His eyes got very hard and his whole manner stiffened and he had a cast to his mouth that was very effective. Sometimes he didn't even have to say anything, he could frighten people with a look if that was what he had to do. As a rule there was nothing on earth more gentle, but if things were going badly, for example if he was being harassed by bureaucrats, he could come on in the grand manner and it almost always worked in his favor. Or if he was being interrogated and he didn't like the conversation he would shut up and run his tongue around the inside of his upper lip expressing such disgust that the people who bothered him soon left him alone. Sometimes I bothered him and I know what it feels like to be repulsed that way, it's devastating, I used to get a feeling in my chest I can still remember when it happened. But he only used these things to frighten people when he did not respect the adversary or the situation, in a little domestic thing for example or, oh, to hell with it, this is a great big abstract bore.

I don't agree with that, but you must be tired, Miss Suzie. I do miss you, but you'll never know it. How can ghosts read? What I really love about all this is that it sets the record straight about so many things and there aren't any dreams in it at all. But it could all be a dream, especially as Fred gets pushed out of it. It's a big monologue of one woman's life. Too bad it has to end! (I don't like being called anything.) —G.G.

⟦ Susan Late at Night ⟧

Art and reality.

I guess there are some things that might be important to me,
let's see. It is after all erotic images and not so much a play or, but
it is a certain charm. Brice Marden shows it sometimes, but say
Kass Zapkus who is not even well-dressed is somehow just exactly
what I like. This may be vicious, I don't really know what to be
vicious is except I know some things that are certainly thought to
be vicious, say, like Andy Warhol, and somehow I know that that
is not vicious at all, and you know what I think, that's not vicious
at all. The trouble is that most people don't know any of these
people and it will never make any difference to anybody except the
people that I've seen. Believe it or not I am a little drunk, or else I
am a little stoned, I'm really not sure, and finally it must be a
combination of the two because truthfully I never feel like talking
much when I am stoned on pot or when I have had three beers, but
when I have done both at once I feel exactly like a little talk.

So what I should do in order to make it more universal or
something is to say what these men do to me physically. I mean
I've never slept with any of the men I mentioned and so, you
know, I really do not know them personally at all, I wouldn't be
able to just describe what I like about them but I mention all this
for a reason, which is that these are people who I think I could
love, or I might have or something. I'm not talking about them
because I do love them, because I don't, and, all things considered,
I probably never will, but I think I might. It's a hard thing to say. I
flatter myself that most other women would never say anything of
the sort out loud, but there's this to consider—I was married very

well at an early age, and now I'm a widow at an early age, among widows, and, you know, frankly I'm not too anxious to get married again but I certainly think about it more than you might think a really loving widow should because after all I'm not at all old and besides I was married at 19 and so of course I'm a great success among women especially considering who I married. I mean like with any luck I'll be quite rich, you know, and while that is a difficulty if you are born to it, if you inherit it sort of by mistake it doesn't affect your manners too much, it is sort of a surprise and you just have it for what it's worth. This is really not true because it really has a huge effect on who you meet after you are as they say free, as well as rich, and that is a definite problem. Under these circumstances you can only like people who you knew before you were in the situation. There is also the possibility that you can marry or just go with a rich man to the manner born, but, I mean, this is hard to do because most of them are so weak, you have no idea, I've met quite a few, really a lot recently, because rich men sort of cleave to strong women, I guess mostly their mothers were very strong women, but, you know, as far as gossip goes, I've only met one strong man who was naturally rich, Tony Stout, as a matter of fact, and of course he's married and everything's fine, and anyway he fits into the category of people I knew *before,* so I mean the people that a person like me are liable to meet are not a very promising bunch. Nobody knows what might happen, but I'm just talking about what I'm doing and thinking, I'm really thinking more than I'm doing, but I guess that's all right too. I'm speaking so slowly tonight! Usually I just rattle it off. I just killed a mosquito, the second one of the season. There will be millions.

This is something I would never say to anybody else but of course I don't have anybody here, I am just sitting here alone and I can hear some birds, probably sparrows, probably not robins, anyway birds that have nothing to do except entertain the dawn that I witness, preoccupied as I am with my future and all, but so then, anyway, for example tonight at the bar I met a very nice Englishman called Allan I don't know what his name was and I do know that he didn't catch my name when I mentioned it, we were just talking and after awhile I asked him his name and I told him my name very briefly because just for a minute or an hour I wanted to just be nobody and it didn't look as if he knew me and we were having a very nice talk, I was enjoying it because we were like two nobodies and it was fine, I mean I don't even know what Prince Charles looks like but you know if he came into the Club I think nobody would recognize him, they would assume he was another artist or poet or something and you know like he might be able to have a very good conversation for ten minutes until somebody spotted him, and then, well, that's the story. So anyway English Allan was coming on to me very fine and all but after awhile he said he just had to pee and so, well, but I guess in the men's room somebody told him who he was talking to and when he came back he was utterly altered. Of course that's a pun, it was like not only did he pee but he had his balls cut off at the same time. I knew right away what had happened. But I wasn't sure what to do about it. I mean I wasn't desperate for him or for anything for that matter, but I was having a good time with him and it looked like he was maybe not an idiot, I mean I don't usually like English people at all, they are all so awful now one way or another, but this guy was different. When he came back from the john he was still different in that way but he was disturbed by the knowledge of who he was talking to. This mourning period is terrible. I sometimes think that it is going to be terrible until I die, like I am condemned to mourning because I really made my luck but I happened to lose my luck and now I'm a girl with a difference, oh it was so much better or else it was worse before all this happened!

That would have been a good time to stop, like I really had a tear in my eye for me, myself, which is not something that I, it just doesn't happen to be the way I act, I don't cry and especially not in public. It's funny the only three times I can ever remember crying were in public. But sometimes I do cry. Once in a while he used to find big round stains on the pillow where I cried almost all night without him, not for any reason, but just simply without him, I mean most nights he wasn't there I thought nothing of it, but the point is that I remember him remarking on the stains on the pillow and being very nice to me for a little while because of it, but I absolutely really do not remember any night when I cried so much

I was wet. I mean shit, it's a terrible thing, I mean not the death so much as the life, I mean the death is nothing it's only the life. You know what I used to wish? That I would die before my parents. Of course that was still when I was in love with them. I haven't thought of that for maybe about ten years. That's all exactly, exactly what I mean.

Change the subject. My mother used to say, Perish the thought. Anyhow I met Brigid coming out of the Club tonight and, you know, I don't even like her, but it was so nice to see her and she is always so nice as long as she doesn't feel bad, and she was just eating an ice cream cone and she smiled and I don't remember what we said but she looked at me and I knew that she knew what I was going through. She didn't look sympathetic as they say she looked positively conspiratorial, how do you say that word, like a friend looks even if she is not a friend. It's very light now. I guess I could go on. I'm sure I will go on some other time. I don't feel drunk or stoned, just sad, which really means that I'm so tired I can't tell what I feel. I had a beautiful day. It's really very difficult, but I mean it doesn't seem hard to me unless I think about it which I hardly ever do.

⟦ Susan's Party ⟧

Reality and work.

One time a few years ago when we were still on 40th Street I came in and he was smiling and laughing a little bit and sort of dancing around. Fred was there I think and some other people too, I don't exactly remember, probably Sammy, I think it was just about the time when they put out the first record, and so of course I asked everybody what was going on and they said he had decided to make a movie about himself. He was kind of busy thinking of what equipment he would have to have in order to make a movie as good as Andy's movies, and where they would do it and whether Andy himself would be in it, of course. After awhile the band started playing and somebody went out and got some food or beer or something and we had quite a party, sort of celebrating his new style and it just happened that a lot of people stopped in, Bob and Nancy and some of their crowd, I think that was the first time we met Ted Castle and after awhile Andy called up looking for Brigid who wasn't there and we told him to come over and after awhile he did and in a way that was the first scene of the movie that was taken, a silent picture of Andy Warhol in those beautiful washed-out green pants of his walking in in the midst of this party that had just sort of happened to us. George had a lot of grass and people kept going out and getting beer. Everybody was really pleased with the whole thing. People didn't stay too long usually but they kept coming in and out and after awhile Fred set the camera in a certain place so that it would show people coming up and talking to Gilbert Green for a minute and then disappearing. Most of the time the band was playing or they played the record when they were tired and so it was very noisy but the people weren't noisy, they weren't rushing around and drinking a lot, they were quiet, sort of posing in different positions here and there, some were in the back room talking about something, I don't remember what it was. Of course we hadn't the faintest idea what we were doing. I was trying to do the lights which as far as I could tell looked all right but it wasn't clear because of course we didn't have any direct experience we were just picking up on things we had thought about but once in awhile somebody would make a suggestion and the strange thing was that we weren't nervous about it at all we just went ahead and did it because that was what we were doing that day.

For one thing we finally had two cameras which were going all the time so that we did have two different versions of the same film, not just shot from different angles but doing different things. This was not a new thing but we were able to handle it better just because we were lucky and we had all been thinking about films for years often without realizing it. This was around Easter on a Saturday night and we finally had most of the people from the Club in the movie for at least a second, and at that time they were mostly very young, pretty nobodies and they certainly dressed up for it.

The political situation was really intense. I didn't understand it all, but one of the main things was that since Gilbert Green had been one of Andy's people some of them really hated him for going off on his own and becoming independent, first of all with the band and then with the movies, and then there were other artists who envied him his success with everything he did, even though he still wasn't very famous, and there were some who just denounced the whole thing as a huge pretentious thing, something nobody would dare to do, that is, make a film about himself when he was really nobody aside from being an old friend of Andy's, and all of this kind of thing was really the subject of the film although it wasn't always too clear what was going on. He made the film as sort of a power play and it really worked because even the people who hated him most came by that day, except for Carl Andre, and they did try to screw things up in minor ways but after all everyone was very excited that something else was going on and as he had figured they would, they thought they could not afford to miss it so they disguised their bitches and came up from the Club and Max's and the Apex Bar and wherever else they were to drop in and pay their respects. Many of course didn't even get into the movie but even they didn't want to miss the scene which they thought was probably going to get very big and important right away.

At first he just stood in a corner but after awhile he went around the room which made it hard for me to keep the lights right, but anyway he went all over and made a lot of remarks about what the different people were wearing. This got a lot of freaks into the film and some of it was very funny because of what he said and how they reacted and I remember at one point he turned to the camera and said that the women in this film were less attractive than the men for the most part and Didi Agee happened to be there then and she said that she agreed with him, and he made an elaborate compliment to the effect that she was the exception to the rule. And then he tried to get them to get some shots of me which at first involved taking some pictures into the lights which was pretty but it didn't show me and then we did it another way with the other camera from behind the lights among which is the best profile that was ever taken of me.

He was the director of the film and the subject of the film, so that in effect the subject of the film was simply its own director. You had had directors before who played parts in their own films but never had they played the part of the director of the film which they were actually directing while they were directing it. This seems a little complex but it really isn't. But the idea was to get rid of the idea that the film or the play or whatever was somewhere else and to just focus on itself as far as possible. Charles Ludlam had done this in a different way in the theatre and Andy Warhol had had some idea of doing it but the problem there was that Andy had to run the camera himself or else it would not be an Andy Warhol film and that was something Gilbert Green wasn't interested in, running the camera himself. After all he was a writer, not a painter.

That day though we didn't really know what we were doing. He probably had some idea but that probably changed as he was going along so that really nothing was ever as clear as it would have been if you saw the movie now. But he did things in such a way that they were essentially visual and not literary which I know surprised him when he saw the film because he never used to like the way he looked but finally he did like the way he looked and that was after all why he called it *The Real Right Way To Dress For Spring*.

After awhile, I don't know what time it was people stopped coming to see us, I think actually the door was locked at some point, I'm not sure, but you get the idea as you watch the film that the world is smaller than you thought at the beginning because people keep reappearing and there aren't any more new faces. At this point I guess there were maybe twenty people there. He asked some of them to stay a little longer, Yvonne Rainer for example, and Frank Zappa and Kass Zapkus and Janet Noble and Didi Agee, and Paul Simon and Dustin Hoffman, and Ondine and Nico, and Dennis Oppenheim and Ted Castle, and Peter Gourfain and David Lee, and Janet Castle and her little boy, and Billy Linich and Fred Hughes, and Viva and Stefan, but they didn't stay actually, and, let's see, Virginia Dwan and Barry Bryant, and the Silver Apples and their girls, but they didn't stay very long either, and Gerry Marsden and Peter Hutchinson, and John Ashbery and Bill Berkson, and Charles Ludlam and Bill Vehr, but they disappeared too, and Stefanie Spinner and Nancy Holt, and Bill Dawes and John Grieffen, and Simone Forti and Robert Morris, and Jasper Johns and Tom Hess, but they weren't there long, and Steve Reich and Karen Bacon, and Jonathan Schwartz and Mary Brecht, and Mary Woronov and Gerard Malanga, and, let me see now, I think Robert, no, he wasn't there either, oh, Morley, Camille, and Lucinda Childs and David Gordon, and Bill Bollinger and Tony Holder, and Claes Oldenburg and Robert Smithson, and Roy Slam and Terry Pease, and Susan Hartung and Max Newhouse, and Abby Shahn and Taylor Mead, and Forrest Myers and Mickey Ruskin, and Allen Ginsberg who just came in and took a look around and left right away, and Paul Morrissey and Jed Johnson and Betsy Baker and Sol LeWitt, and Mike and Dave and Ron, they were the cameramen, and Andy Warhol and Gilbert Green and me and Fred and that was about all.

As I say not all those people stayed all the time and there were some at first whose names I never knew and I probably forgot a few but as you can tell I might just as well have said that everyone was there but I wanted to see how many names I could remember once I got started on it so I did that instead. Now of course I remember some more, David Craver, Eric Davis, Charles Marches and I don't know but anyway what I wanted to do was talk about the way it was made.

It was raining that night for the first time in weeks although it was the middle of April. People weren't prepared for the rain or for the film, and therefore some of their poses were a little drenched and their hair was not quite as perfect as usual. Also it was exciting, the rain and the movie-making. They came in laughing from the street and shaking themselves off. The movie itself was very simple. First there was quite a bit of coming in and petty conversation, then there were some really good conversations, some of them serious and some of them power plays and most of them centered around and about Gilbert Green. Even at first, he would occasionally correct the way people were standing and stuff, but after awhile he told some of the people to go home and he began rearranging their costumes. The band played once in a while not all the time. He first took somebody's hat off and put it on himself then gave it to someone else. Most of the clothes he took off other people he tried on himself before putting them on other people. Some of the people didn't like this, and if anyone resisted him he either told them to go home or he realized they were playing with him and often he went and got something for them to put on. Some of the other people began doing this sort of thing to each other somewhat but if people were laughing too much or getting out of hand or trying to rip clothes off he usually told them to go home. Some of the people were quite surprised and a few who he dismissed told him off or swore at him or tried to pick a fight with him, but he never let them get control of the situation. He didn't shout at people generally, he just spoke to one and occasionally two at a time. He seemed to be in his element, as they used to say. The clothes thing was getting pretty funny because everybody had exchanged shirts and pants and coats and most of the more exhibitionistic ones had nothing on or almost nothing. There was some dancing and the clothes exchange went on, with Gilbert Green walking around and changing things and telling little jokes and generally keeping everybody happy. The crowd was getting smaller and smaller all the time and some of the people who were left didn't play the game they just sat down along the blue wall and smoked and drank and talked and watched. At one point there was a fight throwing beer at each other, but that was quickly calmed when Gilbert Green took the beer away from them and tried to make the ones without many clothes on dress up again which didn't work very well because they mostly wouldn't, but it actually worked out okay because then they took all their clothes off which is what they had wanted to do all along. Then it almost got out of control again because the people who were naked decided that everybody should be naked and Gilbert Green was not naked and he was opposed to everybody doing anything in particular, he insisted that the people who wanted to undress should and the people who didn't should except he did keep trying to dress the ones that were undressed so that after awhile he was tackled by a couple of his old friends and it turned out he didn't have any underwear on but just then he told me to get in front of the camera and start talking and I did. I told a long story about my childhood. I was speaking right into the microphone so that the noise wasn't too great and when they noticed that the cameras weren't on them anymore the people who had been horsing around didn't do so much any more and they began to try to find their clothes and things like that, it was obvious that the party was breaking up. I went on and on with the story I was telling which was maybe not too good a story but it came off beautifully in terms of the way the film was, and I kept on talking until one of the cameras ran out of film. By then there weren't too many people left and Gilbert Green had them use up the rest of the film in the other camera taking abstract shots of piles of clothes and the floors of the place and the walls, and during this bit some of the people said goodbye and things and found their shoes and whatnot and just toward the end of the film Gilbert Green put on a record of some pornographic poems by some poet and so there was this orgy stuff on the soundtrack of the film of the empty room and glasses.

⟦ Susan on Gilbert Green & Childhood ⟧

Reality and memory.

The most beautiful thing about Gilbert Green was undoubt-
edly his hair, it was so soft, and so long, and so full, and so
generally well-behaved, and it even sometimes developed a
beautiful wave in it depending on whether the relative humidity
was up or down, I forget which. I guess you would have to say it
was brown hair, but there was a lot of red in it and a lot of white
but it didn't look white it just looked great. It was so beautiful that
half the people in the world thought he spent most of his time in a
palace of tonsorial art but as a matter of fact when I knew him he
never went to a barber of any kind, once in a while I would just
trim the ends of it a little, and it generally got longer and longer
because I didn't cut that much off. But he did take great care with
his hair, he washed it a lot and massaged his scalp and he really had
a little ritual with two or three different kinds of shampoo, and
there was no doubt that he was a little afraid of getting bald
although as he said he had decided not to get bald. Once in a while
he would turn to the next person next to him and ask in a
distracted way, "How's my hair?" If this happened to be a person
who didn't know him very well, or someone who didn't like him,
there would be a little awkward thing where the person gulped or
laughed or something, but he would smile too, I think he used that
to put people at ease because people were often scared of him and
there was something about his just mentioning his most beautiful
feature, and the way he did it, that was very disarming. Of course
if somebody really detested him and he did that in their presence he
left himself open to their ridicule, which always irritated him
immensely because it was such a clear case of people taking

advantage of him and he always despised people who did that and he was always leaving himself so open that anybody could have taken advantage of him at any time and sometimes they did. He didn't tolerate it one bit. He usually wrote them a letter telling them what they had done and what it all meant and what he thought of them personally. These insults were quite a bit like compliments because usually they were so helpful to the person who received them that he would improve his whole state of mind and might even become a good person of some kind but he could be sure that at any rate Gilbert Green would never have anything more to do with him unless it was unavoidable. This only happened once or twice a year, so the technique of leaving oneself open to be taken advantage of was one that worked pretty well for him but that was because he was so completely successful in really everything he ever did although not always in things that were done in his name by the others who would always surround him begging for work or suggesting things that he ought to do. But anyway what I was going to say was that his hair was his crown in every sense, almost like a valuable decoration, and at the same time he used it as a sign that he was completely vulnerable and that he was leaving himself open to abuse and even damage. One time I met a guy who had proved in an article that Gilbert Green had a castration complex, as he called it, and this guy was all excited because this was the first thing he had ever said and the whole thing was really however that he wanted to meet Gilbert Green because he was in love with him. I told the guy that he could meet Gilbert Green anytime he wanted to and he did and when he mentioned his proof to Gilbert Green, Gilbert Green just said you mean a Samson syndrome, and turned back to whatever he was doing. The guy was crushed but he later proved helpful in different ways, he used to write reviews of things that Gilbert Green had a chance to correct before they appeared although he never corrected opinions he just corrected observations and facts. I can't remember his name anymore but the guy gave up psychiatry completely and then he hung around for awhile and then he disappeared. He maintained at one time that Gilbert Green was the only good psychiatrist in the world, which was just about as ridiculous as anything else that he said. I never liked him. But it was true that Gilbert Green could deal with just about anybody. And his crown helped him and his native grace and his lovely mind. He had started out, a few years before I met him, by completely shaving his head. His hair before that had been sort of ordinary as far as I could tell from the pictures I used to see occasionally just sort of a good haircut thing I guess, but probably not at all white at that time since he was still very young. One time he wanted to do something drastic and he had just been reading about some old Greek, Democritous or Demosthenes I guess, and this guy had lived in a cellar and taught himself how to write or speak or something he couldn't do very well and got very good and he shaved half his head so he would be ashamed to come out. Anyway Gilbert Green went to a barber and had him cut all of his hair off and the barber was very scared to do it because he thought that Gilbert Green was mentally unbalanced but anyway he did it for him. It was about the time I think that Gilbert Green refused to serve in the Army and it may have had something to do with that, what he did was he said that he was a fag and sort of behaved strangely and looked weird, with no hair on his huge head and I think he wore a red shirt to scare them but anyway it worked out very well. I didn't know him then but he told me the story one time because it was the beginning of his success. After that he just let his hair grow, he really never had another haircut except just trimming it up from time to time and as I said it was the most beautiful hair I have ever seen or ever hope to know.

Reality on film.

The weather was always gray when I was very little. The house was kind of a big old wooden house with four different porches and two separate attics and a cold dark damp cellar and it was very quiet there except when it was raining and when it rained you couldn't hear the rain in the cellar but you could sort of hear seepage. Seepage does not sound like dripping it sounds more like your stomach rumbling as they say but it is not a low sound it is a very little light sound. It was pretty easy to get lost in the cellar and as a matter of fact I was not allowed to go there because it was imagined that there were rats there and I was certainly very scared of rats though I had no idea what they were and I am certain that during all the time I was secretly down in the cellar looking for rats I never saw one or heard one and a few years later when I actually saw a rat once, somebody pointed it out to me, it was a dead rat, and I argued with them saying that I knew rats very well and that was definitely not a rat but of course they were right and I was wrong because I had never seen a rat I had just imagined them so clearly that I knew them even if I didn't. It is not possible that there was so much rain and clouds as I imagine that there were, it was not in a tropical climate or anything it was just in Pittsburgh, but I suppose we could have had a very cloudy summer one time maybe in 1948 and that was the summer when I was interested in the weather so it just took hold of me and gave me the idea that it rained every day when I was very, very young. Most of the time I was very dressed up. I must have liked to dress up but I think they had a lot to do with it they thought that little girls should always be very pretty and comb their hair and all that sort of thing, actually I was not a pretty child at all as far as I can tell, except maybe when I was a little baby about two, but I remember always being dressed up and getting new clothes all the time, I don't remember going to stores to buy new clothes except when I was of course ten or twelve but when I was little new clothes always came in a box, usually about three or four new dresses at a time. Now when I think of it it seems to me that they came every day but of course that isn't possible but I did have a hell of a lot of clothes. I just ruined them. I would never become dainty just because I was a little girl and all dressed up. I just went out and played in the mud and ruined my clothes. This used to irritate them but they didn't do anything to stop me so I kept it up and as a matter of fact it wasn't very long ago when I had just gotten a beautiful new costume for some big party or something and I got such a kick out of it because afterwards it was raining and there was a taxi strike or something so I just walked home in the rain and ruined the costume. The next day I just picked it up, took a look at it, it was white silk, and then I just threw it out because it was ruined. I spent a lot of time alone and one thing I remember is the apple blossoms in the spring. The house was in the city but it was on a little hill and it was on the site of an ancient apple orchard that still had a few old trees most of which were half rotted and just about every year another apple tree would finally die but I remember when there must have been almost a dozen of them left and one huge cherry tree that was not so old, and when these trees were in bloom it was something to see. The house was huge and rambling and white, but not a farm house at all, a city house very definitely, and it was surrounded by all these gnarled black old trees that were all covered with parachutes. I remember very clearly that I was always interested in parachutes, and I didn't understand what they were for until later but I loved them very much, one time they told me that that was one of the first words I tried to say and it used to come out as "proots," and I guess I called anything like that proots, but anyway I confused things like that and there was something about cauliflower too, I don't exactly remember what, so what I was talking about was these beautiful trees in the rain and the blossoms. It is the most beautiful scene I can see when I think back on all the beautiful things in my life. Later they sold the house for $50,000 and built a modern one that was very admired and written up and photographed by strangers, but it was never beautiful. A couple of years ago I did a very stupid thing I went back to Pittsburgh in the spring and I found the old house and that was really terrible because there was only one apple tree left and it was completely dead and rotten and the place was a slum and had a hundred families living in it and there probably *were* rats in the basement and bats in the attics and some of the windows were broken and the lawn was all muddy and full of junky old cars with bashed fenders and lots of rust and it was a beautiful day, it was practically hot and all the hills were green as green and you could see for miles ahead and all around and I climbed up on the nearest hill and looked at all the pretty new houses that were so pretty and ugly at once in the sun and I had a feeling of great dejection and I was mad at myself but maybe it was all right too because I learned what people always have to learn, namely that you can't recapture things and times and places, slowly everything is changed. I didn't cry at all I just felt mad and at the same time I was somehow happy too and I walked all the way downtown from way the hell out in Shadyside where I was and not one person recognized me or looked at me very closely or spoke to me at all and I don't think I will ever go back there again. I might but I wouldn't try to recapture my youth. Maybe I'll live there when I'm old, oh, dear, this is disgusting, I have to think of something else. How many more minutes? Isn't that funny? That's what I said in the movie when I was telling this story and you know what? It turned out to be absolutely the last thing I said on the film.

side three

Waring's Long Song

Susan's Sad Song

Waring in the Sticks

Gilbert Green & Fred at Work

Lucky Wary

Fred & Susan at Home

Waring in Love

Susan Looking

Waring in the West

Susan in Love

War the Beau

Susan Scheming

The War is Over

A.D. 1968

⟦ Waring's Long Song ⟧

Wary was still wary, but some things changed with him quite suddenly. One day he said to Fred, "You see me now at my lowest point." When Wary made the remark, Fred was not too interested in Wary's conversation and he didn't know what it meant. Fred was only interested in Gilbert Green whom he had just met by accident. He was trying to figure out a way to interest Gilbert Green in Fred. Wary was not interested in Gilbert Green although he had met him at a party once. Wary was interested in himself, and he had been deceived, perhaps for the last time, by Fred, who had given off the air of being interested in Wary for himself. As soon as Fred met Gilbert Green he forgot about Wary, he actually wanted to get rid of him, but he still liked Wary and he didn't know how to get rid of him without offending him so Fred tried to live two lives at once, in imitation of Gilbert Green, but Fred was not so good at that as his new boss so finally Fred decided to go and live with Gilbert Green. Fred didn't understand what Wary said because he was thinking of a way to break the news to him, and he was not doing too well because Wary was looking extremely beautiful and he had such a delicate expression around his eyes and he was obviously very sad about something and Fred picked up on all this as he always had from the first day he met him, three years before.

So there they were, they were sitting in the two chairs in the large plain white room with painted windows where they often sat as it was their only room and they were close together and far apart. Wary was thinking that Fred depended on him and Fred was thinking that Wary depended on him. They both looked sort of sad. Fred looked distracted and a little nervous, and Wary just looked sad. Fred knew what he was going to do and felt excited about the prospect of finally doing something definite, and Wary did not know what he was going to do but he knew he was going to do some things he had always wanted very much to do and he knew too that he was going to do these things without Fred whom he loved very much. All this naturally made him quite sad but that wasn't the main thing that made him so sad on this occasion it was more saddening that they had found out that they couldn't really share each others' lives and that although they had lots of good times together and they knew each other very well indeed, almost from the inside of their minds. Wary got up and made Fred a nice Martini drink which he thought that he would like right then which was exactly what Fred wanted though he hadn't had such a drink in a long time and he didn't know he even wanted it. This gesture suddenly made Fred sad but he was glad too to have the drink. They sat in silence for awhile in the middle of the light. In his solitude, Fred tried to remember Wary's last remark and then to make the nice gesture of rejoining it with some other remark but he couldn't exactly remember it or if he could he couldn't think of anything to say against it. Fred was not accustomed to being cast in the role of the bad man. But he felt very bad, he felt wicked. He didn't know that Wary could read his mind and he couldn't read Wary's mind but he did sense that Wary had the upper hand since he had made the drink that was making him, Fred, feel a little better all the time. The light was beginning to fade as the sun retired from the day. They sat in silence for a longer time than they had ever sat, Wary looking at Fred and Fred looking at himself and at the floor. Silently Wary made Fred feel horrible. Nothing happened for a long long time. Then Wary went over to where he kept his things which happened to be behind Fred's back where he was sitting, and threw some clothes into a bag that he had once given Fred and took a couple of books, and then he went into the bathroom and shaved and took a shower and changed his clothes, and then he checked the amount of money he had with him which was $176, and he found his checkbook and looked at it to find that the balance was $2708. It was dark now and the only light on was in the bathroom.

Wary sat down on the floor by Fred's foot and took one of Fred's cigarettes and Fred lighted it with his lighter. Wary started to say something but he stopped because there were tears in his throat and he didn't want it to show. Wary grasped Fred's nearest leg at the calf and held it against his head very tight. Fred didn't move, he decided not to pat Wary's head. Instead he said, in an offhand way, "You going somewhere?" and Wary said "Yeah."

Then Fred said, "So am I." He got up and went into the bathroom and took a leak and brushed his hair and checked his wallet, which contained $4, and then he came out into the room which was dark but since it was all painted white it was still somewhat light and he stood for a moment and looked at Wary as he sat on the floor, and then he said, "You better give me some money." Wary took out his wallet and tossed all his money on the floor, and then he took $10 of it back, and put the wallet in his pocket. Fred went over to a table and took the last bit of his drink with the olive at the bottom of it which he chewed.

"Susan won't like this," said Fred to himself.

"Who's Susan," said Wary to Fred.

"A chick," said Fred without looking.

"Do you think he'll keep you," asked Wary.

"Yeah, I don't know, I think so," said Fred.

"How did you know," asked Wary.

"I didn't, I just took a chance," said Fred.

"Just like that," said Wary.

"Not exactly," said Fred.

"What?" asked Wary.

"Does it really matter to you?" asked Fred.

"Okay," said Wary, warily.

Suddenly Fred was quite scared to be alone with the man he had loved for three years and he wanted to run away but instead he decided to hurt him, not to hit him, because Fred could never have done such a thing, but to have the last word. Fred stood his ground as Wary got up. They were unable to see each other except in very general terms. They were standing about ten feet apart. They were separated by a small pile of money. They were rather mixed up but they were older than ever before. They were aware of what was going on and what they were doing to each other. They were excited and sad. They were just on the point of laughing because the tension was so great and the scene was so ridiculous. They were both deciding to play the scene out, each in a different way, just like a duel or a battle in the old days. They were both sentimental and hard-hearted, but Fred was more hard-hearted and Wary was more sentimental. They were of unequal height and they had different ideas. Just as the stance was becoming boring, Wary approached his great friend across the money. Fred stood his ground and felt his heart go. Just at the moment when Wary was going to embrace his departing friend, a tape recorded message came out of Fred's mouth and sundered the air like a shriek: "Get lost," he said, "Get out of my life." The heart of the unexpected was asked for and split just a bit in time for Fred to reach down and take up most of the money and turn on a well-turned out boot toward the door that was waiting for him seventeen feet to the left. This short trip was a long one under the circumstances, but the courageous Fred took it in stride without pausing or rushing or turning around to see what was going on at his back. With a sense of elation, he heard the door close with the dull thud he awaited and he walked slowly downstairs although he wanted to run. Back up inside the old room, Wary was stunned and elated. He picked up the remains of the money, $41, stuffed it in his pocket, and went over and opened one of the windows to catch a breath of fresh rain.

He washed his mouth twice and still felt that it wasn't clean but he knew better than to do it again. The rain descended in torrents and Wary stupidly hoped that Fred wouldn't find a cab and would have to ruin his new boots walking all the way to Gilbert Green's. For awhile he was quite confused but he didn't have to do anything except not answer the telephone when it rang exactly eight times. He thought vaguely of destroying some of Fred's stuff but then he realized that there wasn't anything of value. A few moments' thought left his wound cauterized and tender but no longer open to the world and its amazing effects. He took one of Fred's cigarettes and was about to light up but then he realized he didn't have a match on him and besides he didn't want to smoke because he had no decisions to make so he threw the cigarette out the window and then he closed the window and then he lay down on the bed in his clothes.

The redness of his vision was intense, like the sunrise through closed eyes. The few little tears were sweet moisture to his ruined throat. The patterns cast upon the inside of their lids by his strained eyes were electrical abstract and wondrous. The sparks flew in symmetrical patterns not at all like sparks that fly from steel and carborundum and they kept this up for some time actually until the rain was almost over, and was mostly just dripping off the fire escape. The bed was by the painted windows. Wary opened his eyes once and saw the room, mainly he saw the ceiling and the patterns on the painted glass and a swath of light from the bathroom that cut across the uneven patterns on the ceiling and looked almost green from eye to nose. He snorted once and turned over putting one hand beneath his pillow beneath his head and the other against his outside leg and dreamt an awful dream.

First Gilbert Green hit Fred twice across the face with a black leather glove. This did not cut Fred but he started bleeding from the mouth. The blood was sort of green. It was not really any color but it was not red at all and it was not water either. Suddenly Fred was dead but he was not dead. He was still moving around, he was actually scrubbing the floor to get off the blood but he was really dead. He was lying down scrubbing. He was not doing too well because he was all bloody and he was not able to scrub much. He was dead but he was not dead. Waring was dead too but he was watching Fred being dead. Waring was more uncomfortable than he had ever been but it wasn't because of his posture or any physical thing he just felt that he couldn't stand being dead for one other minute. Waring wasn't anywhere, he was dead but he was watching Fred being dead. She called to him to remember to flush the toilet and turn out all the lights in the bathroom and he went to speak saying *mama, no, mama* but instead he couldn't because he was dead. He didn't think he was dead he just felt it all over because nothing would work. He was completely ashamed of himself. His mortification increased and heightened and flattened out and sailed away on the wing of a wish that happened to come from behind the door where they were hiding with plenty of noise. It happened to depart on time according to the watch that hung from his throat. He was real glad not to be dead for a minute. He consulted his timepiece again and listened to it click as the plane raced along the paved run. They were in the air in a hospital where Waring was dying again. Then he got out of bed and got dressed and although he anticipated trouble from the guards they simply said *good morning sir* to him as he went outside into the grass that was very long grass and all wet from the rain and very squishy underfoot. He found an old boot abandoned by Fred when he died on the lawn that was all overgrown. *Do not do this dream in color or you will ruin it.* The walk walked on through the walk that walked the walker through his death and back into his death again which he could not seem to get out of, simply a silly little death without an end and no place to sit down or rest his ruined feet upon. The deadness of his vision was intense and red as green. He turned over in his sleep and opened his eyes on his darkness and felt his sweat on his neck where it was wet. The chick came across the room and sat down beside him and played with his prick until he told her not to do it any more and then she wept, accusing him of treason to his reason and a lot of other funny rhymes that made no sense and didn't laugh or wink but cried a lot of unaffecting tears and left him with a sinking feeling. The water left the tub with a final gurgle and he realized that he was chilly. He dried himself with powder and prepared his make-up for the evening. He chose silk trousers and a hat made of feathers and patent leather shoes. He entered the room with a bang and everything stopped dead in its tracks. It was very effective. He almost felt dead again but then he knew that it was his turn to sing and he made up a beautiful song that was funny and sad all at once and he danced to the tune from his grisly breast and he beat out the time with the taps on his shoes and his toes were pinched but he felt like a bird. And it sang.

Washed the dishes yesterday with a real fine kind of soap then talked to the telephone until I got some hope for the future of our little minds and the livelihood of all mankinds. It was a dusty vision there I had in bed with rusty things I couldn't clean and little things I didn't mean. It all made sense and I changed tense and tension flew away to come again another day. The flowers drooped and I felt pooped but we watered them once more and I leaned against the door. It broke down and I went down to town where I stole me a bike and started on a hike. I did not go five miles but the trooper caught my tail and we chased each other at a very lawful pace. Soon it was all over and I ran for cover in a field of corn that was where I got born. Two shots were fired right by my tires and I let her spin clear and she ran the other way, the dear. I lay flat and let them search the grass for grass and let them find me if they could and let them bind me if they would. The stolen property was seized right next to my ear and I supressed a sneeze and they lost interest in the trail and later on I saw a quail. She flew before me like a sight in a very fading light and I stumbled on across the roots and wrecked both of my boots. I still had a lot of money and in the morning I found some honey and I lay there in the sun and decided I would have some fun. It wasn't long before I knew that I could do anything I wanted to and I started out to win my life free from stress and full of strife.

Waring got stung once on his right index finger, the one that was slightly crooked and had always been that way, but he had never had real honey before out of a tree and he always liked something sweet for breakfast and so it didn't bother him at all. The sting was even sort of sweet itself. He took a look at his boots and one of them didn't have a heel anymore and the other was coming apart at the toes where the sole had ripped lose. He thought maybe their shots had taken the heel but he didn't remember and he didn't care. He looked around for some water but he didn't find any right away so he just kept on hobbling along and finally, which wasn't too long, he came to a paved road and he started walking along north on it and there wasn't a car in sight, it was however sort of a hilly road and after a few minutes a little pick-up truck came along, it was not too old but it was very muddy, and the guy stopped and picked him up. He was a young guy but he was very big and he wasn't curious, he just asked him where he was going and he didn't say another thing and Waring wasn't scared at all, he was just happy to have a lift and when they got to a little town that had a store Waring said, "Hey, thanks a lot," and left the guy who shifted into first and drove away without a thought. He went into the store and had a tunafish sandwich and two Cokes on toast and then he looked around at the few wares they had there and he bought some very tough black work boots that would last a lifetime and go through anything just as fast as he could carry them. Then he bought a red shirt that was real wool and some dungarees and three pairs of underpants and he asked them if they had a good leather jacket but they of course didn't have things like that they only had a rubber one, a yellow rainjacket, but it didn't look like rain, so he skipped the coat. Then he gave them thirty-five dollars and some change and asked them for a couple of rubber bands. He took his package out in back of the store which was a junk heap with old washing machines and a few tractors and cars and stuff and an old greenhouse with no glass left and lots of weeds in it. He took off his clothes and stashed them in one of the washtubs nearby, except he kept his socks and his undershirt because he had forgotten to supply himself with them, and the shirt was a nice one anyway it wasn't one he really wanted to throw away, and then he put on his new clothes which fit real good and smelled real new and looked bright red and darker blue. Then he put the two extra pairs of underpants in the box left over from his new shoes and tied it up with the rubber bands, breaking one of them as he did so, and then he came out around the house, I mean the store, well, they probably lived there too, and walked through the town which wasn't far to go as it was only a matter of fifteen or twenty old houses that were not all lived in anymore, and he kept on walking. It was a little warm in the sun but it felt good and the grass grew silently on both sides of the little road. After a mile or two he began to think again which he hadn't done very much and when the next car came by it was a woman driving a station wagon and she wouldn't stop of course she just whizzed by and as she did he made a little gesture with his hand imploring her to stop and, what do you know, she did stop a little further on and

Waring ran fast as he could run and hopped in her car and thanked her very much. He was all out of breath because she hadn't stopped very near him at all and she laughed because he was so red in the face and chest. She drove on not saying anything. He told her he wanted to go to a big town with a post office and she told him she was not going quite that far but she had time to take him to the post office and he said, "Oh just leave me where you stop," and she said nothing and pretty soon they passed a lot of automobile dealerships and gas stations and hamburger stands and cocacola signs and drew up in front of a neat brick post office. He got out.

⟦ Susan's Sad Song ⟧

Susan was very sad but she didn't know just what the matter was. She wasted the whole day sunning herself under a gentle sun in Battery Park. A lot of people looked at her but nobody tried to pick her up. This did not specifically make her sad, she was just sad in a sort of general way. She took the ferry at the end of the day and she noticed that two or three men on the crowded boat would have picked her up if she had looked at them the right way, but she didn't like office workers and little kids anymore, and she really just needed to be alone. On the way back she was all alone and she stared out the window and looked at the waves and the balancing doves, I mean seagulls, and at the buildings and at the Statue of Liberty and at the shore.

She went home and cooked herself a hamburg and ate it and looked in her purse to find out that she had 11¢. Then she called up her friend who had married a man in Boston and left him, but she was still living there, and she heard a little about a couple of men her friend could not choose between. Susan advised her friend not to do anything rash, and they talked a little about how exciting the Spring of 1968 seemed to be and how unusual it was for everyone to be excited and active all at the same time all over the country, and her friend asked her what the matter with her was, and she said she was sad and her friend asked her why she didn't remarry Gilbert Green and she said she didn't think Gilbert Green would do it and she had no wish to push him and she absolutely refused to beg him or anything like that because he hated that so much. Her friend told her to take it easy, and she said, yes, and her friend asked her what she was doing otherwise, and she told her friend a little about a movie Gilbert Green wanted to make that was going to be a very silly movie about everyone giggling because they were stoned on grass and they were going to try to show what a giggle is like and how it builds up and gets funnier and funnier all the time, you know, she said, and her friend said it sounded like you would have to get the audience high too, and Susan remarked that Gilbert Green thought he could do that with the movie and they wouldn't have to actually be high they could just get sort of a contact thing, and her friend was of the opinion that it probably wouldn't work and Susan said, "Well if he goes through with it, it probably will work all right," and her friend said maybe so and then said good-bye because one of her friends had just arrived to pick her up for dinner.

Susan hung up the phone and took a walk around the room, admiring the way her body felt and sort of imagining the way she looked when she was sad and looking at her pants flopping prettily around her shoes. Then she turned on the radio and ran a hand through her pretty curly brown hair and found that it was rather dusty and there were some bits of grass and stuff stuck in it too so she decided to wash it and she got out a towel and took off her shirt and answered the phone.

It was Yvonne Rainer calling her to ask her to be in a piece, sort of a demonstration, she was designing. And Susan said she wouldn't want to have to dance and Yvonne said, "Oh, you wouldn't have to dance, I like the way you move," and Susan asked her how much she would pay and Yvonne said she hoped to be able to give her $200, and Susan said that she wouldn't rehearse it, Yvonne could just tell her what to do, couldn't she, right at the time of the show, and Yvonne said that they always liked to rehearse and rehearse and Susan said, why, and Yvonne said that practice made perfect and Susan said that she was always practicing and that she was always perfect and she would be glad to do it if there were no rehearsals, and Yvonne said she would think about it and she asked what Gilbert Green was doing and Susan said, "Oh films" and thanked Yvonne for calling and hung up the phone.

"What a bitch I am," she said out loud to herself and began to wash the dust out of her hair as she thought of what exactly she wanted to do. She decided not to go to the Apex because she would probably have to get picked up by some creep who had or had not picked her up before there and then she thought of calling up Fred but then she thought that Fred was probably at Gilbert Green's place and she didn't want to talk to Gilbert Green on the phone and then she thought that she wished someone would tell her what to do and she decided to go to Gilbert Green's and ask him to tell her what to do because she was so sad and her hair was all wet and she got the soap out of her eyes and she stubbed her toe on the table and said, "shit" and then she went into the other room and changed her clothes and put on black underwear and a sort of coverall with buttons down the front and a silk sash of bright blue and then she decided not to go to Gilbert Green's but to go to the Club and she did that.

⟦ Waring in the Sticks ⟧

Waring smiled and waved at her familiarly as she drove off, then he mounted the steps of the post office, which was ten steps exactly, two at a time, and went in and spoke to the man about some envelopes and some paper but the man said that the post office did not have any paper and so Waring said okay and just bought some envelopes. Then he went to one of the stands and tried two ballpoint pens before he found one that worked right and used the pen to tear open one of the envelopes so it made a flat piece of paper with ragged edges and he wrote a little note to his banker in New York instructing him to close out his account and send him a whole lot of ten dollar traveler's checks in care of General Delivery at the post office from which he was writing to him, and thanking him very much for all his services over the few years that he had known him not very well. Then he signed the note and put it into one of the other envelopes, addressed the envelope to the banker whose name was Harry S. Craver, ripped the ballpoint pen off the desk and put it into his box with the other five envelopes he still had left, broke the other rubber band trying to put it back on, and sent the letter through the slot marked PACKAGES. Then he had to do the whole goddamn thing again because he had forgotten to enclose his personal check for the balance of his account without which the banker would be entirely unable to oblige him however willing he might be. In the second note he mentioned his mistake so that the banker wouldn't think he was off his rocker, but Waring was a little rattled over having made this stupid a mistake and he thought he was probably not as well off as he thought. He was pleased though that his luck seemed to be holding up very well. He walked out of the post office, down the steps rather slowly, and sat down on a little bench which was provided for a bus stop. He took out half a dozen checks from his checkbook and then he put only two of them in his wallet and threw the rest of them with his checkbook into a handy trash barrel and then he counted his money which was only about $50 but he thought that that was probably enough assuming that the banker was as good as he thought and as good as his word and as good as his gold and "jesus H. christ I better walk around or something" he said out loud to nobody that waited for the bus and stood up and gave his head a good shake and pushed back his hair and jumped up and down twice or three times and picked up his parcel that now rattled once in awhile and stuck the ballpoint pen into the package of underpants so it wouldn't and started walking down the street of the downtown of the little town. For the first time in some time he smiled to himself and then he smiled out loud and somebody saw him smiling and they said "Hello" in a friendly way apparently mistaking him for the son of one of their friends and he just said "Hi" and kept on the street.

The bakery was a little shop that smelled real good and he bought a dozen shortbread cookies and two chocolate eclairs and left the shop with a little tinkle, and then he stopped in a drug store that served as a news stand and bought a crummy bikeboy magazine and a package of Marlboros, and, as an afterthought, their most expensive cigar that was not too fat, it was really quite black and slim as a rod. He put all his stuff in his box and then asked them if they had any rubber bands but the man at the cigar counter didn't like the looks of that boy so he said no he didn't have none so Waring said well then gimme some string and he looked the man hard in the eye and the man pulled some string off under the counter and practically threw it at him and Waring said "Thanks" with a growl that visibly scared the old man and he left the drug store alone.

When he got out he saw a kind of a big hotel that was yellow brick but he didn't want to sleep and he didn't like the look of the hotel that said cocktails all over it anyhow so he walked on and he found a little park with bad grass and a puny little fountain that was pissing fitfully.

It was too shady there and he didn't like the noise and the seven old bums who lived there by day were much too curious about him and his looks and his box so he took himself off and went for a walk. Although he looked around five times before he did it he pissed into a hedge in a suburban neighborhood, I mean he didn't care anymore, it wasn't suburban, the village wasn't big enough to have suburbs but it looked suburban and he had as much right as their dogs. He walked as far as he had to until he was sort of in the country, the houses were quite far apart and there were still a few fields and he walked into one of the fields and walked right into the middle of it and it was not too near any house although he could see a couple of houses a little bit, and he sat down and ate an eclair and then he wished for some water and he got up and looked around but he didn't see where he could get any except at one of the houses, so he sat down after taking off his shirts and read the magazine and smoked a cigarette and chewed on some of the grass and shooed away the flies.

He passed two to three days roaming around in the town and out, sleeping in a field in the daytime and after one night out when he spent half his money on beer and passed out in an abandoned car, he stayed two nights in a cheap joint near the abandoned railroad where they even had a god-awful whore who tried without luck or hope of success to get him to talk to her three different times. Then he went up to the post office again and asked if there was something for him and identified himself with his driver's license and was given a thin letter from the banker, saying he was sorry he could not send traveler's checks because the person had to sign them at the bank but he was enclosing a bank check which would be as good as cash at any bank for $2695.74 which was the exact residue of the account that was closed, thanks, and wished well with a hope of success in any endeavour. Waring stashed the envelope and the letter in the post office waste box, took the check to the bank across the street, the Delaware County Bank, as a matter of fact, and after numerous amounts of identification claptrap and other inquiries, he was very polite and well-spoken and his clothes were still new if not good ones, he had a couple of fat wads of traveler's checks in his pockets and a hundred bucks and change in cash and that was all that he had in the world except the trash in his board box at the hotel which he decided to abandon right there and not pay the day's bill and he went into a store and bought a canvas carrying bag that was not very big, it was round and brown with brown plastic handles, and then he went next door to a men's store and bought some underwear and socks and some thin black leather gloves and a great black leather jacket with nothing written on it and no lining to speak of so it wouldn't be too hot unless it got real hot when he would have to take it off and carry it in the brown bag and then he remembered to get a plain wide black belt that was really very cheap considering that it was exactly what he wanted. Then he took off his red shirt and put it in the bag with the other stuff he had bought and he put on the black leather jacket and the belt and paid the man and asked him where the bus stop was, and the man said, "The New York bus?" and Waring said, "Do they go anywhere else?" and the man said "Yes to Binghamton on the other side of the street." He went and waited awhile and went in the luncheonette there and had a cup and asked when the bus was and then it whizzed in and he ran out and in an hour and a half he was in a depot at Binghamton buying a ticket for Chicago and he read magazines and slept all the way to Cleveland and between Cleveland and Chicago he looked out the window at the fields and all the other cars and he didn't think a thing. At the huge depot in Chicago he went to the mens room and put his checks and some other valuables, some identification and things into his brown case and stored it in a locker and bought a comb and combed his hair and took a shit and walked out on the big town he had never seen before.

⟦ Gilbert Green & Fred at Work ⟧

In the Spring of 1968 when roses bloomed and everything was fine in spite of the fact that there was no rain or because the sun always showed every day, Gilbert Green was at the apex of his right angular career. He was busier than he had ever been, which was very busy indeed, and he had several people working for him which pleased him very much and he was quite famous then, he was at least as famous as Joseph E. Levine but he was much younger and he was not as rich. His first two movies had already made some money although not very much but they had only cost $3,000 apiece including everything except the distribution prints because they had only taken one night to film and there wasn't much waste in them at all. The next movies were going to cost more because he was going to pay all the people in them $100 for one night's work, and he was going to make one of the films in Hollywood, which involved a lot of travel expenses and hotel bills and things and that one was going to be called The Hollywood Film and probably be his best picture of all. He was going to use his fame to get two dozen professional movie stars to work for five minutes for which he would pay them $100 apiece, and he was going to use his regular cast, Susan and Geoffrey and David and Paul and maybe Lucinda, and two cameras and two screens, and he was just going to ask his people to ask them questions, he guessed maybe Fred would think up some questions, but what he wanted was if Susan thought of something to ask Elizabeth Taylor or somebody, she would just ask her and talk to her about this one thing for exactly five minutes, and one of the cameras would be on Susan all the time and one of them on Liz, and he thought the movie might take a long time to make because everybody wouldn't be free all at once. But he thought they could use four cameras and, but then that would be too much, and at any rate there were a lot of problems with it, and he found it very interesting to think about. Then he thought he hadn't seen Susan in a couple of days and he called out "Fred?" but somebody else answered that Fred had gone to the Club to have dinner with somebody's agent or something, and Gilbert Green said, "Oh, yeah, that guy from Universal," and then he thought he better not go to the Club. That night his people were painting one of the rooms all blue in order to get ready for the smoking movie, and they were working away in a sort of slow way, and one of the things that Gilbert Green had always hated to do was any kind of painting walls and floors and especially furniture, and once in a while they called him to ask him something or report a piece of gossip, and one time he decided that none of the furniture should be painted at all, he thought it would look too surreal if it was all painted the same color as the room and they had already painted two bookcases blue and Gilbert Green said that was all right but not anymore of the furniture, he read a couple of underground newspapers, one of which had a terrible story about a guy who had some money stolen from him by a couple of spades who he thought were his friends, and the terrible thing about it was that after the mugging the guy still had five dollars left somehow, did he keep five bucks in his shoe or what? and he took a cab to the hospital. "Do people really do things like that?" thought Gilbert Green. And then he decided that the writer had made it all up out of a dream.

Fred was sitting in a swivel chair talking on the telephone. It was obvious that he was making love to Susan on the phone. Gilbert Green felt that this was an intolerable situation but he couldn't figure out how to scare Fred so that he wouldn't make love to Susan on the phone any more. Then he thought it was kind of nice of Fred to take care of things for him so he wouldn't have to make love to Susan on the phone himself. Then he was talking to Susan on the phone himself and all she was saying was nonsense and he kept saying to her, "I don't understand what you're saying," and trying to hang up but he couldn't figure out how to hang up the phone.

⟦ Lucky Wary ⟧

The police in Chicago are a shifty lot, they are very suspicious of everything unlike the police in New York which is entirely different in almost every possible way, the police in New York do not care too much, they try to do their job, but the police in Chicago just about hate any young man who is not wearing a tie and they have been known to advise short haircuts in the interest of health, very sarcastically, and in short they are all bitches. Waring caught this out of the corners of their eyes as they scrutinized his dress and his walk and his long blond hair that fell so beautifully just by his ears and slightly onto his collar. Waring was always lucky and the reason for his luck was in his eyes which were of a very innocent blue hue and very wide eyes that always sparkled pleasantly and with no malice and even with much intelligence when he was talking with his eyes. Also he was not too tall although he was not exactly short and although he was big enough for his height he did not have a threatening or imposing body and he carried himself with grace. This was the verdict of the people of Chicago who stared at him as he walked along the sunny, shadowed streets of that huge old home for addicts of all violence and greed. He thought after awhile he would test his luck a little so he went up to a cop and asked him how to get to the corner of North and Clark, which was the only location he ever remembered having heard of because of Oldenburg's monument that was designed for there, of course it was not built because it was an upright baseball bat spinning at the speed of light which is wholly impossible to build.* So the cop says to him "What do you want to go there for kid, there ain't nothing there," and Waring smiles at the unfortunate cop, and says, "Does that concern you?" in a nice voice, and the cop says "No I guess not" and tells him where it is. So Waring feels that he is again and forever lucky, except on certain days that can be easily determined by such innocent tests of power, unless you forget to test and then do something big on a bad day when it is bound to fail or fall into an error or be damned.

It turned out to be a nondescript place jammed with little shops and one big department store and lots of busy women. He asked one of them which direction the lake was in and she pointed out to the East and he went over in that direction. It was pretty windy on the shore and it blew his hair around and it looked at the seagulls and the vast skyline of apartment houses and probably hotels and it was very vacationing to be there, there was nobody around at all, and then clouds came and covered up the sun and it did not look like rain, but it wasn't nice at all and it was huge, it was really big, and there were so many cars going by and Waring felt as if he was in pure space someplace even though it was very noisy what with all the cars and the small waves that were breaking entirely unlike the ocean of his home, and he just stood there and he looked around and felt like getting on a boat and going back to Europe where he had never been either, and then he laughed at that thought and he thought that he wouldn't like to live there but he might as well stick around awhile and if he was going to do that he had better find someplace to live, he thought (as he climbed across the parkway on a footbridge) for one week, all paid in advance, and he had no idea where those cheap rooming houses must be and he would certainly never ask directions anymore, not in Chicago, he would just find his way and he had better hurry. When he got to a regular street he took a bus and then he took another bus somewhere and then he got off and walked some and then he got on a bus, and got off and took another bus, passing a few places he had already been to, and then he got off on a street called Milwaukee and walked around, it was kind of a crummy place but it wasn't too run down, it was filled with all kinds of foreigners, he didn't even know what kinds, but he found a place there on the

* In 1979 a stationary bat was built in front of the United States Social Security Building in the middle of nowhere. —G.G.

fourth floor of a rooming house that smelled profoundly of cabbage and he didn't pay for the food, he said he would eat out.

This week in Chicago was a very long week that lasted four months. He had always been sort of rich although now he was living like he had always been poor. He spent absolutely as little money as he could spend so that he wouldn't have to work. At the same time if he wanted anything he bought it, and mainly what he bought was two beautiful shirts and a sweater of imported green and gray. After two weeks of scrambled eggs in diners and luncheonettes, and occasionally some meat loaf that was about uneatable and some horrid hamburgs which, however were cheaper than in New York, he was depressed at the thought of his next meal and he hadn't met a soul and he had seen more black people than he had ever imagined he would ever see and he had had ten bucks stolen from him as he was walking along one night without his wallet which he hardly ever carried anymore, not because he was afraid of it but because it made a big bulge in his back pocket. This situation was the worst of his life although he was completely free and he still had a lot of money. It began to occur to him that he would buy a bike and go out West which he was kind of afraid to do. But he knew that if he bought a bike he would then automatically meet a lot of people on the road and at garages and places like that, and he really wanted to meet someone. But it occurred to him at the same time that he was living in a nowhere part of town and he looked very tough even though he was not very tough he was just very lucky and extremely gentle, so what he did was to buy some brown corduroys and some city boots and he put on one of his nice shirts and he really looked quite different and he started frequenting the wasteland around the University, there were a couple of bars there with a lot of people younger than himself but he fit in all right although they were surprised that they did not know who he was. The second place he went into was a mistake, because when he ordered a beer he was asked to prove who he was and when they were satisfied that he was 21 and a stranger in town (he was actually 26) the bartender gave him a beer without charging him for it and drew him around where there were no other customers and spoke to him in a very fatherly way, he came on real nice and all, but what he said was, "This is not a fag bar and don't let me catch you talking to anyone here." With that Waring turned on his new heel and left and he felt like he had been slapped in the face. But he really wanted to meet someone, and he was not easily daunted. He walked about ten blocks with the wind in his face, it was not cold but he was, and he saw a bar that was a neighborhood bar of some kind and he went in and ordered a beer. The woman behind the bar brought it with a fine smile for his hardened heart that warmed him up and slipped down his gullet into his toes and spread through his face with a bright eye and a loose tongue. He felt good for the first time in a long time and to show his pleasure he played the juke box, asking the woman what she wanted to hear, at which she laughed, and then told him to play the songs he liked best, and if he wanted to, number J4. He pushed that first and it turned out to be a rather revolting song called *Everybody Loves Somebody Sometime* and then he pushed two more at random since he didn't want to choose anything from the probably very limited selection and anyway he wasn't interested, he didn't care what he heard just then even that song he played for the barmaid seemed to be great the way he felt. He had several more beers, and the place filled up some, and he got interested in looking at two girls who had just come in with really astonishing hairdos, they still had the pink and green plastic curlers in their hair but it wasn't at all that they hadn't had time, he figured out after awhile, and looking at their fingers he saw it was a sign that they were both married and not really available now. Then he looked at the barmaid's finger and there was a pretty little ring there too but it wasn't a wedding band like the other girls had so he thought maybe he would give it a try.

Little Boy Blue
has lost his shoe
and doesn't know where
to find it.
Hey diddle diddle
said the cat
with the fiddle
and Little Miss Muffet
sat down on a spoon.
Humpty Dumpty
went a bad mile
and Wee Willie Winkie
ate a big pile.
And all the King's horses
and all the King's men
couldn't put Little Jack Horner
back in his corner again.

This is funny. —G.G.

⟦ Fred & Susan at Home ⟧

In the Spring of 1968, Fred was the only one who felt really happy because he had a lot of power over all of Gilbert Green's affairs except his money and he was sort of in love with Susan and Gilbert Green at the same time and he was extremely busy arranging things for Gilbert Green and thinking up ideas for him and doing things to make things easier and more possible for Gilbert Green and he really enjoyed being of service and hundreds of people knew he was the one to talk to if one wanted to influence Gilbert Green and so he was very much courted everywhere he went although he was not recognized in the street by strangers the way Gilbert Green had come to be. He hadn't made love to anyone in a long time but he was so busy with all of Gilbert Green's affairs that he didn't really care besides he was sort of afraid that if he made a play for someone they might have some designs on Gilbert Green and try to influence him, Fred, through sex somehow and besides everybody thought he was Gilbert Green's lover and he liked that reputation quite a bit, he even liked it very much because it wasn't true. Once in awhile, Fred felt like moving in on Susan, and they shared a couple of glances that indicated that it might come true, but he didn't know what Gilbert Green would do about it if it happened and he didn't really want to run the risk of finding out because everything else was going along so smoothly.

Fred was waiting at a table at the Club for some flunky from Hollywood and strangly enough nobody came over to him, he just sat there looking at a paper, and thinking all his thoughts and stuff, and he read an article putting Bobby Kennedy down. He lighted up a joint and smoked it fairly quickly because he thought that the guy from Hollywood was probably going to not want any grass and probably be quite offended if Fred offered it. Then he happened to think of Wary for the first time in a long time, and he thought it was strange he hadn't gotten a postcard from him in a long time, and he thought of the first time they had turned on together and felt quite wicked and very much in love. Then he turned a page of the paper and saw a picture of Lucinda in an ad for the party movie that he had designed himself, and he thought that the typeface should be bigger where it said which theatre the movie was playing at. Then he looked at some of the other ads for the big Broadway movie houses, including *2001* at Loewe's Capitol and *The Graduate* on 57th Street, then he thought he didn't remember how much money he had in case the guy from Hollywood wanted to go out and he took a look in his wallet and found $56 and thought that was enough. He closed up the paper and started thinking of some other stuff, including how horrible it would be if they got busted while they were doing the smoking film, but he decided not to worry about it and just not tell anybody who they asked to be in it that it was going to be that, then he thought that would be silly and he thought why not just do it with a small group of people it would probably be better anyway although it might get boring but they could try it that way and if they had to they could fake it later. He was amazed at the way he was able just about to think like Gilbert Green and it crossed his mind if Gilbert Green died he could probably step right into his shoes, and he didn't like that thought but he did, but he didn't like that thought at all, and he thought of how much trouble it would be to be really famous and not just well-known like he was at the moment and then he thought of Gilbert Green's black patent leather dancing shoes with taps again. He ran his hand through his hair once or twice and he made the sound that he felt when he rubbed his hand on his smooth shaved face and he took a look behind him and saw Susan walking across the room.

"Where is he," she said.

"Home, I guess," said Fred, standing up. "Do you want to meet one of our co-workers from Universal International Films?"

"Where is he?" she said.

"Who?"

"The guy from Hollywood."

"I don't know, I was supposed to meet him. He's late."

"Is he alone?"

"I guess so, I don't know, what do you mean, is who alone."

"Oh, is he alone at home."

"I'm easily confused today, I guess, do you want something. Gee you look great."

"Is he alone at home or not?"

"No they're probably still painting the room."

"Oh, what color."

"Blue."

"Oh. Light blue, huh."

"Yeah. Do you want something."

"I don't know."

"You got a little sun, huh."

"Oh I was out in the park all afternoon. It was great. I'll just sit down till he comes, contribute a little something to the whole scene."

"Thanks."

"Can I have a Coke?"

"Sure."

"Somebody called me up to be in a dance, isn't that funny?"

"Is it, I don't know."

"But I was bitchy I told her I wouldn't rehearse so I don't know if she'll use me after all."

"Who."

"Yvonne."

"Sounds great," said Fred absent-mindedly, "I'll get you a Coke." He got up and moved in the direction of the coke machine but he noticed that someone was already playing it so he said, "Hey bring us a Coke, Jeffrey" and went back and sat down.

"Maybe I should talk to him," said Susan, "What do you think."

"He's in a pretty good mood but he's all tied up about how he's going to pull off this Hollywood thing and whether or not to be in it himself." The guy brought them two Cokes and declined a gesture to join them and blushed when Susan smiled at him for the first time.

"I guess I'll skip it," she said and she snapped the top off of her Coke. "Here he comes," she said, looking up.

The guy from Hollywood looked very nervous and Fred went over and met him and brought him over to Susan and endured a few apologies and found out that the guy did not want a Coke or a beer or some milk, which was all they had at that part of the Club but it was free there, so they couldn't afford to give booze away, or grass either, he added with a glance to guess what the fellow thought of grass, and guessed right and asked Susan to join them, who declined, and took the guy from Hollywood downstairs to the real restaurant to get a double Bourbon on the rocks.

⟦ Waring in Love ⟧

Waring had never lived with a woman before except for his mother who didn't quite count although she had been the most important thing in his life. He had certainly gotten laid quite a number of times and there had been at least two girls who had wanted to marry him but he never could trust them not to betray him although he didn't quite know what all that meant. He had always run away just in time. One of the things he loved about Rosalie was her smile and one of them was the way she wore her tits which was not exhibitionistic at all but it was clear it was not at all hidden or covered up and one of the things was her hair which was long and curly and brown like his mother's would have been if she had let it grow, and another thing was her voice which was rich, it was almost deep, but she was not as beautiful as Waring himself, she was plain, and above all, which was the most peculiar thing of all, she was really quite rich because of the bar which she ran for her father who was quite sick for a very long time; in short, he had retired and gone crazy. Although he had not noticed, when Waring walked in, she, Rosalie, had been at her wit's end because she had just divorced a philandering husband who spent all the profits on really revolting beautiful women who he had taken to all the big clubs because at one time he was supposed to have been a great white jazz musician but somehow it never worked out, and besides, in order to save money she had been living with her father who really was crazy and did nothing but read the newspapers five times every day, calling his daughter a whole lot of names whether she was present or not, and, believe it or not at one time trying to rape the maid, not that he could have but he easily scared her.

Waring accumulated all this information not at first glance but it was what he came to know over time. The first night, he just got sort of drunk and talked to her about everything he had thought of for a month without anyone to talk to, and then, the most amazing thing of all, she closed up the bar and asked him to drive her car home and did not ask him to come in or kiss her, it was not a pretentious house either, but told him to take the car home with him and come to the bar the next night or whenever he felt like it, not next week, she added, but anytime tomorrow. She didn't even ask his address but she said he had a beautiful name and got out of the car and went into the house.

He was sitting in a running car in front of the house where a woman that he loved lived and he got lost twice trying to get back to his place on Milwaukee Avenue but he made it finally without asking directions at all and he liked the car which was a dark red Mustang '67. He went into the house where he had been so unhappy. He lay down on the bed and slept dreamlessly and awoke with no hangover and very excited. He packed his few things into his case, left without saying good-bye, and drove to the bar after noon. It was not open yet and he waited, somewhat scared, for his love to return to her place of business.

When it was opened by an older man not her father a few minutes after he arrived on the scene, Waring had a bit of a scare because the man was very unfriendly to strangers, but as soon as he mentioned Rosalie, the man gave Waring a sandwich and a beer and told him to wait as long as he wished. She appeared herself about an hour later, smiled beautifully, and set about doing some business with a salesman who had also come in. She only asked Waring what drink he liked most of all and he said dry Rhine wine and she ordered some and told the salesman to bring it himself before dark.

When she left the salesman she said she was late because she had to do some things and among other things she had gotten Waring a new place to live. She just told him the address and gave him the key and said he might want to look at it. But he didn't, so they had a Martini and after a while they went out to dinner which Waring paid for, explaining that he had plenty of money.

Rosalie was an unusual woman in that she was always full of surprises. She was not very neat around the house either, and although she loved Waring very much and very well, she never understood him. Rosalie had been married at 18, which means that she was a great success on all three levels, but she didn't have any children, which bothered her, and she frankly wanted to have Waring's child, which bothered him. He felt sort of used, but on the other hand he recollected that he had always felt sort of used by the women he had known, and he had finally refused to be used by his mother and all his other girls, and he thought that for once in his life he would just go ahead with it and see how things developed. The little furnished apartment was not grand but it was in an old building on the ground floor and it had a garden that got quite a bit of sun, and it was elegant in a small way although it was not well furnished. One day as Waring was taking the sun in the garden, reading some more trashy magazines, it occurred to him that he was a kept man. He didn't like the thought of it.

He liked the way his skin was tanned even though he had never before been too much interested in sunning himself. Every morning he took a long walk and every afternoon, when the sun was out, he sat in the sunny garden and read pornography which in most cases was not very pornographic. Every evening he went to the bar and usually he and Rosalie would go to one or another of various restaurants, three of which were Italian and one of which was French and one of which was Lithuanian because Waring had once mentioned that his grandmother, whom he had never known, had come from Lithuania. Rosalie never asked him what he did all day but he often told her what he had seen on his walk or about something that he had read or something he had thought of so that she generally knew what he was up to. If it was busy at the bar, Waring would be the bartender for as long as necessary but he didn't like being on his feet all the time and he came to despise the conversation of alcoholics, even though the customers at the bar were almost all very "nice" people. He decided after listening to innumerable conversations that everyone was really vicious, and then he thought that he was probably vicious too, and Rosalie and Fred and Gilbert Green and his mother and everyone. This depressed him because he did not like to reach such a devastating conclusion, he would have preferred to be much more hopeful. He thought he had better stop thinking.

One night at Gino's Rosalie pulled another surprise. She said that she knew a way he could make quite a bit of money if he didn't mind doing it, and he asked her what it was in sort of a joking way, saying that as long as he didn't have to kill anyone he probably wouldn't mind. She asked him if he ever smoked pot and he said sure but I never go out of my way for it and she said she had had some but it didn't seem to do anything for her, she guessed she was a little old when she first had it. "You mean selling grass?" he asked her, and she said "Yes" and he said "Well, I could do that." She said it is sort of dangerous because the cops in Chicago were very busy about grass at the time, having nothing better to do than harass war veterans and college kids. "But," she said, "as a result it has become much more profitable, the price is higher now because of the cops." "I think it should be free," he said, and she laughed and said that he thought everything should be free, and he laughed and said, "Well that's about right I do." She lovingly called him a hopeless romantic and he accepted her accolade.

Now his morning walks were about the same but he had a lot of stops to make, not a lot really, about five, because he was in the position of supplying other salesmen. Sometimes they asked him if he could get other stuff but he always said no even though he probably could have because he didn't want to get involved in other stuff, stuff he wouldn't have taken himself, stuff that made you sick and weak rather than gay and free.

In two months, he made $11,000 off pot. One day when he realized how much money he had, he deposited some of it, about $2300, in Rosalie's bank account since he was doing an errand for her at the bank anyway. She wouldn't have taken it if he had offered it to her, but he knew she would notice that he had done it because she always watched her money and would always check to see if the bank had made any mistakes. She never mentioned the money but the next day she went out and bought him a lovely ring of antique turquoise set in silver which was not too expensive and very beautiful and he had never really had a ring before and he liked it very much. Those were the only actual presents that they ever exchanged.

When he was thinking about money, it occurred to him that in a year, if things went on as they were going, he could probably make about $80,000 tax free. He couldn't think of what he would do with the money. He already had so much money that he didn't know what to do with it. He bought a few more clothes and he bought an old MGTD that was in perfect shape and had a special engine in it. In a flash it occurred to him to build a house for his family. He was shocked. He had begun to think of himself as married and a father, and he had never permitted himself to think in such a way because he didn't think that such a hopeless person as himself should ever raise a child. Of course, he thought, trying to calm himself, there is practically no chance that Rosalie will ever have a baby, after all. He felt a little better but he had really shocked himself and he took a drive in the noisy city to distract his thoughts. Suddenly he was stopped by the police. He had failed to signal his intention to turn right, but that is not what they were after. They made him get out all his identification. They asked him what he did for a living and where he lived and why the car wasn't registered in his own name. They were very sarcastic. Then they ripped all the upholstery out of his car. He was very mad at them for this but he had nothing to hide and so he remained calm. He took down their badge numbers and told them that he would submit a bill for the damage, which of course he never intended to do. However they were affected by this technique, and they suddenly became very friendly, almost intimate, and implied that they enjoyed meeting him and almost invited him to come around for a beer sometime and they would forget all about his failure to signal his intention to turn. One of them even offered to shake hands with him, and of course Waring declined this final indignity with a smile.

The events of the day, especially the police, shook him up quite a bit. He carted his ruined upholstery to a body shop that had an upholstery shop attached to it, left the car, and walked home. His schedule had been disrupted. He had no more criminal appointments until the following week since it was a long Fourth of July weekend. He almost considered taking a trip with Rosalie but then he thought of all the traffic. They could have a quiet weekend at home. "Goddamn it," he thought, "I really am married." He tried to read something but he couldn't focus. Then he lay down and uttered a soft long low groan, and he pounded his closed fists on the bed. Then he lay there for a few minutes and pondered his quandary. He still couldn't understand why he had to do things in the same ways all the time. Then he said, "To hell with it," into the mattress. After another minute or two he got up, and he felt very excited because he had just decided to take the next plane to L.A. He could hardly believe it, but he had just freed himself from all his responsibilities that were weighing him down. He worked fast. First he called American Airlines. Then he took a look at his clothes and put most of them in one of Rosalie's suitcases, a plaid canvas thing. At the same time he dressed in a beautiful dark blue suit with white stripes in it. Then he took some names and addresses from their place underneath the record player and burned them in an ashtray. Then he took off his ring and put it on the table and then he put it back on. Then Rosalie pulled another surprise.

She never usually called him up, and she had probably only called him up once before in the three months they had been living together, but the phone rang and he picked it up and she said, "Oh! I'm so glad you're home!"

"What's the matter?" he said.

"Oh nothing it's just the most marvellous thing!" she cried.

"Are you all right?" he asked.

"I don't know!" she said, hysterically.

"What's going on, for Christ's sake," he demanded.

"Oh! I forgot to tell you I'm going to have a baby!" she said and apparently began to cry.

"That's great," he said sincerely, "I'm so glad."

"You have no idea!" she sobbed.

"Where are you?" he asked.

"At the bar, oh dear, I feel so weak!" she cried.

"Sit down," he said sternly.

"All right," she said weakly.

"Is Mike there?" he asked.

"Uh-huh, oh my, oh my," she moaned, and then she said in a voice that was so small he hardly recognized it, "I just wanted to thank you, that's all," and she started weeping again.

"Everything's all right," he said very evenly, "Everything's all right."

"Okay," she said, sniffling her tears.

"Tell Mike to heat you some milk and put some brandy in it," he said.

"Okay," she said, "Are you coming down?"

"I've got some things to do," he said and he was pretty sure that she was so elated that she wouldn't detect the quaver in his voice, "I'll see you."

"Don't be too late," she said and hung up. Rosalie never said good-bye not even on the telephone.

Waring hung up the phone and sat still for a minute reconsidering his plans in the light of this development. Then he got his money together, and looked through his wallet and took out the car registration which was in Rosalie's name and put it next to the phone. Then he took out an old blank check he had and wrote on the back of it as follows: "The MG is at the Ajax Body Shop because the police ripped out the upholstery looking for grass but they didn't find any. It will be fixed in a week. You might as well sell it since you don't like to drive it. There's nothing here in the house at all, so don't worry. I did get scared but that isn't why. I'm very happy for you and I wish I could share it but I can't, I just can't. You are a fine woman and I am sure you will be a great mama and I envy the kid already. All this is nobody's fault. You gave me some of my best times. I am going to L.A. right now but don't try to find me because you won't be able to and you will just get yourself all upset. Don't try to understand it, just take it. You will be very busy. If I am ever in Chicago again I will come and see you. W." He read the note once, picked up his bag, turned out the light and leapt out the door with a bang.

⟦ Susan Looking ⟧

Just at that moment, in the active season I call the Spring of 1968, Susan Dial Wentworth Green, to give her all her names for the first and last time at once, felt completely alone. She was completely alone. Everyone else who was at the Club was either downstairs in the restaurant or across the hall in the music room playing pool. She was surrounded by fame and beauty and freedom and money, all of them somewhat potentially great, but she was completely alone. She was surprised to find that she was completely alone just at the time when she would have thought that things were beginning to work out all right, the time of which she had dreamed for four years, when every dream would come true. She thought over her possessions in her mind, she did not tick them off, she sort of revelled in them and threw them out. She had nothing of value to preserve. She sat down and sipped her Coke. She leaned far forward on the table as if she was whispering to its farther edge where no one sat and no one wished to sit though there were many at that time who would have died a little bit to be there. She embraced the left edge of the red plastic table with her left hand and the can of Coke, that was so icy cold and wet, in her other hand and she reached a decision to fall in love with the next man she saw. This audacity frightened her and she glanced around and was quite pleased to notice again that she was alone even as her loneliness had frightened her before. She shifted her position in the folding chair, crossed her legs and imagined how she looked. She looked a little frail, quite tall, especially charming, slightly flushed, very well dressed, and absolutely captivating. She forgot she was bored and she decided not to read the paper, so that she should not appear to be occupied when the next man came in sight. It occurred to her briefly that she hoped it would be Gilbert Green, but she crossed off that possession immediately and relegated it to the category of things owned but unwanted. Her heart was beating like mad and she did not feel one bit hungry or sweaty or uncomfortable. Everything fitted her just fine and she fit the season with an occasion that she would invent right then and there, not knowing whether she would succeed or not, knowing that she was cared for otherwise and it didn't give a damn. After all, she thought, after all my foot. She almost smiled, which gave her face a very lyrical look, and she looked down at her shoes which were bright patent leather vinyl yellow, which gave her a reflective look as well and she was sitting in a pool of light cast from a receded fixture overhead and just at that moment Kass Zapkus and Ted Castle strolling together smiled into the room and came clomping toward her very pleased to see her radiant.

"Hi Kass," she said, selecting him without a meditation or a pause.

"Well," said Kass with a very pleasant smile.

"Hello Susan," said Ted.

"Hello," she said, "I was just wondering who was going to come through the door, I'm glad at last to know."

"Have you been waiting for us very long?" asked Ted with an amused look.

"About an hour and a half," replied Susan directly to Kass who had not gone to get some beer.

"What a wait," said Kass in general, "Do you want a beer, oh, you have a Coke."

"No, I don't like beer," she said.

"I don't like beer either," said Kass, "But I've been having some trouble with my stomach and Mickey's changed his brand of wine, so I guess I'll have a beer for a change," he added simply.

"Does it hurt?" she said.

"Sometimes. Not very much. You look wonderful," he said.

"You don't have ulcers do you," she said.

"Not exactly. It doesn't bother me very much. Don't worry."

"Oh, I never worry," said Susan with a lovely grin.

"Well," said Kass sitting down and changing the position of the table and the subject all at once, "I haven't seen you in a long time."

"I've been pretty busy but now I'm not," she said forthrightly.

"I think it was Green's first movie, wasn't it, that party you had," he said.

"I've seen you since then," she said a little enigmatically.

"Oh yes, I remember one night at Max's when you slapped somebody or something. That's a long time ago too."

"Not long enough."

"Not long enough?" asked Kass with a quissical look.

"Everything is different now," she said.

"Oh I see," said he.

Ted did not return because he had gotten involved with someone in the music room, Terry Pease, it turned out, as a matter of fact, and after awhile Kass went in and got a beer and winked at Ted and went back to the table where Susan was pleased with her success and they had a long talk about an interest that they shared and Kass told some pretty involved information about his paintings which Susan had also been attracted to although she didn't understand it and she was certainly glad that there was a lot of information and she liked the way the voice of Kass caressed his information huskily and cleared his throat once in a while and smoked a truly great deal and didn't drink too much and didn't have beautiful fingernails and wasn't too well dressed and liked his hair and the mind out of which it grew forthwith.

〚 Waring in the West 〛

Except for his suitcase which was soon stashed in a locker at the
Southern Pacific terminal in L.A., Waring gave the impression of
being very rich when he arrived in the capital of much industry.
He had at least $500 on him in cash and he was carrying $1000 in
$100 traveller's checks. People who are carrying $1500 and have a
lot more somewhere else always look different than people who
have $42.50 until payday next month. They carry themselves
better. They often dress better too. But they look different even if
they are not well dressed because they feel very confident, and
the main thing they have to watch out for is developing an insane
fear of robbery which does sometimes develop. Waring couldn't
possibly have feared robbery, he would practically have welcomed
it. He didn't really dig being rich but it was a new experience and
he realized that he wasn't too rich at all, it would be easy for him to
spend all his money if he wanted to. In fact, as he attracted the
glances of all the avaricious people in L.A. and Hollywood, which
has a very high concentration of avaricious people, almost as high
as that of New York or Paris, he decided to spend all his money
somehow in a month or so.

First he rented a room at the Biltmore Hotel and he made them
show him to three different ones until he found the one he liked
best, it was not too high up and didn't have a view to speak of, but
it was an interesting view unlike most vistas out of hotels, you
could almost see people doing things from the sooty terrace. Then
he had a nice hotel dinner that wasn't very good and he certainly
noticed that people thought he was very rich and perhaps even

famous because everybody kept staring at him. Then he went down and got his bag and brought it into the hotel himself and went in and hid all his money. Then he said to himself, "That's silly," so he unhid it, and he took a shower and changed his clothes.

Then he took a cab to a club called The Factory which he had once heard Rosalie describe from a description she had read of it in some magazine. He wanted to test his luck in L.A. just as he did whenever he arrived in a place. The Factory was a private club and theoretically you had to be a member and have a card or something to get in there just to have a drink and be looked at by a lot of avaricious people. When he got there, the doorman said hello to him although they had never seen each other before, and inside the door the woman there who was checking things had to confess that she did not know him, and she asked his name. Waring Johnson, he said with a beautiful glance. He had decided that it would probably enforce his luck to adopt for a moment the name of the President of the United States. He didn't find out if that did it, but she consulted a file card system, and in a second she said, "Oh, yes, Mr. Johnson, How do you do?" He smiled at her even more beautifully and almost winked and pretty soon he was drinking a very expensive drink in a very unusual glass, it was blue cut glass, sort of a faceted goblet, it was very heavy, it was one of the ugliest glasses he had ever had occasion to use. He was using it in an atmosphere that was supposed to be an imitation of Andy Warhol's studio in New York.

Waring had never been to Andy Warhol's factory but Fred had told him about it once and he was certain that the place where he was was not a very good imitation of it. About the only thing that might have been about the same was the way everything in this club was literally covered in tinfoil, which was all crinkled up first, the whole place was entirely silver and the light was rather bright and very even and completely white. The music was horribly sentimental and the customers were very rich. Unexpectedly, after fifteen minutes or so, Waring decided that he liked it all very much, even the glass and almost the music. Then suddenly it occurred to him like a spark that he was playing the part of Gilbert Green in L.A.

"Are you Mr. Waring Johnson?" she said coming over to him sort of looking at him right in his eyes. "Yes," he said, "I have used that name too," and she said "I am so glad to hear it" and he said "The name or the fact," and she said "I don't know. May I sit down?" and he said "You can sit down if you can find a chair or you could possibly use mine but then I wouldn't have one," and she said "Why don't you just call the girl?" and he said "Okay," and he raised his fingers to his forehead in sort of a weak military salute and she sat down. "It's so strange to see you here like this" she said, "It certainly must be, since I have never been here before," he said and she said, "I don't mean that," and he said "I'm glad to hear it," and she said "That's my line but you left out a word," and he said "So I did," and she said "What's the word you left out?" and he said "Goodnight," and she said "Oh, don't go," and he said "Okay, I won't but I do have to go home," and she said "Are you married Mr. Waring?" and he said "Oh no, well I was," and she said, "What a shame," and he said "Excuse me" and stood up and turned around and started to take a leak on the floor but he found out he couldn't, so he rebuttoned his trousers and sat down and said "Excuse me again." "That's all right," she said and he said, "What's all right," and she said "Nothing much, it was nothing," and he said "You're right there, would you like to dance?" "Dancing is not permitted in this room," she said and he said "What a shame," and she said "You certainly do do that, don't you," and he said "Yes I guess I do it quite a lot," and she said "That's all right," and he said "Stop saying that," and she said "That's more like it," and he said "Ye gods almighty," and she said "What a strange expression, I don't like men who swear," and he said "Fuck off," and she said "I love men who swear, don't you?" and he said "Yes I do." "It's a pity you don't come here more often, it is so enjoyable to see you," she said and he said "Your earrings must have been quite expensive," and she said "They were not expensive at all, they were made in Japan out of nothing," and he said "Please take them off," and she took off her dress instead and underneath it she was wearing one exactly the same but it was probably made of a different material or color or something like that.

"Are you sleepy, sir?" said a waitress, "Would you care for some expresso?"

"Yes I would, no I wouldn't," said Waring, shaking his head.

"How about another drink," said the waitress eyeing him familiarly.

"All right," he said, "What time is it?"

"Quarter after twelve."

"Have you got any pot?" he said.

"Smoking is not permitted in California, not even in a private club, sir, sorry," she said. She left to get another drink. She returned immediately with a silver telephone on a long cord. "Are you Mr. Johnson?" she said.

"It couldn't be for me," he said, "It must be for some other man."

"Sorry," she said.

"Oh, skip the drink, okay?" he said.

"Okay," she said.

He left a ten dollar bill in his empty blue crystal glass and was wished good night by five different people as he slowly walked away from the place.

The view from the terrace in the early, early morning revealed a very cloudy rainy dirty day, and Waring felt disgusted with himself. He decided never again to play the role of Gilbert Green no matter where he was. He stood naked at his windows staring out at the passing roadways and the distant hills and the grayness of everything around him. His head was clear and his mind was sharp and his clothes were strewn all over his room. He took a shower and dressed in his blue jeans and a white knit cotton shirt and made a little pile of his valuables. He took all his traveler's checks out of his wallet and put them with the others that he had. Then he tossed a fifty dollar bill onto the bed he had soundly slept upon. He put the wallet in his pants pocket and pulled on his motorcycle boots. He wrapped his valuables in his underwear and wrapped them in his red shirt that was somewhat faded from the sun, and tied the bundle up securely. He took another look around the room and found an aligator belt he loved and wrapped that twice around his bundle. He put on his black leather jacket. Then he combed his hair and stuck the comb in the pocket with the wallet and walked out, leaving the door wide open. He walked down seven flights of fire exits and out the back door of the hotel into the parking lot and kept on walking. The rain felt good. He whistled sharply, there was no wind, the light rain accumulated on his long eye lashes and from time to time he wiped his face on the bundle that he swung along with.

His mind was a race of images and sights from all the lives that he had led until so recently as fifteen minutes to the hour of eight. He didn't see another solitary walker, or a bird or an animal, a few trees and some little bits of grass and lots of garbage cans and five million cars all going in the same direction. He was not going anywhere. He thought of his mother when she was young and he thought of himself when he was young, and he thought of himself and Fred as they had been young artists starting out together three or four years before and he thought of his nap at the nightclub and the lewd Chicago cops and the stereo he had abandoned in New York and the pornography he had abandoned in Waterville, and he took a look at his wet silver ring and thought of Rosalie in tears, and he thought of his mother in tears as she lay dying on East 54th Street, and he thought of a song that Fred had written about the real right way to dress and he whistled it a bit, and he thought of David and he thought of Susan, and Rosalie, and David and his mother and Susan and Rosalie, and of David and Fred, and David and David, and Fred and Fred and Fred and Fred and David and Fred and Fred, and he whistled the song again very slowly and with lots of feeling and the rain stopped and the sun did not come out.

He walked five or six miles in the general direction of downtown L.A. and he was getting nowhere at all. His feet were beginning to hurt and he caught himself beginning to look for a cab. He felt good. He felt very placid. He was not too wet. He wasn't going anywhere. He didn't want to take a cab. He started walking backwards along the street with his thumb out for a ride. Hundreds of cars passed him up. Trucks passed him up. And one motorcycle rider stopped.

"Hi. Where you goin?" "No place. Where you going?" "Down to Sal's. Want to go there?" "Sure why not." "You can hang on to me, she's a little rough at the start, you better tie your thing on, okay." "Thanks." "You get used to it, you got a bike?" "Not now." "What?" "Not right now." "Got bread?" "Some." "I might sell this baby, the new BSA Spitfire is something else." "What?" "I'll tell you later."

They sped along at the speed of machines and even then it took twenty minutes to get to where they were going and wonder of wonders they were not arrested once because Waring didn't have his helmet on, he didn't even have one with him.

Sal's was a snack bar that seemed to be on the edge of some town but everything in L.A. seemed to Waring to be outside of town except he knew he was not in or too near Hollywood. Waring's new friend was called Frank by a few people, but he was known universally as The Buster, not just Buster, and anybody who called him Buster always got kicked in the balls. The Buster explained his name "because I used to be a narco." This gave Waring a story to tell and an early bond with Frank The Buster. Frank The Buster insisted on buying Waring a vanilla malted for breakfast and it was a milkshake that tasted very good to both of them. Frank The Buster had lots of friends at Sal's, but since it was still early in the morning, there was only one other customer in the place, a retired couple out of a green Chevy with Iowa plates. "I always come here for breakfast," Frank explained, "And sort of open up the place." They ate another milkshake each.

"You travel a lot, huh," said The Buster when they finished.

"Yeah, I have been," said Waring.

"Going to stick around?"

"Dunno."

"You got some grass on you?"

"You wanna bust me, go ahead, no, all I got's bread and stuff."

"Bread's bettern grass. It's all one," reflected The Buster beautifully. "Nine-thirty, better charge."

"You work someplace?" asked Waring not wanting to be left.

"Not exactly," said The Buster with a little smile, his first.

"Can I go with you," asked Waring with his eyes.

"I'll drop you if you want. Where you goin."

"Noplace."

"Okay, hang in," said Frank swinging outside the glass door and holding it for Waring, "Say, you better get a topper, I lost my extra one. They're real tight here now."

"Is there a place around here," asked Waring taking a look.

"Nah, but we're not far, I'll take you down to S.A.G. it's almost on the way. Is that thing gonna break loose."

"No, it's alligator hide."

"Pretty."

"Yeah."

On the way down to S.A.G. Frank talked about his bike, a Harley-Davidson knucklehead bought in Seattle for very little and in worse shape and fixed by hand and tooled by trade and dint of hard work and some friendship, afterwards a pretzled rim and reamed bearings and what not, I lost the gas cap, the new inverted V's, the crummy Jap wheels and worse English, a set of shocks, and no fairings never.

Waring went into the store and bought the cheapest helmet and some goggles and looked at leather clothes while Frank The Buster waited outside the store and talked with maybe a mechanic and jumped up and down on the seat of his bike to illustrate his point about the shock absorbers. As an afterthought, Waring bought a little vinyl handbag and an elastic strap to tie it on the bike with and he was given a card with the name and address of the store on it, the South America Garage, Joe Fellow prop.

"You got some glasses, huh," said Frank as Waring repacked his bundle.

"Yeah, I always wanted some," said Waring.

"Hate em," said Frank, "Too hot, you know."

"Well," said Waring.

"You all set, let's go."

"This is not my home," said Frank, "I'm from Kansas, Topeka."

"How long you been here."

"Coupla years."

"I've been here a coupla days," said Waring, "It's the end of the world."

"You said it, it's the end alright, the ass end of the world. You get sort of used to it though, I do, it's pretty free and like that and it's not too bad. How much bread you got."

"A lot," said Waring, warily, and then throwing caution to the wind he added, "I guess about ten grand more or less."

"Wow, I had figured you for a poor boy, wow, ten grand, that's almost as much as we've got altogether. You got it on you."

"Yeah."

"You got guts."

"No I don't, I just don't care, that's all.

"You better hide it somewhere I don't know. I get high sometimes and well you know."

"You want it you can have it. You've been nice to me."

"Hey man, take it easy, it's all right."

"No it's not."

"Well, you're right there, that's right, it's not all right, but don't go giving all your shit to a guy you don't know."

"Okay, I won't."

"How old are you, 25?"

"26."

"I'm 29 and getting older all the time." A pause and then Frank added, "26 and 29 and getting older all the time, ha, ha, ha" he laughed without cracking his lips. "You know what, between us we're fifty five years old. Jesus christ."

"Forget it," said Waring.

"What're you gonna do with all yr bread?"

"I don't know, can't you think of anything else?"

"Ten grand is ten grand."

"I guess so. I think about it half the time myself."

"And the other half you think about yr prick, right?"

"Yeah."

"You're normal."

"Thanks."

"What a life. You want some beer."

"Okay."

"I don't have any grass, and maybe I don't even have any beer."

"You got a chick?"

"Yeah, there's one left, that's a beer, no I've got two, they're sisters."

"Wow."

"When you get to be my age you have to stay in constant practice or else it all falls away."

"Huh, I know that already."

"Don't put me down," said Frank handing half a beer to Waring, "I'm the king."

"I could just shut up."

"Oh, she's a bitch too, huh."

"Sometimes."

"You've really got the blues, don't you."

"Yeah."

"Chicago does that. I was there two months one time. Had the best time of my life but I hadda run away from there. That's a real depressing place."

"I know what you mean, but this is hell."

"The more you travel the worse you find."

"At least you've got a lot of friends and all."

"You must have hundreds, you're so beautiful," said Frank blushing slightly at the ears.

"They don't like me for it though," said Waring looking at the floor.

"Oh yeah," said Frank, "When you're not pretty yourself you forget about that, yeah it must be tough."

"Don't rub it in," said Waring.

"Take it easy kid." They looked at each others' toes and at the floor between them as they sat in a little silence. "I believe in luck," said Frank, "What do you believe in."

"Nothing."

"I mean I think I was supposed to pick you up out there this morning and we can stick together and stuff and do things because it happened and you well you asked to come along, I don't talk very good sometimes."

"Do you have good luck?"

"Yeah, I'm lucky."

"I used to be."

"Yeah."

"I'm still lucky, but, I don't know what it all means, I mean, well, I mean, where does it all get me? I don't get it that's all."

"Young and rich and beautiful and sad and here. What you need is a piece of ass. I'm going to do the dishes."

"Oh, no," said Waring lightly and lay back down on the floor with his right arm over his eyes. Frank The Buster and the King went all around the room gathering a lot of plastic glasses and coffee mugs and a few plastic plates in a paper bag. Then he took it into the bathroom and dumped it with a clatter into the bathtub and turned on the water full blast. Then he came out and went around putting trash like newspapers and cigarette butts and beer cans and milk cartons, one or two, and some dried up flowers and an empty ketchup bottle and some other stuff into the same paper bag and when it was neat he opened one of the four windows and dropped the bag out and looked out and said "Bull's eye" and closed the window and went into the bathroom and turned off the water and took a leak and flushed the toilet and sloshed around with the dishes in the tub and turned the water on and let the drain out and rinsed the dishes and tossed them in the sink, one by one, and came out and sat down on a bed with a magazine, and then tossed it onto Waring's stomach where it rested and picked up a copy of *Life* and lay down on the bed and looked through it a bit. And for a while they both took a nap.

Waring dreamt of being on a motorcycle in back of nobody although he could not reach the handlebars, it was like the rider was invisible but he could feel the muscles of his stomach and he wasn't afraid exactly but he thought there was something wrong and he woke up with a completely numb arm.

Frank dreamt sort of amorphously about a lot of parts of things, bodies and nuts and bolts and clutch plates and shock absorbers that were more like jack-in-the-boxes than shock absorbers are, and Waring's ring, and a huge mess of parts of things that were made of plastic or aluminum or something very light and trying to get the grease off his hands that were covered with grease and his face had dirt all over it because what he wanted to do was to kiss and what woke him up was Waring flushing the toilet. Frank sat on the cot and shook his head. "Do you dig your dreams?" he said.

"Yeah, sometimes," said Waring, drying his hands.

"So do I."

"I just had a dream about riding with you but you weren't there, it was funny."

"It scare you?"

"No."

"I just had trouble getting all this grease off my hands," said Frank.

"What grease."

"Oh, in my dream."

"Oh. Where is everybody anyway, I mean do they come in later or what? What do you do with yourself anyway."

"I get by."

"Yeah."

"I get high with the help of my friends."

"Yeah, where are they."

"What do you care."

"Maybe it's all a lie, I don't know, I mean a man's got to do something."

"Work?"

"Forget it, I don't know what I'm talking about. Things happen too fast."

"You said it."

"I'll buy you a steak, you want a steak?"

"I want to get one thing straight."

"Okay."

"Nobody buys me anything, ever. I take care of myself. I take care of other people too. I take care of them all the way. I'll take care of you too, one way or another, and I won't buy you a steak, you buy your own, I'm going out."

"Where you goin, ma, can I go too?"

"So you're smart too, well, that's all right, I'll take care of you."

"No it's not, I mean what do you want to take care of me for, I mean you can't shove me into a bag like that, you may be the king, but I'm not a piece of shit."

"I love you, Wary," said Frank abruptly, and he reached around and took some keys from a nail on the wall and threw them at Waring which hit his stomach with a tinkle and landed in his hand, and in two steps he was out of the door and in two kicks he charged off with a roar.

⟦ Susan in Love ⟧

Over a period of a few weeks, Susan became as busy as everyone else had seemed to her before, she was making two films and rehearsing a dance and conducting a time-consuming love affair which was the first intellectual love affair she had ever undertaken, and she was at first quite surprised, at their second meeting she had been ready to jump right into his bed, but he kissed her tenderly outside her door and didn't even get out of the car or anything, he just looked fondly after her as she locked herself in for the night, and then drove off to his house.

She had really fallen very hard in love and she accepted everything he gave her and she wanted no more and she was rather miserable at the thought of him and rather overjoyed at the sight of him and rather instructed by him to exercise her brain. Yvonne's show was called "The Mind is a Muscle" too. Susan realized for the first time that she was fairly smart, not because her lover told her so but because he was able to make her mind respond so well to his. They often went to one of three very good cheap restaurants, one in Chinatown that was not as cheap, and one called Caffe Puglia that everyone but Kass called Pulio's, and a Greek restaurant called The Paradise which Susan liked best of all. They only went to Max's once in a while to dance, and from time to time they showed up at the Club or at the Apex Bar for talk and drinks with friends of his. Once in a while on a weekend they had dinner at Ted and Janet Castle's house on Front Street which was always a very good dinner with lots of talk and a very pretty baby that they had. At one point after a few weeks of this, Fred said to her, "What's happened to you, you are so scarce," and she smiled and did not respond because she knew he knew the answer.

Every night, for the first couple of weeks, Susan desired to be made love to by Kass and then she decided that it didn't matter, she was having such a good time as it was and she better not push her luck, but she always made her occasional kisses as warm as they could be for being very brief, & then of course one night he took her in the middle of a recording he was playing for her of his favourite synthetic music by Milton Babbitt, in which at the time she was completely lost and utterly surprised and completely pleased and grateful and winning and devoted and beautiful and rich and even though he was a little shorter than she was, and warm and rich and resonant and rhythmic and related and all puffed up and utterly deflated and sleeping very soundly in the protection of his head.

In the morning she got up first and made him quite a nice little breakfast of eggs and some French sausage, salami really, that he had and parsley and toast and coffee, and then lay down again and just held on to him while he read the book reviews. Later they went to a big demonstration against the war, a little war in Central Park that was extremely crowded, and then he took her home and said "goodnight" although it was only the end of the afternoon, and they laughed a little and he kissed her tenderly and she felt so good that she no longer wanted anything.

⟦ War the Beau ⟧

In the months that followed, the famous Viet-Nam War was not yet being brought to a close due to domestic pressures that were out of control and threatening to overturn the economy and everything else, and Waring was doing a very strange thing for him to do, he was the chief assistant of a king and what the king did, it turned out, was run a real live theatre, and Waring directed it. They staged stuff and the audience was everyone, the cops included, and the universities, and some of the stores, and a few bars and especially the newspapers and media of the day which always ate the whole story whole. They all followed their progress with delight and anguish and much hope, and candy bars and beers and beers and upset timetables and righted wrongs the wrong way and wronged rights properly.

Waring got a new name which was very romantic, namely War The Beau, and of course the whole theatre thing was very sentimental but it did get stuff done that had never been done before and would never have been done otherwise. Los Angeles County was not the same place at all, it was a field of action that left the world of the day breathless and in tears and giggles.

The troop of them was ultimately very large for a group but as a matter of fact it was actually very small, being limited to six big wheels under Frank The Buster. Each of the six, except Waring, was a big-shot in some other sphere of activity which could in turn be activated to do a demonstration if that was what was called for. Do not get the idea that this was a real live bureaucracy as well as a real live theatre, it was a little club of six powerful young men which could be used to mutual advantage whenever there was a desire to do so. Frank The Buster was the most powerful of all of them because he could command all six armies if he wanted to and he never abused his position. I am also not talking about alliances among groups of outlaws, or bike gangs or fight gangs which might be familiar to newspaper readers. This group, which, for example, did not name itself, was not like anything else.

It was a long time, at least two months, before Waring quite understood the whole thing and even for months after that he was always learning a new detail or two of which he hadn't suspected. Waring was filled with admiration of the modesty with which the grand play was carried off, and he loved Frank more intensely than he had ever loved another soul on earth. One of the interesting aspects of the whole thing was that none of the seven of them had ever been in the Army, for one reason or another, so that they had never had a chance to develop a formal sadist routine, and, as a matter of fact, one of their problems was holding in line all of their friends who had been in the Army, and when it came down to it what those guys always thought of to do if they got mad or even annoyed was to blow the whole thing off the face of the earth, and for that reason no guns were permitted at all, and no explosives of any kind, except that Frank had a gun just in case but nobody but Frank had ever laid eyes on the gun and Frank himself never admired it. Frank never mentioned it either, and Waring only found out this detail for example in something that one of the others once mentioned in the line of a joke. One time, however, they did use a sort of explosive, they filled all of the serious theatres in Los Angeles County, which does not have many serious theatres, eight actually, with fumes from burning sulfur and drove all their audiences out in the street where a fireworks display was displayed in the sky, thrown from a helicopter owned by the police which Frank had sort of suddenly borrowed. I mean that they weren't scared of explosives but Frank knew what such danger could lead to. After all he had started out as a cop.

That trick was more useful in keeping guys from the Army in line than anything else Frank had ever done, and he thought and he once mentioned to Wary that if things got real bad they would do it again but then to all the movie houses, night clubs and so on, of which there are literally hundreds in town. One of the marvelous aspects of all the demonstrations they staged was that each one was both a trick and a treat, depending on one's point of view.

Waring never even saw most of the people who were somehow associated with Frank The Buster, but Frank did, he tried to know everybody and that was how he discouraged disloyalty, because even at the farthest reach of his influence, he had actually met all the people who ever might sometime help out. Thus the other big shots would never be quite able to muster their troop for an open revolt because Frank had all the proles in his pocket. But Waring did get to know the big shots quite well and really that was his main job, to keep them happy and find out what they were thinking about. At the outside limit, the whole thing maybe amounted to 500 people.

Charles The Bold, who was the guy who thought up the name of War The Beau, had started out as a linguistic philosopher associated with the University of California at Berkeley, where, when the student revolts were invented, his imagination was captured and he put his pedantic pursuits to one side and conceived for the first time in his life a great admiration for apparent disorder. He was able to steal some of his students who had already been thrown out of school and take them to San Francisco State College where he was ultimately unable to do as he wanted and thus he gave up all his illusions. He started mimeographing a little paper about the philosophy of violent non-violence and Frank happened to pick up a copy of it off the street where it had been discarded and he liked it a lot and he went to see Charles. Charles was the oldest and best educated of the lot and his name of The Bold was a euphemism because he was really the most timid of all of the kings, but he was also one of the smartest and he always knew exactly what he was talking about. His troop were philosophic disciples, mainly ex-students, who had respectable but uninteresting jobs in dry cleaners and bookstores and supermarkets and snack bars all over town, and they met quite a bit and they talked a great deal and they were mostly interested in history and stuff like that, and some of them were girls.

Joe The Pizza King, who was the only one who was really called a king, except when Frank had to pull rank, was entirely different. He started out in Mexico but was brought to La Jolla at an early age and wound up stealing enough money from his foster parents there to set up the South American Garage which had definitely prospered in the heyday of bikeboys and made Joe fairly rich. He was rich in a way but he never had any money, he was somebody who had all the best stuff, he had an Aston Martin, he had excellent food and very good wine and he lived in a small house on the beach of his own design, not the beach but the house, with his sister who was really Mexican and spoke nothing but Spanish, and he was the only one of the kings who practically never came to see Frank at his house but they talked every day down at the garage that was always called S.A.G. Waring was often a guest at Joe's house because Waring, like Joe, really dug all the best stuff, and he even taught Jane, Joe's sister, some English. Joe's troop was small and composed of Chicano mechanics and a certain number of free agents, lone wolf bikeboys who did errands for Frank once in awhile. If they needed a real legitimate front, Joe was it.

Hieronomous Bosch was the only one who didn't have a the in his name and he didn't use his real name at all and Waring never found out what it was but he was always called Bosch and sometimes he was called Bash because he had a habit of throwing something down on the floor and walking out on to show his disgust and when he returned he had usually thought of a really good trick or a treat for the audience. Bosch was supposedly a poet but he never wrote anything, it wasn't even certain that he knew how to write, he was an orphan from an infant and he was ethereal, he was tall and skinny and had almost white hair that was always a mess and he had no visible means of support and at one time he had been Frank's only friend when they were both like sixteen. His poems were tirades and he was the most passionate of all of the kings he didn't drink but one glass of wine but he was always stoned on the things he had in his head which came out once in a while just like Niagara Falls. Bosch troop was about ten or twelve friends who he lived off of and they were all different kinds of people, some were rich and some were poor and some were nothing of the sort, and they didn't know each other much and Bosch troop was the largest of all, because all of these friends had in turn friends of their own so Bosch was a really big king and even Frank didn't quite know the extent of the influence of Bosch but he trusted him absolutely unlike the others so Waring had less to do with Bosch than with the rest.

James The Bad was actually a criminal, and he was never called The Bad and he was never called Jim, he was always called James The Bad or just James. The extent of his criminal activities was never exactly known to Waring, but he found out that James had got together with Frank The Buster because when Frank busted him for selling dope James was able to convince Frank not to turn him in, but rather to punish him in his own way, and the way that Frank chose was to make James the first sub-king of all because although he already knew Bosch, there was no such thing as a king until James made the deal. James troop was all kinds of criminals, and James was not his real name, and Frank still had an aversion to criminals who had got caught, but he was able because of his police training to joke with the best of them and let them know that he was their friend indeed. Frank did not make much use of James troop himself, after all they had their own things planned, but if he really needed money which he sometimes did he would have them take some for him, but when Frank stole it was always from an institution like a chain store or an airline or something fairly big, but never a bank or a railroad or the government because they were so vindictive against thieves. Frank's idea of the ideal robbery was against a non-profit foundation but unfortunately they never had any cash and Frank never stole anything other than cash and never more than he needed right at the moment. Waring was much occupied with cheering up James who was liable to get quite disgruntled and this involved going out and getting drunk with him at least once a week.

Ralph The Man was a pillar of the community, he was actually one of the officers of a rather small bank which did however have fourteen branches around different places, because his skin was so light, and Waring could only guess how he had happened to become one of Frank's troop, it was probably just due to the accident that one of the bank's branches was located across the street and down a bit from Frank's house in South Pasadena and maybe Ralph had been in training there or something like that, but at any rate it was Frank's bank whenever he had to do anything with a bank which was rare indeed but they did mortgage his house once upon a time it was said. Ralph was hardly ever called Ralph The Man but he was sometimes called Ralphie and he was more devoted to his wife than he was to Frank but he was utterly loyal just because she was utterly loyal, and she was called Juanita and sometimes Frank called her John, and she never came to Frank's house in the evening but Ralph often did and in effect Ralph was a front for his wife. He was also good because he made a lot of jokes and he never thought it was the end of the world no matter how bad things seemed and sometimes he would sing a song in a big deep voice and a big wide white smile and all that helped everyone out. Juanita was a very ambitious woman and she had some damn good ideas and she talked beautifully and she had been a personal friend of the late Stokley Carmichael back where they came from, and Frank's wasn't the only deal that she was involved in. About once every two weeks or ten days, Juanita called Waring and invited him to dinner, which meant she was inviting Frank too and one other guest, usually Bosch, and then they had a lot of strange and wonderful food and talked and talked and talked and it was what Ralph loved to call the executive council although he himself was never there after the coffee was served. Juanita also had a Mexican maid called Juanita and these dinners were always held on the maid's night off. Juanita was older than Charles although she was still extremely beautiful and she had two grown sons in another country.

Frank's own troop was first of all all the kings and all of their men and then he had sort of another kind of a following which were sort of inferiors, people he had met over the years and vaguely discarded but he never completely broke with anybody he had ever known, and in addition he really did have two chicks who were sisters and who even Waring never actually met although they sometimes called Frank on the phone, and if there was ever any need of having women around which after all there certainly was, Frank always got them for them so in a way Frank was also a pimp. It was sort of like as if the sisters ran a girl's auxiliary or something, but they didn't ever get very active, they just supplied the needs of the entire empire directly through Frank, and the girls were the only people with whom Waring himself never had anything to do except once when he could have, it was only a few weeks after Frank and Waring had met, and Frank told Wary he could probably get him any girl in the world and Waring told Frank about all his different women and Frank confided some of his experiences to Waring, and at the end of the conversation Waring told Frank he didn't want a woman and Frank really understood what he meant.

Waring's troop was essentially just Frank himself and he never ever abused all that privilege.

⟦ Susan Scheming ⟧

The next day, the next day after that, the next week, the next month and the month after that, Susan, although very busy, became more and more dissatisfied. She was not sure what she wanted but she thought that she would probably be able to decide pretty soon. She was having a very unusual love affair with Kass Zapkus, she was being mean to Fred in little petty remarks that she knew would probably hurt him, and she decided that what she really wanted to do was to get Gilbert Green's attention back again. This might have been easy since she saw him every day, but he never paid her much mind and she thought maybe he was having an affair with somebody although except for Fred maybe she didn't know who. "Nonsense," she thought to herself.

She loved Gilbert Green so deeply that she could never do anything to hurt him, even a little small thing, and she was still grateful to him for having spotted her and taken her along with him wherever he was going which was definitely very successful no matter where it might lead. Then she received an unexpected visit from Stefan Brecht who told her how much he admired her and brought her some flowers and said the most intelligent thing that had ever been said about her, which, however, she was unable to remember after he left and she began getting the impression that she could probably have any man in the world and it was too bad that she didn't want anybody but Gilbert Green who evidently didn't want her anymore. But she thought she would give it a try in quite a complicated manner, which involved trying to get Kass Zapkus to marry her and going ahead and doing that if that didn't attract Gilbert Green's attention.

Then Fred started coming on strong. "Oh, this is too much for me," she thought, but it wasn't. Fred was feeling very, very powerful because of Gilbert Green's successes, and he was definitely jealous of Kass Zapkus who had completely involved Susan in the intellectual way that had always been Fred's function and forte, and since he was feeling so powerful, he thought she had no right to ignore him, indeed almost to insult him every time they met which was still quite often indeed, so he decided to make a play for her. His ace, of course was his position as Gilbert Green's major-domo.

"What's the matter with you?" he said to her one night at the Apex.

"Nothing, I've never felt better," she said.

"Don't lie to me," he said and looked hurt.

"Oh, Fred, I'm sorry," she said and she pressed his upper arm warmly.

"Don't lie to me," he repeated, but this time with a smile that showed her how much he was in love with her.

"Oh dear," she said to herself, "Well, let's, I mean, good heavens!" she exclaimed, "I can't even talk."

"I can't even figure out what you're trying to do," said Fred with a very straightforward look.

"Let's sit down." They went in the back and sat at a table. "Wow," she said, "So much has been happening!"

"Oh? I didn't know."

"Yes you did," she said a bit narrow.

"I mean I could guess something, but," he said.

"All right," she said to herself and plunged. "I'm going to marry Kass."

"Really?" he said with a terrible grimace, "I don't believe it."

"I don't either sometimes."

"Why? Why would you want to do that?"

"You know why," she said eyes down, and thought, maybe that's a mistake.

"Well, I certainly don't," said Fred, and then someone came up and spoke to them and Fred told them to go away. "Did you tell him yet?"

"I'm telling him now," she said with a wink.

"Wow," said Fred, "I think you've got balls, he won't like that one bit."

"I haven't even told Kass yet," she said, relenting.

"Well, that's a sign of something, I don't know what."

"You asked for it," she said.

"So I did. Wow," he said again. "Look," he said, and she looked, "I mean, I know that you were lonely and all that, after all he's got to have time sometimes to make up his mind, just like Napoleon, I mean he was always postponing decisions, you know, and . . . "

"No, I never knew Napoleon," she said.

"Stop it right now!"

"I'm sorry."

"Well that's what I really want to say anyway, I mean stop it, for your sake at least if you don't care about him anymore."

"I want a husband not a director."

"You've got about five husbands right this minute."

"I only want one," she said and started to cry.

"Good god," said Fred. "You must really be in bad shape," and he handed her a handkerchief and held her hand chummily.

"I guess so," she said recovering.

"Look," he said a bit desperately, "Why don't you come and stay at my place. That way you can be in closer touch with things. You can type up my stuff like you used to do and . . . "

"Oh, Fred," she said with tears in her eyes. But the tears were tears of thanks and acceptance and success and surprise.

Susan did not believe that her life could be as eventful as it apparently was. The fact that Fred was taking care of her in the name of Gilbert Green made her feel that things were going to be all right. But it was going to be a very tight schedule and everything depended on Gilbert Green, no, everything depended on Susan because Gilbert Green was going to do nothing. He was just going to sit there becoming more beautiful every day while she languished with some of the most desirable men that had ever been built. First she wrote a note to Kass Zapkus telling him where she was and to call her and saying that she loved him very much. Kass did not call her immediately, but he did call her the next day and they arranged to go out for dinner. He was so pleasant that she forgot her sorrows for a while and they went dancing at Max's and had a marvellous time and cut Viva (who was also not speaking to them) and laughed a great deal and conducted a conversation at the top of their lungs which wore them out with all of their laughing and dancing, and stayed until the end of the night which was exactly 3:30 in the morning. When they got in Kass's car she looked at him as if she wanted to be kissed, but he wasn't looking right then, he was taking a look at Andy Warhol who was just getting into a cab. He drove her to her house, which was really Fred's house, after all, and he kissed her goodnight and said he had had a very good time indeed, and drove away and she let herself in and she felt very mad at herself and she felt quite frustrated and she felt that she wanted to hurt someone, and she knew it wouldn't be Fred this time, and she decided to go through with the rest of her plan.

She ran upstairs and turned on the radio and found a note from Fred saying they had just had to go to Hollywood suddenly but they would be back in two days and a night and he was leaving a check for two hundred dollars and a kiss. She looked at the check and found that it was not Fred's check it was a check from Gilbert Green and it did not have a kiss on it but she imagined it did. She sat down on the floor and wriggled around to the music and took off all her clothes one by one and rolled around and sang a little bit and got up and danced some and then just lay there during a slow Dylan song and thought and listened and then they played ''I Want You'' and she moaned and she almost wept but she was too excited and she turned off the radio in the middle of the song and went to bed but she couldn't sleep.

After an hour in the bed with the stars, Fred had painted some stars over the head of his bed, and she wriggled around so she could see them, she got up and scrambled some eggs and ate them right up and looked at the dawn which was quite definitely blue as blue. She had on Fred's bathrobe which he never used himself, as a matter of fact, which was also blue. She took a piece of blue paper (Fred used different colors of paper for his letters) and she started writing a letter to Kass. It occurred to her after she had finished the first sentence that she might just as well call him up, but she thought that he would hate to be waked, so she kept on writing with the letter, which in a couple of minutes she threw on the floor and immediately took another sheet and wrote to him very fast.

"I can't sleep and I want you so much," she wrote, "that it hurts and I don't know what I shall do but I guess that you must not want me and so I will probably never see you again. I would never be a threat to your life. Ours may be just a passing affair, but if you want me to I will marry you." Then she paused for a very long minute. "I don't mean to pressure you," she continued, "but it seems to me that I am enduring so much pressure that I have to pass some of it on, I mean you must know what pain you are causing," and then she crossed out causing and wrote, "creating, or else you are just insensitive which cannot be true, I know it's not, you are the tenderest person I have ever known. How strange it seems to love someone and to want to understand him. You have taught me a great deal, and I am very grateful, but I am so sad I do not know how to express it. I try not to cry but I fail. I must have made a mistake somewhere," and then she paused for another long pause, "but I refuse to believe it is true. I want to have my cake and eat it too and I know that can't be done but I know that that is what I want, and I want you, and you must believe that I never lie and that I am in pain for you and please help me for my sake."

She read the note over about fifteen or twenty times and looked out at the bright sunrise and put on some jeans and a shirt and addressed an envelope and went outside and mailed the letter and took a short walk in the sun and then went to bed and slept it off.

Later on the next day he responded to her letter and asked somebody to go and find her and give it to her personally.

"This is a bluegreen letter. I refuse to be loved as I refuse to love. I can't possibly be an active love object. First I'm not an object and will never be shaped into one. I am not an affair nor can I be a passing. I am not a canal, not a road, not a destination, not a dead end and not a live end. I am complete—I begin and finish within my own skin which is never shed. I may assume a more outward or inward shape, but I never penetrate it. I don't really believe in anything & not love. To be loved means to be summed up, or to pretend to be summable. The sum of everything is nothing. There are no great men however there are what might be called great men. I disagree with you on that and several other points, but I do enjoy agreeing with you on many other issues that others disagree on.

"I am complete in my aloneness although I sometimes partly act out getting together. Others find themselves to be together so I guess they can be. I generally avoid that issue—but when I am asked to act out togetherness I must admit that I can't, because I'm not ɑ ɩ actor. (I did study acting for several years to no avail.) I do tell the truth. I love to investigate other thinking—communicate. But, communication's ends are not love. Nothing is the end of something else. I am not cruel or kind. I am honest in a gentle manner. Some people find truth painful—I never feel pain though I do feel uncomfortable at times. I never feel it because I despise it and I don't inflict pain on other people. I am sorry when people use me painfully.

     K."

Collaboration, collusion, incest, sodomy, art. —G.G.

⟦ The War is Over ⟧

For months Waring and Frank had been sharing the same house, eating many of the same meals, sharing the same secrets and telling each other about each other. They loved one another and served each other, each accordingly with what the other wanted. Waring was not happy but he was busy and Frank was not happy either. About once or twice a month they found themselves with a nice day and nothing much that had to be done. Then they got into the habit of getting on the bike and riding out someplace in the hills and sort of exploring around. At first Frank always rode in the number one spot, but after Waring got used to the bike sometimes he got up first. When they got wherever they decided to go, which was never exactly repeated or ever decided in advance, sometimes they hiked around in some fields or they just lay down in the sun and talked and thought things over and tried to get a little distance on the whole scene they were making.

On one such late summer trip, Waring was up front and Frank was holding him tight from behind. It wasn't too hot but the sun was out, it was actually fairly late in the day because they had been up late playing a trick the night before, one that hadn't worked out too well actually, they had tried to put red vegetable dye in 400 selected swimming pools, and they had done quite a few of them all right, but by the time the trick was over sixteen of their people had been arrested for trespassing, ten of them had been shocked by electric fences and one had been seriously wounded by a watchdog and one had had his hand shot off by the owner of the house he was assigned to "poison." The last thing was the most depressing accident that had ever befallen Frank in the course of his many exploits and Waring was visibly shaken, and both of them were very silent as they rode to get away from it all.

When they got somewhere nice, it was outside a little town, and there was a little collection of trees pretty far away from the road, Frank nudged Waring, and he drove the machine into the field and up toward the trees and stopped it behind a little clump of bushes where it probably wouldn't be noticed by curious police cars cruising along the road with nothing to do but to harass law-abiding citizens. Frank carried the bottle of Rhine wine they were going to share and they walked silently into the little wood and found a sunny little meadow in the middle of it. Waring opened the wine with a folding corkscrew from his pocket, handed the bottle to Frank, and sat down, at the same time pulling off his shirt and throwing it aside. Frank took a swig and handed the bottle to Waring, took off his shirt and put it down on the ground and then lay facing Waring, propping up his head with one arm. They didn't say anything for a long time and the wine didn't taste very good either.

"I think that rear bearing is shot," remarked Frank at length.

"What?" said Waring who had not been listening.

"Nothing, oh it was just nothing," said Frank. "You know what? We're dressed exactly alike," and it was the first time that Frank ever really smiled at Waring all the time he had known him.

"Different shirts," said Waring, and he laughed to see Frank The Buster smile for once in his life.

"Yeah but we're not wearing them," said Frank and he stared at the side of Waring's face until Waring looked around and they looked into each other's eyes like animals for a full two or three seconds, and then Frank said to the eyes in a voice that was slightly husky, "I want you."

A hush descended and they could almost hear each other's hearts burn with different emotions. After quite a long hush interrupted by birdcalls, Waring took a big breath and looked back at Frank and he said, "I didn't want you to say that."

"Well," said Frank, shifting his posture, "There it is isn't it."

"This is too good a thing," said Waring, "It might just disappear and . . . "

"I don't get it," said Frank.

"You said so yourself the other night at the house you said something like well if all this was just for sex well then it wouldn't be worth it."

"I wasn't talking about that," said Frank, "I didn't mean it that way."

"I don't know," said Waring with a hitch in his voice, and he rolled over and lay on his stomach which was prickled by the grass and pounded by his heart.

"Still Wary, huh," said Frank. Waring looked up at him and smiled a beautiful smile, very quickly.

"I can't smile," said Frank, "I feel sick." He took a swig of the wine and set it down by Waring who rolled over and had some too. Then Waring took the bottle by its neck and tossed it out across the field and the bottle tumbled over and over in the air spilling the remains of the wine as it lurched and landed with a thud not too far away. Frank got up, brushed off his pants, took up his shirt and ran down to where they had left the bike and Waring followed slowly and got up behind Frank and they went home in silence and sadness.

Charles The Bold and Charles troop revolted from Frank because it was one of their people who got shot and although Frank gave them some money and swore to become, in effect, more intellectual, start up a few more papers and things like that, they said they didn't need Frank anymore though they thanked him for his help in the past. This was the boldest thing that Charles The Bold had ever done and he was so scared when he did it that it was hard for him to speak, but Frank just looked hurt, and told him quietly to get the fuck out. Charles offered his hand, which was not accepted or looked at and Waring walked Charles to his car, putting his hand around the man's shoulder which was shaken loose and then said good-bye.

Inside the house, Bosch and Ralph sat with Frank and all of them were depressed. Waring came back in and opened a beer and another (Bosch and Ralphie never drank beer) and then Bosch threw a book on the floor with a bang and strode out the door. "That's a sign of health," said Ralph but nobody smiled including himself. It was dark in the room by that time and nobody moved and nobody spoke. Ralph crossed his legs and closed his eyes and prayed silently. Waring stared at the floor. Ralph stared at the ceiling. Frank finally spoke. "Every thing is no good," he said darkly, "I guess it's the end of the life."

"Don't say that," said Waring.

"If I want to," said Frank.

"Okay," said Waring.

"Shut up," said Ralph. They sat in silence a couple more minutes and then Bosch came back with a bang. He had ripped all the rear view mirrors off all the cars in the street and he brought them in and laid them on the floor with a crash.

"Jesus Christ!" said Frank, and then Bosch stood there in all the debris and told one of his tirades which began very slow.

"The end of the world is a bright crash of light and it moves and it speaks and it gets ready for nothing, nothing at all, nothing at all, it is nothing at all, it is nothing, it is no thing at all, it is just light and nothing. It makes me sick to see you like this, sucking your thumb and crying for mama in the middle of a mess you can't even clean up. Screw you Frank. Screw you Wary. Screw you Ralfie. Screw Big Frank The Buster. Screw everybody. You think the world's gonna wait for you to grow up, you think there's sun in the air out there, what's a blood bath to you, what's a bubble bath either, it's all new and improved like the tide on the beach out there in the morning when the sun don't come up any more, so we all freeze, and our cocks shrivel up first and then our head and our hands and our feet and our heart, and that's it, there's nothing left it's all gone. This was the life. It wasn't much of a life. It was just life and we lived it up. It was so freeeeeeeeee!"

And he stooped over and scooped three mirrors and threw them one at each wall except the wall at his back. Then he paused, picked up another mirror and threw it through one of the windows which dropped with a crash outside.

"All right everything's no good anymore, so stop playing games. Kill yourself. Or kill off a dozen movie stars and then kill yourself. Or put some cyanide in the smog and sit around and get sick and die like a fly. A real terror has got to be real. Cut out this decorative shit. You're all fags anyway, you'll never have any guts, Jesus ain't it pretty tonight, goddamn right it stinks here in heaven and the higher you go the harder you cough. What's another catastrophe, another one for the books. Go. You got to take it. You got to go. You got to take it. You got to take it, you got to go, you got to go, you got to go, you got to go, you got to go, you got to go . . . ''

And as he repeated ''you got to go, you got to go, you got to go'' he started kicking the mirrors around with his feet then he got down on his hands and knees and stopped everything and then he began to weep silently, and then he laid down on the floor and sobbed loudly and nobody moved and nobody spoke.

Early in the morning Waring awoke from a fitful dream that didn't make sense and he felt like he was still in the dream and there was a weight on his head the size of a steel ball the same size and he didn't have to dress because he wasn't undressed and he went out into the chilly morning that was damp from the night before and he got onto Frank's bike and charged through the streets with reckless abandon about 80, and he went further and he got on a highway and he got off the highway and he went through some more streets and he rode down Hollywood Boulevard and he came to a big hotel that had a big tall neon sign on the top and he couldn't even see the sign but he knew the place and he flew into the parking lot and almost banged into a car and locked to a stop. He stood on the bike for a second and shook his head once as if to try to get rid of the weight that wouldn't roll off, and then he kicked the stand down and jumped off and looked around, found the door, walked into the hotel by the back way walked through the lobby and came out at the front. He looked around again and went back in the hotel and got in a self-service elevator just before the night bellboy caught up with him and took the car to the top. When it opened he was in a hall full of doors and he looked up one wall and down the other and saw the sign marked EXIT and went right through the door and up a flight of steps and stepped out on the roof and there was a man there with beautiful hair and he was smoking a cigarette. The dawn was still blue and gray.

"Wary!" said Gilbert Green, "Aren't you Fred's friend Wary? What are you doing here?"

The ball rolled off Wary's head and split his consciousness below the belt where he sat on a tarred and pebbled roof right down and looked at the surface of the roof and replied, "I don't know."

"How did you know we were here?"

"I don't know."

"What's the matter?"

"I don't know."

"We just came out to make a movie. I couldn't sleep, and, what's the matter with you, do you want to see Fred?"

"I don't know."

Waring stood up and he felt as free as air and he moved very slow he felt weightless and he felt nothing and he moved around but he didn't do anything and he didn't look up and he didn't look down and his movements were almost like a dance and Gilbert Green stood hypnotized by the gray apparition moving around and making no sound until Waring hopped up on the ledge at the edge of the roof and continued his dance and Gilbert Green said "Watch out Wary" because it looked like he might fall, but he steadied himself and continued his dance and Gilbert Green followed him along the edge of the roof until Waring stopped dancing and stood there facing Gilbert Green in the dawn and cast a glance over his shoulder and saw the parking lot far below and couldn't see a thing, and Gilbert Green said, "Come off there Wary, you might fall." Wary said, *"Take yr hans off me gilbert green."* And Gilbert Green carefully got up on the ledge and moved toward Waring very carefully and slowly, not saying anything but staring each other right in the eye and when he got about a foot from him he put his arm around Waring's shoulder and Gilbert Green said "Okay now" and Waring kicked hard off the ledge And there wasn't a single more sound.

〖 A.D. 1968 〗

I awake from my dream in a revery of past successes with real tears and imaginary laughter to find an intention forming in my brain—I wish to re-member it.

>In the morning and the evening
>Red and blue the objectable colors
>The motion picture of my mind.

Jumping up and down on the bed, playing sisters playing Lana Turner and Maria Montez (which is better?) and screams a little under the unused eyepockets and the well-washed hair.

>In the morning and in the afternoon
>As a short nap may lengthen into a long speech
>Yet another comic image
>Transmitted inwardly.

Do not say fuck it is a dirty word fuck fuck it bats against the eyeballs and creates a scene in the nursery that never was so green as never could only be you see it isn't dirty it is just there another word among the pages that we relie on to tell how it was with us that year.

>In the morning and at midnight
>A silver point among the clouds
>Remembering how many dollars we had today
>And what we had to eat and sleep.

Life passes lively in dreams and suchlike compositions you have good luck I cannot reach it would you hand it too thankyou I regret that I regret that I regret, no thanks, no exchange, and, all anticipation, it was a big green tree I fell the swing was white strawberries are in flower now, okay.

—G.G.

- 235 -

⟦ Postface ⟧

This book is my surreal novel about the extraordinary year 1968. I wrote it during the winter and spring of that year, finishing it on my wife's birthday, May 10th. She and our son Jesse were visiting her parents in Chapel Hill, New Jersey at my suggestion. I wrote the last part particularly quickly and had to work on it ten or twelve hours a day without interruption, because the book was writing itself and I had all I could do to keep up with it. The day after I finished it, I had a drink with John Ashbery who at that time was my editor at the old Art News magazine. I told him I had just had a remarkable experience—I had finished writing a tragedy. He asked me how it ended and I told him it ended with the words, *And there wasn't a single more sound.* That was about eighteen years ago, and today I finished editing the manuscript.

The fact that *Gilbert Green* has spent so long underground has something to do with my first book, an epic novel called *Anticipation,* which McPherson & Company published in 1984, eighteen years after I had completed it. Without joking, I used to call *Anticipation* "the great book" because I realized that at the age of twenty-eight I had summarized my youth in epic form, something few young writers can boast. Very excited, I ran to all my friends to show them this wonderful book and have it published. I went to Boston and visited my friend David Neck White and his wife Ruth Jenkins at their house in Cambridge. While White was curiously perusing this text which I, like all young writers, thought was the best book of all time, I glanced over at Ruth who was reading the current issue of *Glamour* magazine. The blurb on the cover ran, "The Real Right Way To

Dress For Spring." I was suddenly overcome with emotion because I thought that I could never hope to interest the readers of *Glamour* in my great work to nearly the extent that they would gobble up this tacky magazine story about spring fashions. There and then I resolved to write a book to bridge the gap; I told everyone that I wanted to write a popular novel.

Stefan Brecht took me seriously. In 1968, among many other things, I received the final notice that the house we had occupied for six years in the Wall Street district of New York was going to be torn down. To ease the blow, which turned out to be one of the worst things that ever happened to me, Brecht offered me a small subsidy and an old farmhouse in Massachusetts, if I promised to write the "popular novel." In fact, I finished it before our house was destroyed. Early in the year I told Andy Warhol that I intended to write three books in 1968, a trilogy. I didn't tell him that the character Gilbert Green was to some extent to be based on him. I wrote the second one, now called *Alaska,* at Brecht's farm. Instead of writing the third book, I went to California alone, to the distress of my family. There I wrote my first epic poem, *America,* my third book of 1968. My wife Janet Blue caught up with me in Chicago where we began another of our several honeymoons. I thought I was going back to publish *Gilbert Green* in New York, but such was not to be.

The publishers who had expressed an interest in *Anticipation*— "we'd love to see your next book"—were rewired back into the circuit, but it didn't work. The world was reeling from the events of the year and people refused to eat raw meat. We didn't even realize that the Events of 1968 amounted to a tragedy of awful proportions. The assassination of Martin Luther King and the abdication of President Johnson are recorded in passing in *Gilbert Green.* The fact that Andy Warhol was killed, as he tells it, and brought back to life a month after this book was written, astonished me. The day after Warhol was shot, Senator Kennedy of New York was shot dead in Los Angeles. The student strikes in New York and Paris had given much encouragement and spirit to the book, but I was no student anymore. The riots and outrages that surrounded the Democratic National Convention in Chicago later in the summer were still raw when I went there in November. The last thing any publisher could imagine publishing was a popular tragedy.

In addition, I was under the influence of what might be called minimal structuralism or conceptual art. This kind of art always describes its own process, and is always in danger of becoming simply tautological. *Gilbert Green* was designed originally as a series of eighty-one texts, nine times nine, and I attributed an obscure meaning to each of the small numbers, one through nine. Therefore, the book might have seemed almost as arcane as *Anticipation,* although it proceeded from very different motives; I had in mind to write a novel absolutely of its own moment that everybody would understand. It was and is a book of dreams, rock and roll music, poetry, sex, drugs, money and death. The publishers didn't get it. There was no such category. The sudden shifts and goings in and out of "reality" were regarded as illegal. I was shocked and crushed. Perhaps I should add that when I wrote this book I had had no experience with drugs more potent than salt, sugar, aspirin, novacaine, caffein, adrenalin, tobacco, alcohol and marijuana. It isn't about drugs, but about dreams.

But where did I get the title *Gilbert Green?* I heard it first as a song played on the radio by a disc jockey called Rosco in 1967. He used to play it all the time, but I couldn't buy the record—I later found out it was never released. It was sung by Gerry Marsden, who had made a big hit with a group called Gerry and the Pacemakers in England and later in the U.S. This was Marsden's first solo effort. What I loved about it was that it was a song about writing a song, and that, at the end, a large orchestra played a romantic version of the song on the same cut without words. I kept looking for a copy of the record. The operative line for me in this song was *Couldn't I write a song about a man who's dead?* I made Gilbert Green into an amalgam of myself and Andy Warhol and what I imagined a great artist and poet might do in those unsettled times.

Two years after I'd finished the book, my friend Tom Robbins brought me an old book called *The Forgotten Enemy,* by Gilbert Green! This man was the youth secretary of the American

Communist Party when it had been (unconstitutionally) outlawed, and in prison he had written this book and others. I read the book, of course, and I flashed on the line in the song *Now we can tell the World that he was right!* I was no more a communist than a druggist, but it interested me that a name I had appropriated had such a history. I'm sure many people have been named the same and I look forward to hearing from their friends. Finally a copy of "Gilbert Green" was discovered by an oldies dealer called Bleeker Bob who asked $50 for it since he had been looking for it for me for six or seven years. I got him down to $25 and went home to savor my find. I discovered from the label that "Gilbert Green" is a song by Barry and Robin Gibb, better known as the Beegees, and that their producer on this cut was Robert Stigwood who later produced the Beegees' movies. All of this somewhat backs up my sense that there is something prophetic as well as documentary about *Gilbert Green—The Real Right Way To Dress For Spring.* I feel it is getting truer as it is getting older, truer to the times and truer to life. I am surprised again by its sense of tragic reality in the midst of utter hopefulness cast in the form of a popular entertainment.

It is perhaps needless to remark that many of the other names in this book, including my own, are "real." I mention this more as an expression of gratitude than as an apology. Of course I could have used Don, Bob and Jane. I had a great teacher of English and French in high school called Don Gay. As soon as he taught me the meaning of the long word "verisimilitude"—fiction being like life—I immediately adopted it as a goal, and this appropriation of realities in my books serves this purpose. All words carry a special charge, and names an extra special one. As my friend Nancy Holt is always remarking, peoples' names coincide with their characters. As I remark at various points in the book, "This is not real, it is just true," and vice versa. I have already mentioned my debt to Andy Warhol, and I must add a word of thanks to my friend Kestutis Zapkus, who briefly appears as a character too. Although years ago when we had a tiff, Zapkus asked me to expunge his name from the text, he has recently encouraged me to remain true to my original work. I have dedicated this publication to my son, who is now at university. When I wrote it, in the Spring of 1968, I set this at the head of the book:

> *To all those who with head, heart and hand*
> *toiled in the construction of this monument*
> *to the public service, this is inscribed.*

It is the dedication of Grand Central Terminal in New York, appearing over the main entrance ramp on Forty-second Street. I think it is one of the greatest modern buildings in the world and I am glad it has been rescued from destruction, just as this my dream book has been rescued from oblivion by this publication.

Frederick Ted Castle
New York, 13 June 1985

This book was composed by The F.W. Roberts Company, and printed by Maple-Vail Inc. Of the first printing, fifty copies have been bound in buckram with marbled endsheets, numbered, and signed by the author.